U0136473

2011 不求人文化

2009 懶鬼子英日語

I'm 我識出版教育集團
I'm Publishing Edu. Group
www.17buy.com.tw

2005 意識文化

2005 易富文化

2003 我識地球村

2001 我識出版社

2011 不求人文化

2009 懶鬼子英日語

I'm 我識出版教育集團
I'm Publishing Edu. Group
www.17buy.com.tw

2005 意識文化

2005 易富文化

2003 我識地球村

2001 我識出版社

最強
英文寫作
Powerful English Writing Techniques for All Purposes
指南

[風靡全球的萬用寫作法]
[五大類文體完全適用]

告別「下筆無能」，
英文寫作前必備的4個步驟！

STEP 1
要先知道讀者是誰：選定文體！

寫作不能信手拈來，寫作前務必知道寫作題目的要求，才能對症下藥！

右圖提供英文考試的常見文體及應用範圍給讀者參考，本書也依照文體編排章節，讀者可針對個別文體閱讀。

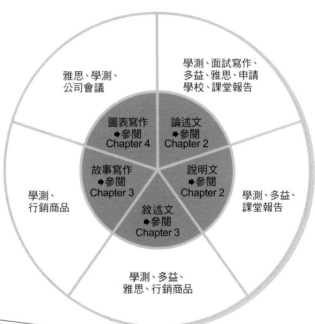

雅思、學測、公司會議

學測、面試寫作、多益、雅思、申請學校、課堂報告

圖表寫作
➡參閱
Chapter 4

論述文
➡參閱
Chapter 2

故事寫作
➡參閱
Chapter 3

說明文
➡參閱
Chapter 2

敘述文
➡參閱
Chapter 3

學測、行銷商品

學測、多益、課堂報告

學測、多益、雅思、行銷商品

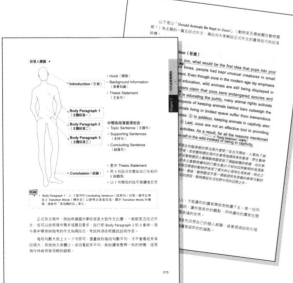

STEP 2
時間和字數也很重要：擬定段落！

正式的英文寫作通常都是五段式作文，寫作前可以先擬定各段落的重點和句數，關於各段落的寫作要點可參閱本書第15頁的「人體圖」。熟悉段落人體圖，寫作時就能掌握題旨、首尾呼應。

STEP 3
派上用場的文法和單字：牢記句型！

英文寫作需要的單字和文法不用太難，不過適當的加入轉折語和形容詞也很重要！本書各章節除了穿插正、反例句供讀者寫作參考之外，並以表格列舉常用的轉折語和中階單字。

> ✗ Talk show discusses various topics.
> *脫口秀討論各式各樣的主題。*

> ✓ Talk show can be in the form of an interview or a simple conversation about social, political, or religious issues.
> *脫口秀可以用訪談或簡單對話的形式來探討社會、政治或宗教的議題。*

STEP 4
讓文章幫你表達想法：活用公式！

寫作的目的不是把自己會的單字和文法全部用上，而是組織一篇每個人都看得懂的文章！以下是本書介紹寫作4大公式，善用這些技巧，你也能在英文寫作上搶滿分！

PEEL 剝皮公式　　　　　　　　　　　　➡ 參閱第 85 頁

Point（論點）＋ Evidence（證據）＋ Explain（解說）＋ Link（連結）

OREO 餅乾公式　　　　　　　　　　　　➡ 參閱第 90 頁

Opinion（意見）＋ Reason（理由）＋ Evidence（證據）＋ Opinion（論點）

FRIES 薯條法則　　　　　　　　　　　　➡ 參閱第 117 頁

Facts（事實）＋ Reasons（理由）＋ Incidents（事件）＋ Examples（範例）＋ Statistics（數據）

Story Mountain 故事山　　　　　　　　　➡ 參閱第 153 頁

主角的特徵、背景→故事的來龍去脈→發生了什麼？何時、何地，以及如何發生→如何解決？對誰造成影響？寓意為何？

　　英文寫作對很多人來說是一件令人頭痛卻又不得不面對的一件事，包括一開始接觸英文寫作的我。起初，我的英文作文卷子上充滿著老師幫我修改的筆跡，自己也非常挫折。但在高中時期有幸遇到舒涵老師，告訴我正確的英文作文寫法，包括令人提起興趣的開頭、中間整體的組織架構、句型以及適時變換單字與片語，到最後以具有說服力的結語畫下句點，經過老師不厭其煩的指導，我慢慢地了解其中的精髓，也漸漸地對英文作文得心應手。老師的教法也幫助我通過全民英檢中高級，以及在學測拿到英文滿級分。到了大學，過去所培養的英文作文能力幫助我在面對大量的醫學原文時，能快速抓到文章的組織架構以及其所要表達的重點，相較於其他醫學系同學也就更有優勢。

　　這本書真心推薦給正為英文作文煩惱的同學，以及想要在英文作文方面更上一層樓的讀者們。

國防醫學院醫學系 三年級 林〇淩同學

　　剛接觸英文寫作時，連該怎麼下筆都毫無頭緒，但在上過舒涵老師的寫作課後，開始認識各種文體的核心概念。從最重要的架構、舉例的細節與方法、到同義詞的比較與練習，在老師清晰且詳細的講解之下，讓我逐步進入英文寫作的世界，也讓我後來在準備其他英語相關考試時，能更得心應手。

　　印象最深刻的是在準備托福時，有一次題目為論說文，閱卷者在看完我的作文後感到非常驚訝，原因是大部分的學生對於結構的概念通常較薄弱，而我卻能在第一次練習時，呈現出讓閱卷者驚豔的標準作文寫法。

　　在此推薦這本書給所有不想被英文作文打敗，及希望進一步了解寫作內涵的讀者，各位必定能重新認識英文寫作，並提升寫作的能力！一起學好英文作文吧！

科技部兼任研究助理 陳〇嘉

以前總覺得單字只要背得多，寫作時用字選最長、看起來很厲害的，這樣作文就會得高分了。但是這樣寫作的結果就是常常得到閱卷者「母語人士不會這樣使用」的評語，因此我對英文寫作有著很厚的心理陰霾。

本書中的教學方式，不全然是讓你能學會更多更艱深的單字片語。對我來說，最有幫助的是，老師用獨到的方式舉例，使得讀者從有趣又生活化的例子了解到，如果錯用了寫作方法，自己的作文可能會變得很好笑，從而加深對詞彙、片語，甚至到寫作方法的印象，而不僅僅是單純一句「母語人士不是這樣寫的」這種缺乏建設性的回饋。

透過書中各種舉例，慢慢地就更能理解不同寫法該如何運用在英文寫作中，並從用詞精確度、句型的變化、寫作的架構上，提升自己作文的程度。兼具趣味與學習成效是本書的一大特色，因此推薦給大家！

中山大學資訊工程學系 三年級 蔡 O 師同學

- -

我於申請香港的港大以及中文大學期間受楊老師的寫作指導，在履歷表以及面試上有卓越的改善。在履歷表方面，楊老師利用寫作法教導我從面試官的角度思考，設想如何在面試官短時間的審核內，呈現一份受人青睞的履歷。

準備英文面試期間，楊老師利用多元的練習題材，指導我如何運用英文寫作準備口試。讓我在團體面試中能有條理的陳述邏輯與想法，並能運用寫作的邏輯思維去聆聽、參與、分析、引導小組討論的程序，製造和諧的雙向溝通，讓考官對我印象深刻。在個人面試環節裡，楊老師也用英文寫作的邏輯提升我對情境題的即時應變能力，讓我了解到英文面試其實可以透過「寫」來準備。與老師多次的先寫作再口語練習模擬後，我在面試當天穩定且自信的表現，使考官留下深刻印象。

我由衷感謝楊老師的指導與英文寫作教學，通過多層關卡，達成十七歲以來的目標。

香港大學與香港中文大學正取生 Janie Hou

「老師，你可不可以推薦我一本書，看完就知道怎麼寫作文？」

與許多厲害的前輩們相比，我還是個超級小菜鳥，但教書的這些年，仍會碰到學生帶著絕望或是充滿希望的眼神來問這些問題。不過使用外國語言書寫文章本身就是一件需要事前**大量的資訊輸入**（input）、反覆練習，最後才會有好的輸出（output）的過程。

我自己也花了很多時間摸索英文寫作，甚至也有過瞎子摸象的挫折感。所以我明白多數考生在時間有限、架構不熟、練習不夠的狀況下，面對英文寫作勢必慌慌不安。

多數學生的困擾不外乎為：

(1) 我好希望有個表格化的 SOP 或是方針讓我遵循！

(2) 時間有限，考試的文體又多，有辦法讓學習過程系統化嗎？

(3) 有個基本盤可以讓我掌握嗎？至少我在面對作文時，不會什麼都寫不出來。

因此在本書《最強英文寫作指南：風靡全球的萬用寫作法，五大類文體完全適用！》裡，我透過**視覺化表格、口訣、公式**等來拆解英文作文。書中集結了無數次我在教學中嘗試後的成功經驗，很多考生們利用這些方法準備學測、語言考試、面試前擬稿，甚至成功申請到國外理想大學。

我由衷感謝我教過的學生們，是你們大量的回饋激勵我去想出更適合臺灣學生學習寫作的方法。謝謝曾在交大指導過我的葉修文教授、孫于智教授、林律君副教授、張靜芬副教授，以及無私讓我觀課的語言中心吳思葦老師，正是這些優秀的學界前輩為我鋪上了層層的養分，讓我得以在教學時運用他們的智慧來設計課程。謝謝我識出版社的編輯團隊，願意給予一位素人機會，肯定我 trial and error（嘗試錯誤法）後的教學心得，並且給予許多能使本書更臻完善的建議。謝謝黃博訓老師在出版的過程中給予許多建議與鼓勵；謝謝知名影評人吳老拍先生，在我思考提案此書前撥冗給予許多寶貴的建議。謝謝親愛的家人在我忙於寫書時協助育兒，並總是給予我無限的支持與鼓勵。

楊舒涵

Chapter 01 / 一切先從經典開始

目錄
Contents

Chapter 02 / 論述文與說明文

Chapter 03 / 敘述文與故事寫作

Chapter 04 ／ 圖表寫作

Chapter 05／比較和對比

Chapter 06／因果關係

Chapter 07 ╱ 佛腳給你抱：
寫作秘笈大公開

〔書中常用縮寫〕

S 主詞	V 動詞	Ving 現在分詞
Vpp 過去分詞	N 名詞	adj. 形容詞
adv. 副詞		

在寫作前，
我們要先知道自己面對的是什麼樣的敵
人——意即文體為何？
思考攻打的模式——如何拆解與書寫文章？
以及寫作的受眾是誰？

Chapter

01
一切先從
經典開始

> "The scariest moment is always just before you start. After that, things can only get better."
> — *Stephen King, On Writing: A Memoir of the Craft*
>
> 「最可怕的片刻都是在動手做之前，一旦開始著手，事情只會愈來愈好。」
> ──美國驚悚小說大師史蒂芬‧金《史蒂芬‧金談寫作》

　　你是不是常常一碰到作文題目就腦袋空白，或是需要用到英文口說的場合就支支吾吾呢？英文的「說」與「寫」是知識的產出，屬於進階的能力，需要大量的資訊輸入並搭配練習才能有令人滿意的結果。不過，練習需要方向，不能像無頭蒼蠅到處亂撞，否則即使閉門練功多時，也無法造就武林高手。

　　在寫作前，我們要先知道自己面對的是什麼樣的敵人，也就是今天題目要求的是什麼樣的文體，才能對症下藥，寫出讀者或是批閱的人想要看到的內容。

Section 01　五段式作文到底長怎樣？簡單圖示讓你秒懂！

　　中文寫作有起承轉合，英文寫作也有段落分配！英文的段落分配，可以用人體的圖形來分解。寫作時，只要記住各段有什麼元素，不管時間多緊迫，腦筋多空白，套入每項元素就不用害怕如何在有時間限制之下寫出合乎英文寫作規範的文章。

　　我們可以把人體的頭部想成是 Introduction（引言），我們遇到別人時，第一眼會先看到對方的臉，所以開頭要能夠吸引人，讓人家對你的文章有好的第一印象，引起別人興趣他們才會想要「讀你」。在 Introduction 這段的最後一句有個關鍵句叫作 Thesis Statement（主旨句），是整篇文章的核心。接下來依序是 Body Paragraph 1、2、3（主體段落），分別代表你的三個觀點或想法。腳的部分則是 Conclusion（結論），功能是為這篇文章做總結。

段落人體圖 ▶

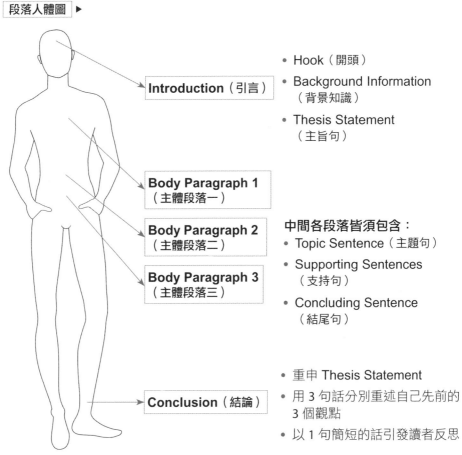

Introduction（引言）
- Hook（開頭）
- Background Information（背景知識）
- Thesis Statement（主旨句）

Body Paragraph 1（主體段落一）

Body Paragraph 2（主體段落二）

Body Paragraph 3（主體段落三）

中間各段落皆須包含：
- Topic Sentence（主題句）
- Supporting Sentences（支持句）
- Concluding Sentence（結尾句）

Conclusion（結論）
- 重申 Thesis Statement
- 用 3 句話分別重述自己先前的 3 個觀點
- 以 1 句簡短的話引發讀者反思

PLUS!
- Body Paragraph 1、2、3 當中的 Concluding Sentence（結尾句）的第一個字記得加上 Transition Words（轉折詞）以便帶出後面段落。關於 Transition Words 的種類，請參照「善用轉折詞」單元。

　　正式英文寫作，例如申請國外學校或是大型作文比賽，一般都是五段式作文，但可以依照寫作需求或題目要求，自行把 Body Paragraph 2 和 3 拿掉。現今高中學測與指考的作文為兩段式，考試時須依照應試說明作答。

　　每段句數大致上 5 ～ 7 句即可，盡量做到每段句數平均，才不會看起來某段頭大，其他地方身體小。各段看起來平均，能給讀者整齊一致的感覺，這是寫作時經常被忽略的細節。

以下是以「Should Animals Be Kept in Zoos?」（動物是否應被關在動物園裡？）為主題的一篇五段式作文，藉此向大家解說正式作文的書寫技巧和段落結構。

第一段 ▶ Introduction（引言）

When it comes to the zoo, what would be the first idea that pops into your head? From ancient times, people had kept unusual creatures in small cages for entertainment. Even though zoos in the modern age lay emphasis on conservation and education, wild animals are still being displayed in captivity. While zoogoers claim that zoos save endangered species and play an important role in educating the public, many animal rights activists believe the negative impacts of keeping animals behind bars outweigh the benefits. ① Firstly, animals living in limited space suffer from tremendous mental and physical illness. ② In addition, keeping animals in captivity also violates animal rights. ③ Last, zoos are not an effective tool in providing meaningful educational activities. As a result, for all the reasons mentioned above, animals should be left in the wild instead of being in captivity.

> Hook（開頭）
> 相反論點
> Thesis Statement（主旨句）

一提到動物園，第一個浮現在你腦海裡的想法是什麼呢？從古代開始，人類為了娛樂，將不常見的生物關在小籠子裡。即使動物園在現代社會裡強調保育和教育，野生動物仍然被關在籠中展示。雖然喜好去動物園的人聲稱動物園拯救了瀕臨絕種的物種，也在教育公眾當中扮演重要的腳色，許多注重動物權利的行動主義分子相信囚禁動物的負面影響遠大於其好處。首先，住在有限空間裡的動物們承受了極大的心理與生理疾病。除此之外，囚禁動物也違反了動物的權利。最後，動物園並不是一個能提供有意義的教育活動的有效工具。因此，根據上述所提及的原因，動物應該生活在野外而非囚禁之中。

▶ 第一段解說

第一段是門面，要夠吸引人，才能讓你的讀者興致勃勃讀下去。第一段同時也是一座橋樑，能架起所有資訊，讓你發表你的觀點，同時讓你的讀者在閱讀時結合自身的經驗，通往你要表達的世界。

開頭的 Hook 利用提問讓讀者先回想自己的個人經驗，接著透過說明引領讀者思考這個議題，潛移默化讓讀者認同你的論點。

「相反論點」則是跟自己抱持相反意見的人可能會提出的論點，藉由提出對方論點，一邊能展現自己有風度，一邊可以反駁這個論點。此外，也可以讓讀者知道對方的立場並沒有強到值得讓他們信服。

編號①、②、③分別代表了作者用來說服讀者的三個理由，並會在 Body Paragraph 中依序呈現，末尾則是 Thesis Statement（主旨句）。

第二段 ▸ Body paragraph 1（主體段落一）

Animals in captivity suffer from stress, confinement, and dullness.
→Topic Sentence（主題句）
Furthermore, animals are often prevented from doing activities that are natural and vital to them, such as running, mating, and interacting with their own kind. According to various scientific research, living in a limited space will cause severe mental and physical problems, for instance, obsessively licking their tails or paws, or pulling out their own hair. Wild animals will also develop abnormal or behavioral problems. Although these animals
Concluding Sentence（結尾句）◂
eventually are adapted to zoo life, they have forever lost the opportunity and freedom to experience life in the habitat.

被囚禁的動物承受了壓力、監禁，以及無趣的生活。此外，動物經常無法從事那些對牠們來說是自然且必要的活動，例如奔跑、交配以及與同類互動。根據許多科學研究指出，生活在有限的空間會導致嚴重的心理和生理疾病，同時，牠們也會發展出不正常或行為方面的問題，例如執著於舔牠們的尾巴或爪子，或是拔自己的毛髮。雖然這些動物最終會適應動物園裡的生活，但牠們也永遠失去了體會在棲息地生活的機會與自由。

第三段 ▸ Body paragraph 2（主體段落二）

We all agree that all human beings are born free and equal in dignity
→ Topic Sentence（主題句）
and rights, and this should also be true for animals. Humans do not have a right to breed, capture, and confine other animals under any circumstances. However, by keeping animals in cages, zoos show that it is acceptable for humans to interfere with animals' lives and keep them locked up far from their homes. Some may argue that by keeping these animals, people are able to conserve these species and to ensure the survival for threatened

creatures. Nevertheless, being an endangered species does not necessarily
→ Concluding Sentence（結尾句）
mean these animals could be deprived of rights.

　　我們都認同人類生而自由且平等，且享有尊嚴與權利，這也應當適用於動物。在任何
情況下，人類都沒有權利繁殖、捕捉以及監禁其他動物。然而，藉由把動物關在籠子裡，
動物園展現出了人類干預動物的生活以及顯示了把牠們從家中抓走並關起來是可被接受的
一件事。有些人可能會爭論說藉由把這些動物關起來，人們可以保育這些物種，並確保這
些被威脅的生物能生存。然而，即使是瀕臨絕種的物種，也不一定代表這些動物就該被剝
奪權利。

第四段 ▶ Body paragraph 3（主體段落三）

Many zoos or zoogoers claim that zoos provide meaningful educational
→ Topic Sentence（主題句）
opportunities, but most visitors actually spend only a few minutes at each
display, seeking entertainment rather than enlightenment. Although zoos
certainly offer the opportunity for the public to see animals up close, does
seeing animals in this way mean that people learn something meaningful?
Seeing animals in artificial environments does nothing to educate visitors
about the species in the wild. Instead, visitors learn with a distorted and
inaccurate perception of the species. Frankly speaking, zoos are more like a
Concluding Sentence（結尾句） ◀
place to provide entertainment rather than education.

　　很多動物園或喜好動物園的人聲稱動物園可以提供有意義的教育活動，但事實上，多
數遊客都只會停留在每個展示區數分鐘，而且尋求的是娛樂而非啟發。雖然動物園絕對可
以提供大眾一個近距離觀看動物的機會，但以這種方式看動物真的代表人們可以學到一些
有意義的事物嗎？在這樣人工的環境下觀看動物根本就無法教育大眾在野外生存的生物是
什麼模樣。遊客反而會以扭曲且不正確認知來獲得對這些動物的知識。老實說，動物園比
較像是一個提供娛樂而非教育意義的地方。

▶ **第二、三、四段解說**

　　在 Thesis Statement（主旨句）中，我們通常會呈現三個觀點，而 Body
Paragraph 1、2、3 的功用就是闡述我們的想法。英文寫作很忌諱在同一段裡
塞入太多不相干的資訊干擾視聽，一段只能專心寫好一個想法，所以三個想法
必須分別在這三段中呈現。

　　Body Paragraph 的第一句中都是由 Topic Sentence（主題句）開始，簡單陳述這段要講的觀點或想法，接著會需要用到 Supporting Sentences（支持句）來幫助你加強你的想法，支持你的論點，讓你想呈現的東西更有說服力。我們可以使用例子、解釋、定義等方法來佐證，這部份在後面會詳細說明。最後會用 Concluding Sentence（結尾句）當這一段的結尾，總結這段，並承接下一段。

第五段 ▶ Conclusion（結論）

　　Animals pay a very high price in zoos for our unwise and selfish decision. It is cruel to neglect the fact that animals suffer from mental and physical illness, especially when they cannot speak up for themselves. In addition, no matter how noble the goal is, we cannot deny that zoos usually favor exotic or popular animals which could draw visitors' attention over endangered species. Furthermore, so far there is no hard evidence to prove that a visit to the zoo adds to the understanding of these creatures. Based on humanitarian reasons and animal rights, no one should ever have the right to put animals behind bars.

　　動物園裡的動物因為我們不明智又自私的決定而須付出很高的代價。忽略動物承受了心理和生理的疾病這件事情事非常殘忍的，尤其是動物無法為自己發聲。此外，不管目標多麼的神聖，我們不能否認動物園通常偏好能吸引遊客的奇珍異獸而非瀕臨絕種的物種。再者，目前並沒有確切的證據證實去一趟動物園就能增加對這些生物的了解。基於人道理由與動物權利，絕對沒有人有權利把動物關在鐵幕中。

▶　**第五段解說**

　　末段能讓你為整篇文章下最後結論、再次展現你的觀點的重要性，以及促使讀者對於這個主題產生新觀點或是反思。這段還有一個很重要的任務，就是必須要重述你的 Thesis Statement，讓讀者再次深思你的觀點，但不能照抄第一段的句子，必須用自己的話換句話說。

英文中有句話叫「Show, don't tell.」意思是要你把心中想表達的東西直接展現出來，而不是一直強調「真的很重要喔！因為很重要所以我說三次喔！」畢竟口說無憑，要讓讀者覺得值得讀下去，就必須讓他們了解「為什麼這個主題值得我花時間閱讀？」所以在寫第一段時，要開門見山地把你想要表達的意見寫好寫滿，而不能迂迴又曖昧的吊人胃口。

Introduction（引言）主要分為三大部分，依序為：Hook（開頭）、Background Information（背景知識），以及 Thesis Statement（主旨句）。

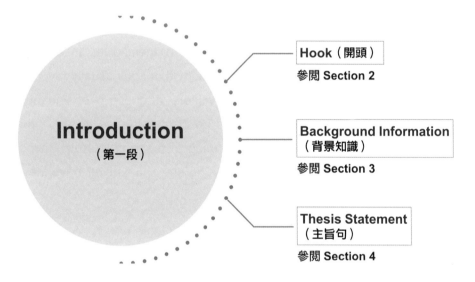

Introduction
（第一段）

Hook（開頭）
參閱 Section 2

Background Information
（背景知識）
參閱 Section 3

Thesis Statement
（主旨句）
參閱 Section 4

2-1 　讓讀者上鉤的 Hook

Hook 是鉤子，釣魚時鉤住魚的嘴巴，獵物就再也跑不掉了。好的文章就像是在釣魚，想要吸引讀者上鉤，就必須提供好吃的餌給他們。在文章的一開頭就必須引起讀者的注意，讓他們被勾住，進而對你接下來要陳述的東西產生興趣。

在這個資訊爆炸的時代，我們每天都會接受並處理海量的資訊。加上手機和社群軟體的盛行，大家都只想用最快的速度知道重點在哪裡，所以好的 Hook 要能讓讀者有想要讀下去的慾望。

■ 寫 Hook 的方法

Hook 的寫法有很多種，我們以「Is Social Media Good for Our Society?」（社群媒體對我們的社會是否有益處？）這個主題來說明，以下提供 8 種寫 Hook 的方法，並說明各種方法的優缺點。

❶ 提問　難易度★☆☆☆☆

優點	缺點
人是具有好奇心的生物，提出一個跟你的主題有關的問題，藉由拋出問題讓讀者必須從你的文章中找到答案，是一個很實用的技巧。如果是需要讀者反思的問題，也能讓讀者檢視自己與你想法的異同之處。	相較於其他Hook的寫法，提問比較容易，但很容易因為時間緊迫，即使是不適合用提問法的開頭還是硬擠了個問題，讀者會困惑「這個還需要拿來問嗎？」或是提出一個沒有辦法引起讀者興趣的問題，只會讓讀者更不想耗費時間去閱讀下一句。

例　What do you usually do with social media, making friends, sharing thoughts, or simply browsing information?

你通常使用社群媒體做什麼呢？交朋友、分享你的想法，或只是單純瀏覽資訊呢？

PLUS!
- 藉由這個問題，讀者一方面會回想他們都用社群媒體做什麼，一方面也會想知道你要提出什麼他們還沒想過社群媒體所能帶來的功用。

❷ 強而有力的聲明　難易度★★★☆☆

優點	缺點
藉由一句強而有力的聲明，可以吸引讀者的注意，加強論點的重要性和可信度。提出聲明還有一個最大的好處，就是無論你的讀者在讀你的文章前，抱持正方或反方的觀點，他們都會因為想知道你如何證明你的觀點，或如何說服他們而往下讀。另外，這個聲明應該要跟Thesis Statement（主旨句）有關，才能承先啟後，讀者讀起來才會流暢。	有些同學開頭會硬塞一句與主題無關的聲明，或者是這句聲明跟主題沒有直接關聯，這個時候會讓讀者很難建立這句聲明與主題的連結。又或者是提出一句邏輯不強的聲明，很容易讓讀者反駁因而失去文章的公信力。舉例來說：「考駕照年齡若下修，會有更多事故發生。」讀者可以輕易反駁你無法證明年紀愈輕愈容易製造交通事故，也無法證明當擁有駕照的人數增加時，事故必然會增加。

Social media enables the spread of unreliable and false information.

社群媒體促使不可信賴的以及假消息的傳播。

- 這句強而有力又簡短的聲明可以讓認同你觀點的讀者探討你為何跟他們擁有一樣的想法；同時，也能誘發不認同社群媒體是假消息來源的讀者的好奇心，想知道你要怎麼為這個觀點辯護。

❸ 事實與數據　　　　　　　　　　　難易度★★★★☆

優點	缺點
事實與數據能讓讀者對主題感興趣，因為這些是真實的資訊，同時也是非常具有說服力的證明。想像你在跟人聊天時，如果突然說一句「有篇報導指出……」是不是瞬間就能為自己的論點增添可信度呢？	有時候因為緊張或時間壓力而掰出不合邏輯的數據或事實，反而讓這篇文章失去可信度。另外在提供這些佐證的資料時，必須確定你提供的資訊是來自一個有可信度的來源（某個領域知名人士或具有聲望的報章雜誌等）或機構（政府機關、大型研究機構等）。

 According to a study conducted in 2016, adolescents who overuse social media may have trouble in maintaining successful relationships later in life because online communication hinders the development of interpersonal skills.

根據一項 2016 年的研究顯示，過度使用社群媒體的青少年因為線上溝通阻礙了人際關係技巧的發展，日後在成人時期較難維持一段成功的關係。

- 讀者在讀完這段文字後，會根據你提供的研究產生疑問：為什麼這些青少年因為社群媒體就沒辦法在成人時期維持成功的關係呢？什麼樣才叫過度使用呢？這時因為有科學研究的支持，而引發讀者求知欲，想要一探到底是哪些原因造就了這個研究結果。

❹ 比喻

難易度★★★★☆

優點	缺點
不管是使用明喻或暗喻，一個跟主題有關的比喻可以讓讀者對文章產生興趣。英文當中的明喻會使用like或是as（像），例如：He is as sly as a fox.（他狡猾的跟隻狐狸一樣。）暗喻則會將A事物比擬成B事物，例如：Laughter is the best medicine.（笑是最好的良藥。）	比喻要能夠對比的巧妙才能讓讀者讀起來覺得有意思，假如沒辦法想到比較適合的譬喻，寧可放棄這種寫作的方法，也不要硬要用，否則很容易弄巧成拙。

 Social media is like a box of chocolates; you never know what you will get.

社群媒體就像一盒巧克力，你永遠不知道你會得到什麼。

PLUS!
- 在這個明喻中，讀者會想知道到底我們可以從社群媒體中得到什麼，又為什麼社群媒體像一盒多種口味的巧克力呢？

❺ 故事

難易度★★★★☆

優點	缺點
不管是從古至今流傳下來的故事，或是說書人這個職業的誕生，就可以知道大家對於故事有多麼著迷。一個好的故事可以讓讀者對於你的主題產生興趣，也可以激起讀者的情緒，引發你希望帶來的效應。不過使用故事前，需要仔細考慮這個故事是否跟主題相關，或是內容是否過長，一方面可能會令讀者一頭霧水，一方面也會讓人因為字太多而看不下去。	好的故事能產生強大的作用，但是故事通常會需要比較大的篇幅來詳盡解釋與主題的關係，如果不小心寫了一個過長的故事，會讓讀者搞不清楚文章的重點到底是這個故事，還是你要論述的觀點，所以在使用故事時一定要拿捏好句數，不要太冗長，搶走了文章本身的風采。

例　Arab Spring, a series of protests that started in the spring of 2011, took place in several Muslim countries, such as Egypt, Morocco, Syria, and Libya.

阿拉伯之春是一系列在 2011 年春天展開的抗議行動，發生的地點在數個穆斯林國家，例如埃及、摩洛哥、敘利亞以及利比亞。

• 人都喜歡聽故事，不管是溫馨的、驚悚的、意想不到，或甚至是悲傷的。因為故事訴說了主角的歷練與解決事情的方法，在某個層面來說可以反映到我們的內心。但也因為故事的描述需要大量的形容詞與句型變化，因此這個寫作方法較適合中上程度的寫作者。

❻ 引經據典　　　　　　　　　　　　　　　　難易度★★☆☆☆

優點	缺點
藉由引用名人的話語，或是帶入相關領域學者或有聲望的人士所說過的話，可以讓你的文章增加可信度，也能說服讀者你的文章具有重要性。引用時記得加上引號，一般來說，使用強而有力且簡短的引言能吸引讀者目光。	寫作考試礙於時間限制，有可能會突然想不到比較好的名言佳句，或是想不出來原句是什麼。此時，可以試著換句話說，把原句言簡意賅地寫出來。

例　"Social media is about sociology and psychology more than technology," said Brian Solis, an author.

作家布萊恩・索里斯提到：「比起科技，社群媒體更像是社會學和心理學。」

• 引用他人話語時，務必要尊重智慧財產權，記得加上引號。使用引言時也必須採用令人印象深刻，而且要與主題相關的。

❼ 俗語或諺語　　　　　　　　　　　　　　　　難易度★★☆☆☆

優點	缺點
在日常聊天時，我們常會說「俗語說……」來加強語氣，或是讓對方產生共鳴。俗語或諺語是自古以來前人留下的智慧結晶，加上雖然俗語或諺語會依照各種文化有所不同，但是所包含的意義卻往往是橫跨各種文化和種族都能理解的。	有時間壓力下的寫作很難找到適合的俗語或諺語，也很有可能因為對語言的不熟悉導致誤用，反而會有扣分的效果。建議平常可以準備幾句常用的俗語或諺語，例如：「Don't judge a book by its cover.」（不要以貌取人。）

例 As the proverb goes, "A picture is worth a thousand words." But does it worth a thousand likes on social media if the content is an inappropriate or a false one?

一張圖片勝過千言萬語，但如果內容是不適當的，或者是假的，也值得在社群媒體上得到一千個讚嗎？

- 從這句話當中，我們可以很快理解「一張圖片勝過千言萬語」的含意，也能很快理解作者為什麼要說那麼這張圖片如果是不適當的，或者是假消息的話，也能說出千言萬語，甚至得到眾人欣賞嗎？善用俗語或諺語的好處就在於其文化含意深遠，而且一說大家就都知道。

❽ 給定義　　　　　　　　　　　　　　難易度★★★★☆

優點	缺點
有時候讀者對於你要寫的主題並不是那麼熟悉時，給一句簡短的定義可以讓讀者馬上對這個主題有初步認識，也比較不會令人感到艱澀而不想閱讀。 通常在科學類的文章中，開頭會給一句關於這個主題的定義，例如：「A black hole is a place in space where gravity is so strong that even light cannot get out.」（黑洞是太空中一個引力非常強大的空間，即使是光也無法穿透。）	如果拿到的題目是比較艱澀的主題，例如科技、醫學、哲學等等，需要在開頭時給予一個清楚的定義，讓讀者不會害怕閱讀這篇文章，或是覺得讀起來很困惑。然而如果你對文章本身不是那麼熟悉，又不能言簡意賅的給予清楚的定義，那麼選擇其他的開頭方式會是比較好的。

例 According to Wikipedia, social media is an interactive technology that facilitates the creation or sharing of information or ideas by virtual communities and networks.

根據維基百科，社群媒體是一種互動式的科技，可以藉由虛擬的社群或網路，促進創造或分享資訊及想法。

2-2 NG！要盡力避免的 Hook

(1) 直接照抄題目

舉例來說，假如寫作題目的說明是：

> 自從科技發展日新月異，人類的日常生活已為我們所居住的地球帶來極大的浩劫。有些人認為這種負面的影響是無法被改變的，有些人則認為只要我們願意，隨時都可以採取行動來改變現況。請就你個人的觀點書寫一篇文章，並闡述你的立場。

有些人因為懶得想 Hook，就直接在第一段翻譯題目的提示：

> 例 Human activity has had a damaging impact on our planet. Some said the situation cannot be changed, while others believe that people can always take action to make this world better.
>
> 人類活動已為地球帶來破壞性的影響。有些人認為這種負面的影響是無法被改變的，有些人則相信人們總能採取行動來讓世界變好。

除非真的是腦袋一片空白，時間緊急，而你又完全沒有想法的狀況下才使用這招。因為這招太過懶惰而且很沒誠意，也會讓讀者對你接下來要講的失去興趣。

(2) 賣弄學問

英文有句話說「be too clever by half」（聰明過頭了），而我們要避免的 Hook 就是讓讀者覺得我們在賣弄學問，特別要避免的是使用「how to...」（如何做……）以及「X ways to...」（做……的 X 種方法）。試想一個這樣的開頭「Do you know how to reduce waste in our everyday life?」（你想知道如何在我們的日常生活中減少廢棄物嗎？）或是「In this article, you will learn 10 ways to save water at home.」（在這篇文章當中，你會學到 10 種在家省水的方法。）讀完之後是不是覺得作者好像在強調自己很厲害，硬要你接受他提出來的方法呢？又或者很有可能讀者對這個議題已經很熟悉或是具有專業知識，而你接下來的內容無法說服對方，這時候就會很像像關公面前耍大刀。寫作的目的是要向多數廣大觀眾傳遞文章當中的論點與想法，因此不能把範圍寫死。

牛刀小試　幫文章起個頭吧！

以下擷取了某個文章的第一段，請閱讀下文，並利用前面提過的方法為此段寫出合適的 Hook（開頭）。

_____Hook_____Perhaps you could make your dream come true by buying yourself a ticket. Space tourism is human space travel for recreational purposes. There are currently few companies that offer such tour packages, such as the Russian Space Agency, Virgin Galactic, and SpaceX. Work also continues towards developing suborbital space tourism vehicles.

_____開頭_____也許你可以透過為自己買一張門票實現你的夢想。太空觀光業是一種人類為了娛樂的目的而到太空旅遊的形式。現在有幾間公司提供了這樣的旅遊套裝行程，例如 Russian Space Agency、Virgin Galactic 以及 SpaceX。他們也持續研發次軌道太空飛行的太空觀光飛行器。

參考答案

1. **利用提問法：** Have you ever wondered what it would be like to travel among the stars and the moon?
   你是否曾經想過在星星與月亮之間旅行是什麼樣子呢？
2. **利用名言佳句：** "That's one small step for man, one giant leap for mankind," said Neil Armstrong in 1969, and now you might have a chance to experience his journey to moon as well.
   「這是一個人的一小步，卻是人類的一大步。」尼爾‧阿姆斯壯於 1969 年如此說道。而如今你也許有機會可以跟他一樣體驗到月球的旅程。

Background Information（背景知識）：
背景知識要給足！

在寫了一個吸引人的 Hook 當開頭之後，讀者這時候會開始產生興趣，想知道關於這個主題你要說些什麼，所以接下來的任務就是提供讀者 Background Information（背景知識）。

背景知識的功用在於讓讀者對於接下來你要探討的內容有初步概念，也許是關於了解這個主題必須要有的先備知識，也許是這個議題的利弊分析，或是跟這個主題相關的資訊摘要。

提供背景知識能讓讀者做好準備閱讀你即將要呈現的觀點，也能讓讀者預測接下來要發生的事情，讓他們產生好奇心，並試圖找出答案。在寫背景知識時，你可以用幾句話讓讀者對這個主題產生共鳴，讀者也能透過你提供的資訊對這個主題有初步認識。

3-1 寫背景知識的原則

寫背景知識有以下三大原則：

(1) 簡短且精準：因為文章內的多種資訊需要讀者花心思閱讀，如果太過冗長，很容易就讓讀者失去興趣。

(2) 和主題相關：提供核心資訊才能讓讀者知道你講的每一句話都和主題是環環相扣的，沒有一句是會浪費他們時間的廢話。

(3) 要體貼讀者：很多人在寫背景知識時經常會犯一個錯誤，就是忘了站在讀者角度思考，或先假設讀者已經熟悉這個主題了，因而輕描淡寫帶過關於這個主題最關鍵的背景知識，有時候甚至會給專有名詞，卻忘了給定義或解釋，讀者讀起來會覺得自己好像門外漢，沒辦法了解內容。

下面也提供幾個問題讓你在下筆前思考一下，就可以避免自己寫得很高興，但是讀者卻讀得一頭霧水這種狀況：

✓ 一個完全不了解這個主題的人，要知道哪些資訊才能看得懂這篇文章？	✗ 避免過長或過短
可以思考是否需提供給讀者定義，以及幾句可以介紹本文的必要內容。	只需要提供閱讀這篇文章時最需要知道，也最重要的細節，囉哩囉嗦或草草帶過對讀者來說都會增加閱讀的負擔。
✓ 關於這個主題，如果是我，我想知道些什麼？	✗ 避免曖昧不清
當我們能站在讀者的立場思考時，我們比較能寫出讓讀者讀起來清楚且有邏輯的文章。寫作時，必須時不時回頭看看自己是否跳過太多應該給予的資訊。	想像一下你很認真聽別人發表見解，但他卻連話都說不清楚，是不是會感到很挫敗又生氣呢？寫作也是同樣道理，針對主題必須一針見血提出自己的看法，並就你的信念努力去捍衛它，不要浪費讀者的時間去猜測你到底想說什麼。
✓ 提出哪些背景知識對我來說是有利的，才能說服我的讀者我的觀點很重要？	✗ 避免扯太遠、跳躍式思考
每個人心中都有一把尺，但標準是可以因為學習到了新的資訊而改變的。也因此，在陳述自己的論點時，應該就本篇文章提出最能打中讀者的心的說明，毫無保留的把最厲害的殺手鐧拿出來。	很多人寫作時會突然想到某個點，深怕沒寫進去無法展現程度，害怕字數不夠而硬塞內容。整篇文章應該要專心一致陳述你所想帶給別人的觀點，以及舉出相關的例子佐證。「去蕪存菁」，其他不相關的事物就勇敢斷、捨、離吧！

看完寫作時的原則之後，我們延續前面的主題「Is Social Media Good for Our Society?」（社群媒體對我們的社會是否有益處？）來示範 Hook 以及 Background Information 怎麼寫。

首先，假如這篇文章我是持反對意見，認為社群媒體帶來的是壞處，我可以這樣開始構思：

Hook 的部分，依照這個主題，我採用「強而有力的聲明」來強調社群媒體對社會有巨大的影響。

接著我們要提供背景知識，可以利用前面提供的問題，思考一下需要提供什麼樣的背景知識，以便帶出讀者的共鳴：

(1) 關於這個主題，我自己會想知道些什麼：社群媒體帶來的影響是什麼？為什麼影響深遠？

→ helps them to expand their social circle（幫助他們拓展社交圈）

(2) 一個完全不懂這個主題的人，我可能需要提供什麼資訊：社群媒體是什麼？

→ a technology that facilitates online interaction between people（促進人與人之間線上互動的科技）

(3) 我的觀點：社群媒體雖然能帶來好處，但是壞處其實更多。

→ There are much more negative effects than you could imagine.（它所帶來的負面效應比你能想像的還多）

根據以上思索過的問題，我們可以這麼寫：

> 例 Social media, according to Wikipedia, is a technology that facilitates online
> →定義
> interaction between people, and it opens the door for interaction between
> →觀點
> people and helps them to expand their social circle. While it may seem that
> social media does good to human beings, there are much more negative
> effects than you could imagine.
>
> *根據維基百科，社群媒體是一種可以促進人與人之間線上互動的科技，它打開了*
> *人與人之間互動的大門，也同時幫助了人們拓展社交圈。乍看之下，社群媒體對*
> *人類帶來好處，但事實上它所帶來的負面效應比你能想像的還多。*

在這段文字當中，首先在首句劃底線的部分給了讀者定義，說明 social media 是什麼。接在 and 後面劃底線的句子則是多數支持社群媒體對社會有益處的人會寫的觀點，而我並不否認社群媒體有這些作用，但也正是因為這些社群媒體帶來的後續效應，使得「它所帶來的負面效果其實是比你想像的還來的多。」

結合一句強而有力的聲明當 Hook 之後，這段就變成：

> 例 <u>There are few inventions in the world that have had such an immense</u>
> → Hook
> <u>impact as social media.</u> Social media, according to Wikipedia, is a
> technology that facilitates online interaction between people, and it opens
> the door for interaction between people and helps them to expand their
> social circle. While it may seem that social media does good to human
> beings, there are much more negative effects than you could imagine.
>
> *世界上很少有發明能像社群媒體一樣帶來如此巨大的影響。根據維基百科，社群媒體是一種可以促進人與人之間線上互動的科技，它打開了人與人之間互動的大門，也同時幫助了人們拓展社交圈。乍看之下，社群媒體為人類帶來好處，但事實上它所帶來的負面效應比你能想像的還多。*

Section 04 Thesis Statement（主旨句）：決定文章好壞的關鍵句！

　　在寫作時，不能只是寫自己開心的內容，在思考下手寫哪些觀點的同時，要問自己「我這篇文章重要在哪？為什麼讀者要花時間在乎並閱讀我所寫的文章？」如此一來，寫作就不會像迷路一樣失去主題，塞了一堆不相關的內容。

　　雖然多數時候我們寫英文作文是為了某種目的，也許是成績、畢業門檻或工作等等，但不管是為了什麼目的，我們都希望讀者知道「我寫的東西有重要性，值得你一讀。」也因此好的主旨句能讓讀者理解我們的思路，了解我們的觀點，並決定他們是否有讀下去的必要。

　　寫一篇文章的作用就在於探討、發展、以及支持主旨句提及的論點，並用事實、舉例，和有邏輯的理由來說明為何我們的論點是具有可信度，而且值得讀者站到我們這邊。

4-1 什麼是 Thesis Statement（主旨句）?

寫主旨句的時候須注意以下八點：

(1) 重要性無敵：因為所有後面的段落、論述和舉例都圍繞著主旨句。

(2) 位置擺最後：永遠放在第一段最後一句。

(3) 句數不必多：通常是一句或兩句完整的句子。

(4) 作用很明確：

　　①能回答題目所要求的答案。

　　②提前預告讀者接下來各段的發展。

　　③讓讀者一讀就能馬上抓到你這篇的論點。

(5) 結構有二三：通常包含兩三個支持你觀點的理由。

(6) 內容要清晰：具體的聲明、個人意見或觀點。

(7) 用字要有力：通常都是強而有力的口吻，避免使用被動語態。

(8) 不用你我他：主旨句不能用代名詞（你、我、他等等），或「In my opinion…」（依我個人意見……）、「I think…」（我認為……），因為不客觀。

■ 主旨句長怎樣？

因為主旨句包含了解釋你觀點的理由，所以主旨句的長相通常是：

❶ 一句能表示你的論點、想法或個人意見的句子。

 ✗ Taipei is the capital of Taiwan.
臺北是臺灣的首都。

PLUS!
- 這句話是事實而不是個人觀點或意見。

例 ✗ In this essay, I will introduce Taiwanese culture.
在這篇文章當中，我將會介紹臺灣文化。

- 文章本來就是讓我們陳述個人想法的，所以不需要特別聲明接下來要做什麼，而且這句看不出來個人觀點為何。

 ✗ What differs Taipei from other cities in Taiwan?
是什麼讓臺北不同於其他臺灣的城市呢？

- 主旨句必須直接了當表達個人觀點，因此不能是問句。

 ✓ Taipei has become the capital of Taiwan since 1895 because of its geographical position, colonial history, and port performance.
臺北自 1895 年起，因為地理位置、殖民歷史，以及港口性能而成為臺灣的首都。

- 整句清楚點出臺北成為首都的原因，可以讓讀者期待接下來的內容。

❷ 一句只能包含一個完整概念的句子。

 ✗ Monitoring the internet usage of citizens is essential for our government, and so are health conditions and phone logs.
監控國民的網路使用情形對政府是必要的，同樣的道理，監控身體健康狀況和通話紀錄也是一樣的。

- 句子當中包含了三個不同的主題：監控網路使用、身體健康狀況與通話紀錄，需要討論的主題應只有一個。

 ✓ Monitoring the internet usage of citizens is not acceptable because it severely violates human rights.
監控國民的網路使用情形嚴重侵犯人權，這件事是不能被接受的。

- 這句話言簡意賅，且清楚點出作者觀點。

❸ 一個特定且明確的的主題。

 ✗ Talk show discusses various topics.
脫口秀討論各式各樣的主題。

 PLUS!
- 主題不明確,看不出來到底脫口秀是何種脫口秀?表演內容為何?討論的主題是什麼?這句話當中的主題不明確也過於廣泛,需要讀者花費心思在文章當中自己拼湊答案,因此不是好的主旨句。

 ✓ Talk show can be in the form of an interview or a simple conversation about social, political, or religious issues.
脫口秀可以用訪談或簡單對話的形式來探討社會、政治或宗教的議題。

 PLUS!
- 這句話明確點出主題是脫口秀,以及次要的相關概念。

❹ 只包含與主題相關的論點。

 ✗ Dogs are humans' best friends because they are the most popular pets. They are faithful, and they bark a lot.
狗是人類最忠實的朋友,因為他們是最受喜愛的寵物,很忠實,而且很常吠。

 PLUS!
- 狗是最受喜愛的寵物跟狗會吠並不是他們成為人類最忠實的朋友的原因。

 ✓ Dogs are humans' best friends because they are faithful, they appreciate everything you do for them, and they will love you as much as they can in return.
狗是人類最忠實的朋友,因為他們很忠實、會感激主人所做的每件事,以及會盡他們所能回報你的愛。

PLUS!
- 句中三個論點:狗很忠實、會感激主人所做的每件事,以及會盡他們所能回報你的愛,都與主題有直接連結。

寫這些論點時，需依順序排列，並分別在主體段落 1、2、3 中陳述。

4-2 主旨句怎麼寫？

主旨句雖然只有一句，但卻是整篇文章的中心思想，也是帶領個段落發展的核心人物。除了在第一段預告接下來各段的發展，也會在各段中分別被闡述，最後則會在結論重新被提出以便讓讀者複習。

主旨句要能夠回應主題，也因此如果題目是「What Is the Best Taiwanese Food of All Times?」（最好吃的臺灣食物是？）主旨句可能就是「The best Taiwanese food is definitely bubble milk tea.」（最好吃的臺灣食物絕對是珍珠奶茶。）使用題目當中的問句，簡單的轉換成主旨句，是考試時常用的方法。

看到這裡很多人可能還是不知道如何下筆，那麼我們就來破解怎麼寫主旨句吧！如果以寫數學公式的概念來看，可以想成是：主旨句＝主題＋個人意見＋轉折詞＋原因（通常有 3 個）。

用「Do Journalists Have a Moral Obligation to the Display of Violent Images?」（記者是否應應該為展示暴力的圖片負起道德責任？）來寫主旨句，假如我支持這個論點，可以按照公式這樣破解：

(1) 主題

→ journalists（記者）

(2) 個人意見

→ have a moral obligation to the display of violent images
（應對展示暴力圖片負起道德責任）

(3) 中間加入解釋原因的從屬連接詞

→ because（因為）/ since（因為）/ as（因為）/ now that（既然、因為）

(4) 原因（為什麼記者應該負責？）

→ ① the display of violent images severely violates victims' privacy
（暴力影像的展示嚴重危害了受害者的隱私權）

② the exposure to violent images may decrease public's sensitivity to violent events
（暴露於暴力影像之中有可能會降低公眾對於暴力事件的敏感度）

③ journalists tend to play to the gallery in order to increase readership

（記者會為了增加讀者群而傾向於譁眾取寵）

那麼我們很快就可以得出這個句子：

例 Journalists <u>have a moral obligation</u> to the display of violent images because
主題　　　　個人觀點
the display of violent images severely violates victims' privacy, <u>the exposure</u>
原因一　　　　　　　　　　　　　　　　　　　　　原因二
to violent images may decrease public's sensitivity to violent events, and

journalists tend to play to the gallery in order to increase readership.
原因三
記者應對展示暴力圖片負起道德責任，因為暴力影像的展示嚴重危害了受害者的
隱私權，暴露於暴力影像之中有可能會降低公眾對於暴力事件的敏感度，並且記
者會為了增加讀者群而傾向於譁眾取寵。

如果觀察這整個句子，還可以觀察到前面提到的重點，那就是「不用你我他」。雖然撰寫文章需要你發表及闡述個人意見，但英文不會用「I」來撰寫主旨句，因為使用第三人稱在英文當中才會顯得有力及客觀。

只要按照這個公式，不論今天是別人出給你的題目，或者是你必須要自己想一個題目出來寫，都可以使用這個簡單的方法讓你快速寫出符合英文寫作要求的主旨句喔！

■ 寫主旨句的方法

當我們學會了簡單的主旨句公式，我們可以進到進階版的兩種寫法：

❶ 主旨句＝主題＋個人意見：原因（通常有 3 個）

前面示範的方式都是使用 Transition Words 來連接兩個句子，例如 because、since 等等，而另一個很方便可以改寫的方法就是使用冒號「:」，我們延續前面「記者應對展示暴力圖片負起道德責任」的例子：

Journalists have a moral obligation to the display of violent images <u>for the following reasons:</u> the display of violent images severely violates victims' privacy, the exposure to violent images may decrease public's sensitivity to violent events, and journalists tend to play to the gallery in order to increase readership.

基於以下的理由，記者應對展示暴力圖片負起道德責任：暴力影像的展示嚴重危害了受害者的隱私權，暴露於暴力影像之中有可能會降低公眾對於暴力事件的敏感度，並且記者會為了增加讀者群而傾向於譁眾取寵。

- 冒號的功用在於說明、舉例，讓讀者可以一看到冒號就注意到後面是重點所在。

❷ 主旨句＝原因（通常有 3 個）＋連接詞／轉折詞＋個人意見＋主題

　　這句進階版的句子在後面的部分需要花點心思寫，不過只要掌握這個公式，把原本的公式整句顛倒，將原因放在最前面當成強調的重點，再加個連接詞、be 動詞或是轉折詞，並將主題移到最後即可。

 The display of violent images severely violates victims' privacy, the exposure to violent images may decrease public's sensitivity to violent events, and journalists tend to play to the gallery in order to increase readership <u>are the reasons to explain why</u> journalists have a

　　　　　　　　　　　→ 連接理由與論點的片語

moral obligation to the display of violent images.

暴力影像的展示嚴重危害了受害者的隱私權，暴露於暴力影像之中有可能會降低公眾對於暴力事件的敏感度，並且記者會為了增加讀者群而傾向於譁眾取寵，以上這些理由能夠解釋為何記者應對展示暴力圖片負起道德責任。

- 關於轉折詞與連接詞，請參閱第 253 頁「善用轉折詞」的章節。

找到了寫主旨句的方法之後，我們來看一些例子。

> *2019 年的四月，在日本有名高齡 87 歲的老人開車撞死了一位媽媽和她的女兒，也因為這件事情，一向十分敬老的日本人開始熱烈討論高齡者是否能繼續持有駕照並開車呢？*

以下我們就用這三個 NG 的句子來看看如何寫一句好的主旨句。

❶ NG 一

 ✗ A controversial issue is whether elderly people should have driver's licenses.
一個有爭議性的議題就是老人是否應該持有駕照。

- 這句話「到底老人應不應該持有駕照呢？」陳述的是一個事實，而非闡述個人觀點；此外，本句中並沒有說明你個人支持或反對老人持有駕照。

❷ NG 二

 ✗ Some people think that elderly people should resit a driver's test in order to keep their driver's licenses.
有些人認為老人應該重考駕照的考試才能保留他們的駕照。

- 同樣的，這也是一句事實，而不是你個人觀點的陳述。句子當中的「some people」也無法代表你個人的觀點或意見，因此不是一句好的主旨句。

❸ NG 三

 ✗ In this paper, I will provide evidence about elderly people and discuss the issue of their driver's licenses.
在這篇文章中，我會提供關於老人的證據，以及探討關於他們駕照的議題。

- 前面提過，雖然主旨句是在闡述你個人的想法和意見，但不能用「I」開頭，直接寫出你的想法即可，不用大聲跟全部人宣告「這是我的觀點喔！」

綜合以上的 NG 點，我們要怎麼改善這句主旨句呢？

 ① <u>People over the age of 65</u> should be required ② <u>to resit a driver's test every year</u> to determine whether they are fit to hold a driver's license.

65 歲以上的老人應該每年重新考一次駕照，來檢視他們是否有資格擁有駕照。

PLUS!

- 從這句改寫過的主旨句，讀者能夠清楚知道：
  ① 所謂的 elderly people 是指年過 65 的族群，給了清楚的定義，讀者才能夠知道所謂的老人是哪個年齡層的人，並決定是否要支持你的觀點。
  ② 你身為作者，認為老人可以擁有駕照，但是必須符合「重新考照並且通過」這個前提才能開車上路。

我們再來看一個例子。

 科學家曾經做過研究，出生的順序會影響人格，因此有人在爭論出生順序如果是老大是否真的比較有領導能力？

以這個例子寫出的兩個 NG 主旨句會是：

❶ NG 一

 ✗ There are some similarities and differences between siblings.
手足之間有一些相同之處，也有相異之處。

PLUS!

- 你有沒有常常在聽人家講話時，內心浮現出「所以呢？ So what?」這樣的心情呢？這句話給讀者的就是這種感覺。因為大家都知道，即便是同一個工廠出產的產品也會有相同和相異之處，所以這句話帶給讀者的只是無限的問號。

❷ NG 二

 ✗ Birth order can affect one's personality.
出生的順序會影響一個人的人格。

PLUS!

- 這句話雖然看起來很有趣，讓讀者會想探討下去，但是後勁不夠。正當讀者內心覺得「出生順序居然會影響格人人格呀？」這個句子就沒了。所以比較好的做法是直接陳述到底出生順序影響了人們哪一部份的人格。

例 ✓ According to various research, children who are first in birth order usually demonstrate better leadership skills than their siblings.
根據各種不同的研究，相較於其他手足，出生順序是老大的人通常展現較佳的領導能力。

PLUS!
- 這句話既有研究的支持，也很清楚的說明主角是老大，而他們相較於其他手足，在領導能力方面是比較優異的。

4-3 主旨句的 Dos 和 Don'ts

Dos	Don'ts
✓ **一句話解決** 只能用一句話點出本篇要講的重點、要評論的主題，或是這篇你想陳述的觀點。	✗ **使用曖昧不清的語言** 例如使用「elderly people」這個名詞，讀者不清楚你文章當中老人的定義是幾歲的族群。
✓ **沒有你我他** 主旨句雖然是表達你個人觀點的句子，但是句中不能用代名詞，例如I、you、we、they、he、she、it。	✗ **不要提出聲明** 例如「In this paper, I will discuss three questions.」（在這篇文章當中，我會探討三個問題。）
✓ **使用精準的字** 例如前面的老人是否依然能擁有駕照並開車，要清楚定義出elderly people（老人）就是age over 65（年過65）。	✗ **提出太廣泛的主旨句** 例如「All insects are annoying.」（所有的昆蟲都很討人厭。）

我們學會了如何寫開頭、背景知識以及主旨句，我們現在已經知道如何組合第一段。最後在這章的結尾，我們來複習一下三種絕對要避免的 NG 第一段。

(1) 只為了填滿空白而塞滿字，卻不知所云的開頭

通常對於考試題目或是被指定的題目不知道如何下筆時，常常會因為慌張或擔心，即使內容看起來很虛，但還是拼命用一些不相干的內容湊字數。

> 例　✗　There are many kinds of healthy food you can choose for breakfast. For instance, fruits and vegetables are good choices. Every kind of healthy food brings you many benefits.
>
> *早餐有很多健康的食物可選擇，舉例來說，水果和蔬菜是一個好選擇。每種健康的食物都能帶給你很多好處。*

　　看完這段後你內心是不是會覺得「我知道早餐有很多健康的選擇，我也知道吃的健康一點會對我有好處，所以呢？」所以即便這段看似文字很多，但全都是沒辦法讓你的文章加分的贅字唷！

(2) 照抄應該不會怎麼樣吧？僥倖心態重述題目的第一段

　　以 107 年度學測題目為例，題目敘述寫著「排隊雖是生活中常有的經驗，但我們也常看到民眾因一時好奇或基於嘗鮮心理而出現大排長龍（form a long line）的現象，例如景點初次開放或媒體介紹某家美食餐廳後，人們便蜂擁而至。」有些考生既沒有換句話說，也沒有加自己的想法，直接翻譯題目：

> 例　✗　Lining up is a common experience in our daily lives, but we have also seen the public form a long line based on curiosity, or simply want to take part in the trend. For instance, we could see from the news that people crowded to a restaurant or a tourist attraction opening for the first time.
>
> *排隊雖是生活中常有的經驗，但我們也常看到民眾因一時好奇或跟風而大排長龍。例如，我們可以從新聞中看到景點初次開放或媒體介紹某家美食餐廳後，人們便蜂擁而至。*

　　很多人經常會覺得考官或批改作文的老師因為看了太多份的內容，應該不會注意到自己照抄題目或提示。事實上這種行為反而更讓你的文章「鶴立雞群」，因為考官即使再怎麼被各式文章轟炸而感到疲憊的情況下，照抄題目反而讓你在茫茫人海中更顯眼，而且是最容易被一秒發現的「偷吃步」做法。前面也提過，除非你真的走投無路了，否則務必要避免這種開頭喔！

(3) 長輩說教魂上身之文謅謅定義開頭

> 例 ✗ A key aspect of this issue which must not be overlooked is that the matter is of significant importance, and the issue deserves our full attention.
>
> *關於這個議題有一個不可忽略的關鍵,就是這個問題有極大的重要性,而這個議題值得我們的注意。*

　　雖然在文章當中,替讀者著想,適時的提供讀者關於一些專有名詞的定義是一種體貼也能提供詳盡資訊的做法,但是如果是想要賣弄學問,或是想要展現專業,給了別人看了只會更困惑的開頭,只會造成反效果。試想有人一開口跟你聊天就說:「根據辭海……」是不是讓人看了就想睡呢?

■ 主旨句的 Checklist

一段好的第一段應該要……	一句好的主旨句應該要……
☑一開頭就有一個Hook來勾住讀者注意	☑一至兩句言簡意賅,包含主題的聲明
☑提供足夠的背景知識給讀者	☑在這句當中可以觀察出接下來段落的走向
☑最後一句必須要有主旨句	☑是整篇文章的中心思想提供者
	☑主旨句只包含精準的文字與明確的論點

牛刀小試　你的句子有肌肉，還是弱雞一隻？

　　好的主旨句能讓讀者一看就能知道文章脈絡，反之，一句曖昧不明的主旨句會讓讀者充滿疑惑，無法瞭解文章接下來的走向，因此學會判斷強而有力，或有氣無力的主旨句能幫助我們在寫作時避免犯同樣的錯誤。

　　請在讀完以下句子後，在寫得好的主旨句前寫 S（Strong），較差的則寫上 W（Weak）。寫作前可以想想，強而有力的主旨句應該要包含主題和原因，有氣無力的主旨句則是寫得過於廣泛、狹隘或是籠統。

（　）1. People who have committed crimes are all bad people; therefore, they should be put in prison forever.
犯罪者都是壞人，因此，他們應該永遠被關進監獄裡。

（　）2. A lot of people will wonder where the waste we produce every day have gone.
很多人都想知道我們每天製造的廢棄物跑哪去了。

（　）3. Implementing bicycle rental policy benefits bike enthusiasts, pedestrians, and our environment.
腳踏車租用政策的實施有益於腳踏車狂熱者、行人，以及我們的環境。

（　）4. Technology has changed our lives in a good way.
科技以好的方式改變了我們的生活。

（　）5. McDonald's provides the best French fries in the world.
麥當勞提供了世界上最好吃的薯條。

參考答案

1. W → 並非所有人都覺得犯罪者都是壞人，也不是所有人都認同他們應該要被永遠監禁。
2. W → 並非所有人都想知道我們每天製造出來的垃圾跑到哪裡了。
3. S → 論點中明確指出這個政策的受益對象。
4. W → 並非所有人都覺得科技對我們帶來的影響都是好的。
5. W → 有些人不會認同麥當勞的薯條是世界上最好吃的。

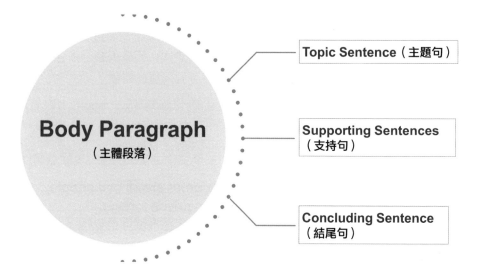

主體段落可以說是為了說明第一段的主旨句而生的，所有在主旨句中所提到的論點都必須在接下來的段落分點解釋清楚。我們可以把段落想像是一篇文章的縮影，每一段都包含了一個獨立的觀點，也因此每一個主體段落就跟第一段一樣，必須要從一句有趣而且可以吸引人的主題句開啟主題，接著由支持句提出能說服讀者的例子，最後總結這個段落，提供一個能順利承接到下一個段落的結尾句。

例如，以「Is Social Media Good for Our Society?」（社群媒體對我們的社會是否有益處？）這個主題來說，我們的主旨句寫的是：

> 例 Social media is good for our society because it allows people to make new friends and expand their social circle, helps senior citizens feel more connected to the society, and allows for quick and easy spread of public health information from the government.
> 社群媒體對我們社會有益，因為它允許人們結交新朋友，拓展社交圈，幫助年長者感到更與社會產生連繫，並使政府的公眾健康資訊快速且簡易地傳播。

因此，在主體段落的部分，我們就必須要來證明我們所說的論點是真的，是具有可信度的。我們在主體段落就應該要解釋：

例 Social media is good for our society because <u>it allows people to make new</u>
　　　　社群媒體如何讓人交新朋友及拓展社交圈？
<u>friends and expand their social circle</u>, <u>helps senior citizens feel more connected</u>
　　　　　　　　　　　　→ 社群媒體如何讓年長者覺得與社會更有連結？
<u>to the society</u>, and <u>allows for quick and easy spread of public health information</u>
　　　　　　　　　　→ 社群媒體如何讓公共健康更快速且容易傳播給大眾？
<u>from the government</u>.

5-1 掌握 131 結構

藉由 131 結構，除了可以幫助你同時掌握字數及句數，還可訓練你將想法控制在有限的句數內精準表達！

1		
一句由主旨句延伸的主題句 →	三句支持句 →	一句結尾句

1 句	Topic Sentence（主題句） • 主題句通常在主體段落的第一句，而且只能有一句。 • 簡單明瞭闡述第一段的主旨句所提出的其中一個主題、觀點或想法。
3 句	Supporting Sentences（支持句） • 用來驗證、說明、舉例、解釋你在主題句提到的觀點是可信的。 • 使用的證據可以是：原因、事實、引言、定義、例子、數據或分析。
1 句	Concluding Sentence（結尾句） • 改寫你的主題句（絕對不能照抄！） • 總結前面寫過的論點

段落的字數通常沒有限制，但落在 50 ～ 300 字最適合讀者閱讀，也不會因為寫得過長而失焦。

在第 15 頁的人體圖，我們有提醒需要在 Concluding Sentence 的第一個字加上 Transition Words（轉折詞）。但是也可以在 Concluding Sentence 之後再加一句 Transition Sentence（轉折句）。

主題句、支持句、結尾句的順序

我們延續前面的主題「Is Social Media Good for Our Society?」（社群媒體對我們的社會是否有益處？）來分辨段落中的主題句、支持句、以及結尾句。請在主題句前面標上 TS，支持句共有三句，請依序填上 SS1，SS2，SS3，結尾句標上 CS。

（　）1.　According to a survey, 30% of teenagers admitted that social media is the main distraction while they are writing assignments.
根據研究，有 30% 的青少年承認社群媒體是他們寫作業時最大的誘惑。

（　）2.　Students who are heavy social media users tend to have lower grades.
重度使用社群媒體的學生成績較低。

（　）3.　The other report indicated that students' scores have improved by 14 percent after the cell phones were banned in school.
其他研究顯示出在學校禁止手機之後，學生的成績提高了 14%。

（　）4.　If students spend too much time using social media, it will lead to lower academic performance.
如果學生花太多時間使用社群媒體，則會導致較低的學業成就。

（　）5.　Another research paper has shown that students who used social media while studying scored 30% lower on tests.
另一個研究報告顯示，當學生一邊學習一邊使用社群媒體，成績比其他人低 30%。

參考答案

1. **SS1**　2. **TS**　3. **SS3**　4. **CS**　5. **SS2**

Section 06 / 好的段落能給讀者這樣的感受

(1) 呼應主旨句

　　讀者已經在第一段的最後一句得知你提出的論點，因此心中會抱著期待接下來在主體段落看到你充分的解說，也因此你有什麼樣的好料就要趁熱端上桌，不要讓讀者覺得希望落空。舉例來說，假如你在「Is Social Media Good for Our Society?」（社群媒體對我們的社會是否有益處？）這個主題的主旨句主張了：

> 例　Social media is bad for our society because it lacks privacy, it entices people to waste time, and it harms people's productivity.
>
> *社群媒體對社會有害，因為它缺乏隱私，誘使人們浪費時間並損害人們的生產力。*

　　那麼接下來三段的關鍵句就要緊抓著這三個關鍵詞不放：privacy（隱私權）、time-wasting（浪費時間的）、productivity（生產力）

(2) 陳述觀點，但要記得點綴

　　吃喜宴的時候，即使是再平凡無奇的一道菜，都還是會取一個好聽又喜氣的名字增添氛圍，讓這道菜上桌前，食客可以在腦海中先勾勒出大概的模樣，上桌時則是靠香氣和口感來更加強化好吃的概念。

　　寫這三段的主體段落時，不能只是平鋪直述的在各段主題句說：

> **主體段落一——privacy（隱私權）**
>
> 例　✗ Using social media is bad for our society because people might share too much private information online.
>
> *使用社群媒體對我們的社會是不好的，因為人們可能會分享太多私人資訊在網路上。*

> **主體段落二——time-wasting（浪費時間的）**
>
> 例　✗ Social media is bad for our society because people will waste too much time using cell phone.
>
> *社群媒體對我們的社會是不好的，因為人們會浪費太多時間使用手機。*

> **主體段落三──productivity（生產力）**
>
> 例 ✗ People will spend too much time checking or using social media while working or studying, and this will distract them from the work they need to do.
>
> *人們會花太多時間在工作或讀書時查看或使用社群媒體，這樣一來會使他們分心於原本要做的工作。*

讀完這三句不需要作者說明你也知道的主題句，是不是讓你對整篇文章失去興趣呢？

(3) 一致性讓讀者讀起來更輕鬆

第一段的主旨句給了接續的段落陳述的中心理由，因此，每一段的開頭都應該要有一句清楚明瞭的主題句，而段落裡的內容只能圍繞著該段的主題句打轉，支持句要能說明為什麼這個論點是重要的，提供相關的細節與資訊，讓讀者能夠買單，認同你的說詞。

(4) 連貫性讓文章不卡卡

連貫性代表了文章的品質，一篇有連貫性的文章能讓讀者讀懂你想鋪陳的觀點和文章發展的邏輯。要讓每段都能連貫，最基本的就是段落中每一句都要跟主題句有關。

句與句之間產生連結之後，整篇文章就會有整體感，那麼你的基本分也就拿到了。有連貫性的段落還能讓讀者銜接先前提及的舊資訊，承接下面要陳述的新資訊，文章讀起來很流暢，沒有任何卡卡或遺漏的地方。

除了句子之間要讀起來沒有任何空隙之外，段落的連貫性也取決於其長度。假如某段文字過多，很容易會讓讀者失焦，而你在寫作過程中也很容易寫到忘記自己是否有聚焦到這段的核心概念上。

反之，假如在這段你就只能勉強擠出兩到三句，那麼你就必須花點心思下功夫，延伸這段的核心概念，或是提供相關的佐證說明。假如當下你真的想不到任何可以延伸寫作的內容，寧可把這段合併到另一段相關的段落上，或直接捨棄。

(5) 有邏輯的排列組合

一段表達清楚的對話能讓人們溝通無礙，同樣的道理，一段精心排

列的段落也能讓閱讀的人讀起來很輕鬆，不會產生誤解。第一段有了主旨句之後，我們其實對於各段該寫什麼內容已有基本的概念了，但是要如何清楚地呈現自己的觀點，則需要運用巧思去安排想法。

(6) 不提不相干的資訊

前面我們提過 131 結構，通常一個段落裡需要 3 句支持句才能完整陳述這些證據是如何支持你的論點，所以在思索要放哪些證據到段落裡時，求精不求多，每一句都需字字到位。

想想看，你是否曾經有跟某人吵架但卻一直不在對的頻率上，雞同鴨講很久，或是讀了別人一長串的訊息，但卻還是不知道對方到底要表達什麼呢？不管是對話或寫作，裡面如果含有太多不相干的資訊，都會削弱作者的觀點，也會讓讀者滿頭霧水。

也因此，能夠判斷什麼是「不該放進文章的細節」能讓文章讀起來沒有太多讓讀者困惑的廢話，也能讓直搗黃龍，讓讀者專心讀懂你要呈現的觀點。

寫作時，下筆前不妨用兩個問題來檢視自己即將提出的證據是否真的能支持你的觀點：

一、我提出的證據跟主題有直接關係嗎？還是讀者要自己聯想，而且還不一定想的到呢？

二、我提出證據後需要進一步的解釋理由嗎？我的理由有強到足以說明我的觀點嗎？

有時候我們會很扼腕，明明想到了很好的支持句，但似乎跟這個段落一點也不適合。這時候不如放棄這個支持句吧！寧可讓讀者在適合的段落讀到恰恰好能解釋主題句的證據，也不要讓讀者讀了整段塞滿很棒但卻感覺凌亂沒邏輯的想法。

■ 如何達成有連貫性的段落？

❶ 使用轉折詞（transition words）

使用轉折詞可以強調各種觀點之間的關係，或發展的先後順序，例如能表達順序的 first、second、third。使用轉折詞也能讓讀者了解你一系列連貫的想法，或是讓他們發現原本可能會漏讀或誤解的部

分，例如表示邏輯關係的 furthermore、in addition，或是 in fact。妥善運用轉折詞除了能為文章增添層次，也能讓讀者在閱讀時快速找到因果關係和文章重點。以下底線字的地方為轉折詞，可以讓各個想法自然地串連在一起，讓讀者讀起來更容易。

> 例 Use a variety of transition words within your paragraphs to create coherent paragraphs. <u>Similarly</u>, making good use of transition words in your writings helps your ideas flow naturally throughout the essay. In these ways, transition words serve as clues for reading. <u>However</u>, don't overuse the transition words, unless you are doing so for a specific effect. <u>In conclusion</u>, good transition words spice up your writing.
>
> *使用各式各樣的轉折詞在段落中可以創造連貫的段落。<u>同樣地</u>，在你的寫作當中妥善運用轉折詞可以幫助你的想法自然地流動於整篇文章中。透過這些方法，轉折詞可以當作閱讀文章的線索。<u>然而</u>，不要過度濫用轉折詞，除非這麼做是為了特定的效果。<u>總而言之</u>，好的轉折詞可以幫寫作增添可看性。*

❷ 重複關鍵詞／句

這個用法特別適用於有定義或是強調某個重要觀念的段落，此時重複關鍵詞或關鍵句能強化整體的連貫性，也能讓整體從上到下都一致，更能讓讀者理解你要陳述的定義和核心觀念是什麼。仔細觀察這句林肯的名言，粗體的部分和畫底線的部分反覆出現，除了可以加深讀者印象，也可以更自然流暢的串起核心資訊。

> 例 You can fool **all the people** <u>some of the time</u>, and **some of the people** <u>all the time</u>, but you cannot fool **all of the people** <u>all the time</u>.
> – Abraham Lincoln
>
> *你可以在一時矇騙所有人，也可以長時間矇騙一些人，但不可能在長時間矇騙所有的人。—— 林肯*

❸ 創造對等的結構

英文當中的 Parallel Structure（平行句式）利用 and、but、or 這類的對等連結詞（請詳閱第 174 頁「那些年，我們一起追的粉絲男孩們」）來簡化相同時態或詞性的句子。也因為對等連接詞只能連接相同類型的東西，例如字和字、片語和片語、子句和子句，所以當作

者使用這種句型時，讀者會被整齊劃一的簡化句型吸引住，也會覺得讀起來流暢。除此之外，使用這種句型能夠讓讀者在這一系列的句子中馬上找出每個核心觀念之間的關聯。

使用平行句式沒有什麼特別要訣，只需要細心的注意到在主要動詞後的每一個動詞都必須要是同樣的時態，或是同樣的詞性即可。

例 My father enjoys taking hikes, jogging, and surfing in his free time.

我父親喜歡在閒暇時健行、慢跑和衝浪。

例 After knowing I got an F on my exam, I went straight home, took a shower, and went to bed.

知道我考試被當之後，我立刻回家，洗個澡，直接上床睡覺。

例 My sister appears to be exhausted, worried, and upset.

我姊姊看起來筋疲力盡、擔憂且沮喪。

PLUS!
- 我們可以從劃底線的部分看出動詞的時態都有一致性（全部使用 Ving 或是過去式），或是詞性都是形容詞。

---

❹ 觀點、時態、數字要前後一致

這三點是很細微但是也是讓文章好讀的重要關鍵。以觀點來說，如果文章當中有時候用比較不客觀的「I」，但有時候卻又用比較客觀的代名詞「one」，讀者在閱讀時會錯亂到底這篇文章説話的人是誰，也會覺得通篇不一致。

時態的部分，一般來説，書寫故事時，因為是陳述已經發生的事情，所以我們習慣用過去式。如果是陳述事實，例如圖表，我們習慣用現在式。但是時態如果不一致，就會讓讀者產生誤解。舉例來説，在故事裡如果時態不一致，一下子從過去式轉換成現在式，主角就突然死而復生了。

數字的部分，很多人在前面提的明明是「a woman」，到了後面主詞卻變成「they」，讀者會被搞混到底是一位女士還是一群女士呢？以上這些沒有一致的部分會讓讀者覺得讀起來不順暢之外，也會讓你的論點變得難以理解。

During the performance, the audience sitting in front of me stood up and ~~drops~~ the popcorn.

→ During the performance, the audience sitting in front of me stood up and <u>dropped</u> the popcorn.

表演時，坐在我前面的觀眾站了起來並打翻爆米花。

6-1 段落時序的排列

　　正如同醫生針對每種病都得開不同的處方籤一樣，沒有一種排列組合是適用於所有文章的。下面舉出幾種常用的排列組合，我們可以依照文體，或是個人比較擅長的寫作方法選擇，最終目的就是在寫作時讓讀者讀起來覺得文章合乎邏輯。也因此，好的文章經常會交錯使用不同寫法，除了能客製化段落以配合自己的文章，也更能讓讀者隨著我們的編排了解我們的論點。

(1) Chronological Order（也稱作 Time Order）：依照時序

安排順序	依照時間先後、事件發生或人物出場的順序
適用文體	故事、敘述文、解釋事件的因果關係
使用原則	通常在描寫故事時，或是解釋事情的因果關係時，會按照時間的推移來陳述，也可以按照事件發生先後，或人物出現的次序來說故事。 如果沒有依照時間先後，或是依照事情發生的次序來陳述故事，讀者容易搞混故事如何發展或因果關係。 跟中文一樣，也有作者喜歡使用倒敘法，這種手法在電影、戲劇，或文學作品中很常見，但是在考試或有時間壓力下的寫作，建議要先在旁邊畫好時間軸，才不會自己先搞混故事發展過程。
常用轉折詞	• first 首先　• then 接著　• next 接著　• later 之後　• afterward 之後　• last 最後　• finally 終於　• in the end 最後　• the following day 隔天　• by noon 中午前　• as soon as 一……就……

Benjamin Franklin <u>was born in Boston, Massachusetts, on January 17,</u> <u>1706</u>. He attended Boston Latin School but did not graduate. Despite the fact that <u>his formal schooling ended when he was ten</u>, but he managed to continue his education through extensive reading. <u>At the age of 12,</u> Franklin became an apprentice to his older brother, James, a printer, who taught Ben the printing business. <u>When Franklin turned 15</u>, his brother founded the first truly independent newspaper in the colonies.

班傑明‧富蘭克林於 1706 年 1 月 17 日出生於波士頓的麻州。他曾就讀於波士頓拉丁學校，但沒有畢業。儘管他的正規教育在他十歲那年就結束了，但是他設法透過大量閱讀來延續他的教育。富蘭克林在 12 歲時成為他那印刷師傅的哥哥詹姆斯的學徒，他教導了富蘭克林關於印刷這門產業。富蘭克林 15 歲時，他的哥哥在殖民地建立了第一家真正獨立的報紙。

PLUS!

- 畫底線處從出生的地點與年份開始說起，接著陸續標記了事件發展的順序：10 歲開始自學、12 歲變成學徒，15 歲哥哥成立了報紙。時間順序的寫作法讓讀者可以漸進式的了解劇情、事件發展，同時也可以把最重要的事件放到最後，讓讀者隨著人物出現或情節演變而有所期待，就像俗語說的「The best is saved for the last.」（把最好的留到最後。）

(2) Climactic Order（也稱作 Order of Importance）：高潮事件先或後出現

邏輯安排	依照事件的重要性
適用文體	論述文、說明文、解釋事件的因果關係
使用原則	依照事件的重要性排列，從最不重要的開始依序排列，把最重要、最刺激的事件留到最後才說。反之，也可以在一開始就把最刺激的事件直接呈現，再逐步陳述事情發生的成因，讓讀者像偵探一樣往回推演。 一般來說，會使用依照事件重要性排列，通常是因為想要營造隨著事件發展而逐漸增加的刺激感，或是想要讓最能被強調的事件在最後被引爆。
常用轉折詞	• first of all 首先 • then 接著 • more importantly 更重要地 • finally 最後

> 例 Justin, not expecting a thing, walked into the pitch-dark room. He heard some strange whispers and sounds. "A thief!" He was on pins and needles and was looking for a stick as a weapon. Suddenly, the bright lights poured the room. All of his friends shouted "Surprise! Happy birthday to our favorite person in the world!"
>
> *賈斯汀在毫無預期會發生事情的狀況下走進了漆黑的房間。他聽到一些奇怪的耳語和聲音。「是小偷！」他如坐針氈地想要找尋一根棍子當作武器。突然間，亮光傾瀉了整個房間。他所有的朋友大喊「驚喜！祝我們在這個世界上最喜歡的人生日快樂！」*

(3) Spatial Order：依照空間次序

邏輯安排	依照空間安排
適用的文體	故事、看圖寫作
使用原則	根據空間的細節所做描述順序之安排。作者描述了可從該一位置所看到的景象、物體。描述時要有連貫性，才能讓讀者搭配著圖片閱讀時沒有跳來跳去的感覺，一般來說習慣從： 上→下 大→小 左→右 前→後 外→內 遠→近 這樣的描述順序能讓讀者讀起來更自然流暢。
常用的轉折詞	• above 之上 • below 之下 • nearby 靠近 • next to 隔壁 • across 對面、另一邊 • on the opposite side 對面、另一邊 • (just) to the left / right （就）在左邊／右邊 • a few meters behind 幾公尺之遠

The inside of my grandmother's refrigerator was a smelly, gooey mess, and it was overstuffed with food for all kinds of recipes and the leftovers from our Chinese New Years' feast. On the top shelf of the fridge were raw meat and frozen food, which had probably been jam-packed for ages. Next to these foods sat moldy fruits and vegetables. To the right of the rotten groceries sat the remains of fried rice and soup that had been served a month earlier. On the shelf below amassed quite a collection of spice bottles, jams, barbecue sauces, and tons of seasonings. None of the food in the fridge was edible, and the fridge had gotten spills and sticky stuff throughout it.

在我祖母冰箱的內部是又臭又糊的一團混亂，而且裡面塞滿了各種食譜煮出來的食物，以及過年大餐留下的剩菜剩飯。冰箱的最上層是生肉和冷凍食品，它們可能塞在裡面數個世紀了。這些食物旁邊是發霉的水果和蔬菜。在這些腐爛雜貨的右邊，有一個月前煮的炒飯和湯的剩菜。在下面層架上積聚了很多香料罐，果醬，燒烤醬和大量的調味料。冰箱裡的食物沒有可以食用的，而且整個冰箱裡都有溢出來和黏黏的東西。

PLUS!

- 畫底線處標記了空間由上而下的次序，讓讀者可以在腦海中想像作者的祖母冰箱當中混亂的場景。使用以空間次序為主的寫法可以讓讀者意象化文字所要呈現的畫面，並讓讀者產生身歷其境的參與感。

前面提到了以有邏輯的方式呈現想法是很重要的，如此一來讀者才能理解你的文章，讀起來才不會有阻礙，下面這個練習請你試著重新排列組合被打亂的句子，並在前面加上編號。

（　）1. When going on a trip, you need to allocate your budget effectively for hotels, transportation, and food.
當你去旅行時，你需要有效地分配你的預算給下榻的旅館、交通費，以及吃飯的費用。

（　）2. Even though you may want to cram everything in your schedule, do not forget that there are only 24 hours in a day!
就算你很想要塞滿行程，也別忘了一天只有 24 小時。

（　）3. Planning your trip in advance will save you plenty of money and makes you laid-back during the whole trip.
提前規畫你的旅程可以為你省下不少錢，還能使你在旅程中從容不迫。

（　）4. Hotels and transportation are extremely expensive during the high season.
飯店和交通的費用在旺季時是極度昂貴的。

（　）5. On the other hand, you need to schedule your time well so that you will be able to enjoy sightseeing and to do a variety of activities.
另一方面，你必須要妥善規畫你的時間，如此一來你才能享受觀光以及做各式各樣的活動。

（　）6. It is essential to plan your holiday trip in advance.
提前規畫你的假期旅遊是必要的。

參考答案

1. 2　　2. 5　　3. 6　　4. 4　　5. 3　　6. 1

Section 01　Topic Sentence（主題句）：主體段落的主題句怎麼寫？

　　我們可以把 Topic Sentence（主題句）想成是電影的預告片，或是報紙的頭條，讀者一看就知道重點是什麼，因為主題句的作用在於點出這一個段落的核心想法，並能支持 Thesis Statement（主旨句）中的觀點。

　　所以當你不知道如何寫主題句時，只要記住一個重點，寫出來的句子要讓讀者一看到，就能大概猜到這段要陳述的概念是什麼。只要主題句能讓讀者秒懂這段大意，剩餘的部分寫起來就易如反掌了。以作者的角度來看，主題句除了能指引這段發展的方向，讓讀者知道這段的重點，此外，有很大一個作用其實也能讓作者在寫作時不會扯到別的地方而失去方向。

7-1　寫主題句的要點

　　前面提到主題句的作用在於讓讀者一眼就能了解這段要講的核心概念是什麼。接下來請看以下這三句主題句：

(1) 主題句一

> 例　Effective communication is a complex process that requires good skills.
> 有效的溝通是一個需要良好技巧的複雜過程。

(2) 主題句二

> 例　Getting excellent education and attending various extracurricular activities are the keys to success in finding a job.
> 進入一所好學校以及參加各種不同的課外活動是成功找到工作的關鍵。

(3) 主題句三

> 例　Global warming is related to humans' activities.
> 全球暖化與人類的活動有關。

　　以上這三句主題句，有顏色字的部分即是所要表達的核心概念。從這些句子中，我們第一眼就能知道該篇文章的作者在某個段落想表達的主題是什麼，心中也會有個大概的想法猜測作者接下來可能會提出哪些觀點來說服我們。

一句清楚明瞭的主題句不但能幫助讀者秒懂主題，也能讓他們有耐心閱讀接下來你要提出來的佐證和相關資訊。

■ 主題句怎麼寫？

以下整理了五個寫主題句的要點以及寫得比較好與比較差的例句：

❶ 主題句提供的內容或資訊必須夠完整才不會讓讀者一頭霧水。

 ✗ Some types of preventive measures should be taken by the government.

政府應該要採取某些形式的預防性措施。

> **PLUS!**
> • 和下面的例句相比，這句主題句用字曖昧不清，讀者必須花時間去找「某些形式的預防性措施」到底是什麼樣的措施。

 ✓ To curb the spread of COVID-19, our government has implemented rigorous hygiene and social distancing measures.

為了要抑制新冠肺炎的傳播，我們的政府採取了嚴格的衛生和社交距離措施。

❷ 如果不是需要讀者深思的議題，就不要吊人胃口使用問句當作主題句，直接點出重點會比營造神秘感還更能讓讀者有興趣讀下去。

 ✗ Should schools provide free lunch for their students?

學校應該提供學生免費午餐嗎？

> **PLUS!**
> • 一般人都會覺得如果能為家裡省錢，學校本來就應該提供免費的午餐，所以看不出到底有什麼理由不提供，也會失去閱讀這段的興趣。

 ✓ Since school lunch is critical to students' health and well-being, it is schools' responsibility to provide nutritionally balanced free lunches to students.

既然學校午餐對於學生的健康和福祉至關重要，學校有責任提供學生營養均衡的免費午餐。

❸ 寫主題句時不使用「I think...」（我覺得）或「In my opinion...」（我個人認為），因為寫這篇文章本來就是在陳述你的觀點，所以不須多此一舉。

✗ I think that it is important for everyone to carry their own eco cups when they go to tea shop.

我覺得大家去手搖飲料店時自備環保杯是很重要的。

PLUS!
- 大家都知道帶環保杯是重要的，讀者會覺得為什麼你要多此一舉陳述一個大家都知道的概念呢？

例 ✓ In order to reduce the use of disposable cups, people should carry eco cups to tea shop.

為了要減少一次性餐具的使用，人們去手搖飲料店時應該要帶環保杯。

❹ 主題句必須能讓讀者秒懂這段要陳述的概念。

✗ History is only a record of past events; we should watch historical dramas, such as *Legend of Concubine Zhen Huan*.

歷史只是記錄過去發生的事件，所以我們應該要看歷史劇，像是後宮甄環傳。

PLUS!
- 讀者看了這句之後沒辦法了解為什麼比起讀歷史，看歷史劇還更能幫助我們了解過去發生的事情，也不知道前後兩句的關聯在哪裡。

例 ✓ High-quality historical dramas that play with accuracy give us a deeper understanding of the past events than do the historical record.

相較於歷史記載，高品質且具有正確性的歷史劇能讓我們對過去的事件有更深的了解。

❺ 主題句必須清楚明確才能幫助讀者預測這段接下來的走向。

 ✗ The subway fare hike makes public transportation ride an unsatisfactory experience in Chile.

捷運票價的漲價使得在智利搭乘大眾交通運輸工具是一個令人不滿意的經驗。

PLUS!
- 讀者沒有辦法理解為何捷運票價漲價會讓搭乘大眾交通運輸變成一個不愉快的經驗，因為兩件事情沒有直接關聯，因此讀者很難去預測這段到底走向為何。

例 ✓ Incapable of providing subway fare at a reasonable price, the Chile public transport system is receiving its lowest satisfaction ratings.

智利的大眾交通運輸系統無法提供合理的捷運票價，因此得到了至今最低的滿意度。

7-2 主題句的位置

　　因為讀者通常習慣從段落的第一、二句來判斷這段的重點為何，或是判斷作者的個人觀點是什麼，所以一般我們習慣把主題句放在第一句，如此一來可以讓讀者一眼就看出我們要講的重點是什麼。

　　但有時也會有例外，下列情況，我們會在主題句前面再加上一句，作用可能是：

(1) 連結前一段主題

(2) 為了提供背景資訊

(3) 營造轉折

例 Given the evidence of animal agriculture's impact on our planet, veganism seems like a practical and feasible environmentally responsible option for consumers. <u>However, not all plant-based products have</u> → 主題句 <u>smaller environmental footprints when compared to meat products.</u> In some cases, small-scale farming is more sustainable than large-scale plant-based food production.

考慮到畜牧業對地球的影響，素食主義對消費者來說似乎是實際可行的對環境負責的選擇。然而，並非所有植物性製品的生態足跡都比肉製品小。在某些情況下，小規模農業比大規模植物為主的食品產業更具永續性。

在這個例子中，我們可以看到第一句濃縮了這位作者在先前所說的觀點：因為前面提供的證據能清楚解釋畜牧業（animal agriculture）會對我們的地球所帶來的影響，所以一個很實際又可行的方法似乎就是吃素。接著後方畫底線處提供真正的重點，也就是主題句，提出了讓讀者會期待的爆點：接下來要講的東西將會違背先前的論點。

如果對基礎的主題句寫法已經很熟悉，或是希望每一段的主題句都能有所變化，不妨試試不同的寫作方法。如此一來可以用有創意的寫法在每一段都鋪陳驚喜，也能夠營造轉折的懸疑感以及增加論點的強度。假如對自己的寫作能力還是很沒有信心，只要把持住一個要點：簡潔有力即可，最簡單的方法就是把主題句放在每段的首句。

7-3 寫主題句的方法

嚴格說起來，寫主題句其實並沒有一定非得要怎麼樣的公式，但是再好的方法重複太多次的話，讀起來也會很拗口又無趣。能夠在一篇文章中採取不同的方法寫作，不但可以讓文章有變化，也可以讓讀者讀起來興致盎然。

一般來說主題句都只會有一句，但是有時候配合文章需求，也能夠增減一兩句來增添內容的完整性。第一句若是做出聲明，第二句的功用通常是引起讀者反思，或進一步詳細說明聲明的內容。

假使主題是「Should the Death Penalty Be Allowed?」（我們是否應該允許死刑的存在？）如果我支持應該要有死刑，在寫第一段最後一句的主旨句（Thesis Statement）時，我提出三個原因說明：

例 Death penalty should be allowed because ① it would serve as a reminder that when someone committed a crime, they have to pay a high price. ② Second, a death penalty will certainly guarantee the killer will never kill again while a life imprisonment does not. ③ Lastly, execution is a cost-effective solution because keeping prisoners behind bars will cost the government a huge amount of money.

死刑應該要被允許，因為它可以當作是一種提醒，提醒人們如果犯罪的話，他們必須付出昂貴代價。對犯人處以死刑的話絕對能確保兇手絕對不會再犯，然而終生監禁卻不盡然。最後，死刑是一個有成本效益的解決方法，因為把人關起來將會花上政府一大筆錢。

因此在接下來的三段 Body Paragraph 中，我們的任務就是要在這三段的第一句分別解釋我們提出的原因。我們可以這樣寫：

Body Paragraph 1 的主題句
例 Most people are afraid of losing their life; therefore, the death penalty is the best discouragement when it comes to preventing people from carrying out the worst crimes.

多數人都害怕失去性命，因此，當提到預防人們犯下糟糕的罪刑時，死刑是最好的阻遏。

Body Paragraph 2 的主題句
例 It deters prisoners who are already serving sentences from committing crimes repetitively.

死刑可以威懾那些已經在服刑的罪犯不要再重複犯罪。

Body Paragraph 3 的主題句
例 If people take into account the cost of the layers of appeals, death penalty is less costly than putting a murderer in jail for life.

假如人們把層層上訴的成本納入考量，比起把一個人終生監禁，死刑相較之下花費較少。

牛刀小試　幫段落起個頭吧！

以下擷取了某個文章的一部分中間段落，請在讀完文字後，試寫出符合這個段落的 Topic Sentence（主題句）。

_____ Topic Sentence _____. For example, learning a new language can improve brain function. Researchers found that teens proficient in two languages performed better on attention tests and had better concentration than those who spoke only one language. Another fascinating reason for becoming a multilingual is that it makes people smarter. According to a study, students who study foreign languages tend to score better on standardized tests than their monolingual peers, particularly in math, reading, and vocabulary. Consequently, there is no doubt that people should invest their time in learning a foreign language.

_____ 主題句 _____。例如，學習一門新語言可以提高大腦性能。研究者們發現，相較於只會說一種語言的青少年，精通兩種語言的青少年在專注力的測試表現更好。成為多語者另一個迷人之處在於它使人們變得更聰明。根據一項研究，相較於那些單語者的同儕，學習外語的學生在標準化測驗的成績有表現得比較好的傾向，尤其是數學、閱讀、以及字彙。因此，毫無疑問地，人們應該投資自己的時間在學習外語上。

參考答案

提供兩個不同的主題句供讀者參考。

1. There are many reasons why people should spend time learning foreign languages.
   有很多理由可以說明為何人們應該花時間學習外語。
2. Learning a foreign language offers several mental benefits.
   學習一門外語提供了一些心理層面的好處。

Supporting Sentences（支持句）：答應別人的，就要做到！

　　如果你在第一段的主旨句中答應你的讀者要給他們牛排吃，那麼在主體段落就必須詳加説明這塊牛排是什麼等級的牛排，口味如何，為什麼好吃，讓讀者的眼睛能大飽口福。接下來要講的就是如何運用 Supporting Sentences（支持句）讓你的讀者覺得他們走進這家餐廳沒有被騙錢，的確吃到了跟廣告主打一樣好吃的餐點。因此寫支持句時，我們就必須要把細節解釋清楚。

8-1 加點調味料，讓你的舉例更有風味：支持句的種類

　　以下提供六種支持句的寫法供大家參考。

(1) 明確的理由：給予讀者解釋為什麼你的觀點是有可信度的。

> 例　The low retirement rate is contributing to the current lack of available job vacancies.
> 低退休率導致現在職缺的不足。

(2) 能被證明的事實：使用可以被證明為真的事件或陳述，加強讀者的信賴感。

> 例　Many young couples in Taiwan now rely on their parents to support them financially because their jobs weren't paying enough for them to live independently.
> 現在許多臺灣的年輕夫妻仰賴他們的父母在經濟上支援他們，因為他們的工作不足以讓他們獨立生活。

(3) 數字會説話：數字能讓讀者對數量的多寡、事情的重要性有概念。

> 例　The UN's work agency warns that hundreds of millions of people around the globe could be jobless due to the impact of COVID-19.
> 聯合國的就業機構警告，全球數以百萬計的人很有可能因為新冠肺炎的影響而失業。

(4) 清楚明瞭的例子：運用明確的舉例支持提出的論點。

> ⑨ America is a multicultural nation, and home to a wide variety of ethnic groups. People around the globe have immigrated here and brought with them their home cultures, which are adopted by Americans and became part of American life. One example is a wide range of foods that Americans enjoy. Sushi from Japan, fried rice from China, and tacos from Mexico can be seen on Americans' dining tables.
>
> *美國是一個多文化的國家，也是各式各樣不同的種族的歸屬。全球各地的人帶著他們的家鄉文化移民至此，這些文化被接納並成為美國人生活的一部份。舉例來說，美國人有非常多元的食物選項，日本來的壽司，中國的炒飯，以及墨西哥捲餅，都可以在美國人的餐桌上看到。*

(5) 引言：有些大家熟知的引言放到文章當中，比解釋千言萬語都還來的有用。

> ⑨ With more than half a billion people watching on television, Neil Armstrong climbed down the ladder and proclaimed: "That's one small step for a man, one giant leap for mankind."
>
> *伴隨著數百萬人在電視機前的注視，尼爾‧阿姆斯壯下了階梯並宣布：「我的一小步，是人類的一大步。」*

(6) 動人小故事：與這個主題或事件相關的簡單小故事。

> ⑨ Last year, he was laid off at the age of fifty. Nowhere to go, he walked along the river to contemplate his future.
>
> *去年，他以五十歲的高齡被資遣。無處可去，他沿著河岸走，思索著他的人生。*

8-2　如何在支持句中呈現證據

　　前面我們提到可以提供證據來讓讀者覺得我們的寫作很有道理，現在則是要實際操作如何在支持句當中呈現證據，使讀者閱讀起來有邏輯，最後被我們的觀點收服。

呈現證據的方式可以有很多種，我們通常會使用文字說明，例如提出數據、舉例、引言等等。但有時候如果因為文章的需要，例如描述趨勢或是數據，也可以使用圖表來解說。

(1) Quotations（引言）

我們都聽過各種名言佳句，當對方的言論字字珠璣時，我們不但會被打動，也會希望下次在談論類似的議題時能夠使用這些當初也打動過我們的文字，來加強自己說話的力道。使用引言時，因為是直接一字不漏使用原作者的話，所以必須要考量在何種情況下要直接全部引用原作者的文字。

■ 何時使用引言最好？

❶ 假如你沒辦法想到比原作者的原文更好的方法來陳述，不要懷疑，直接引用吧！

❷ 假如原作者的文字當中包含了原創的想法，或是能協助你解釋某個特定的字，與其花時間想出新詞，不如直接借用作者的話吧！

❸ 如果這位作者本身對於某個議題有很強烈的立場，讀者一讀就會知道你在說什麼，那麼也可以直接引用。比如說近日為了環保議題而抗議的瑞典女孩——桑柏格（Greta Thunberg），假如她的所言更能引起讀者的情感，那麼不妨直接引用對方的話吧！

(2) Paraphrase（換句話說）

有的時候在使用我們心儀的作品或名言佳句時，解釋的過程中，考量到讀者可能對原作品不熟悉，所以我們既需要透過文字傳遞原文之美，但又不能遺漏原文中的重要細節或證據。此外，在避免一字不漏抄襲原文的情況下，我們必須經過消化和理解後，以自己的方式重新詮釋原作者的話。但是要注意的是，改變原文順序，或是替換幾個字不是換句話說喔！為了能夠妥善換句話說，避免被說是剽竊，最好的方式就是先把原文擱置在一旁，思考一下，假如現場有個觀眾，你要如何把消化後的內容解釋給對方聽呢？一定都是用自己理解後的方式來重新說明，而不是背出作者原汁原味的作品吧！

而換句話說又跟寫大綱（summary）有很大的不同，因為換句話說只需要專注在某個特定的重點，通常長度比較短，只會是一個短句或是

小段落而已，但是寫大綱必須在短篇幅裡詳盡涵蓋原文所有意思。

■ 何時使用換句話說最好？

❶ 假如你想使用某個作者的觀點或立場，但是你認為對方的措辭不夠強烈或是特別到能引起讀者興趣，那麼不妨自己換句話說。

❷ 假如你只需要原作者某個特定的觀點來支持你的論點，或是需要批判對方的論點，那麼就只要把需要的部分換句話說即可。

❸ 假如原作者是某個領域的巨擘，或是提出的論點至今仍被奉為圭臬，那麼可以把原作者的論述換句話說，再放在自己的文章當中。

(3) 數據與圖表

有時候使用數據和圖表反而比文字來的有力，也可以是論點很好的佐證；但也因為數據與圖表可以隨著作者偏好的角度詮釋，所以提出這些資料當證據時，必須把這些輔助的資料和自己的論點連結，才能讓讀者理解這些數字或圖表和論點之間的關係。

我們以新冠肺炎（COVID-19）的死亡數來說，下方是以該國居住者中人口的死亡數比較圖，從圖中我們可以清楚的看出每個國家死亡人數以及嚴重程度，比起單純用文字描述來的震撼許多。

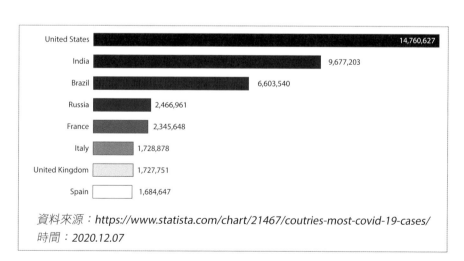

United States	14,760,627
India	9,677,203
Brazil	6,603,540
Russia	2,466,961
France	2,345,648
Italy	1,728,878
United Kingdom	1,727,751
Spain	1,684,647

資料來源：*https://www.statista.com/chart/21467/coutries-most-covid-19-cases/*
時間：*2020.12.07*

辨別哪句才是支持句

能分辨哪些是與主題相關且有效的支持句是很重要的，因為這樣可以避免加入不必要的支持句讓讀者混淆，也能在寫作時加入最切中主題的支持句來說服讀者。

有了一句清楚的主題句之後，我們會使用各種證據：舉例、事實、數據或描述等方法來增強我們的論點，也因此所有的支持句都必須只切合主題。請你從 A、B、C、D 四個選項中，選出無法支持主題句的支持句。

1. Teens should not be allowed to take driver's license test until they reach the age of 18.
    青少年在滿 18 歲前不應該被允許考駕照。

    (A) Teens can act on impulse sometimes.
        青少年有時候會衝動行事。

    (B) Teens need their parents to tell them how to drive safely.
        青少年需要他們的父母來告訴他們如何安全駕駛。

    (C) Teenagers' brains are not fully developed and mature enough to handle the decision making required to drive a car safely.
        青少年的腦部還沒有發育成熟到可以應付安全開車時必須做出的決策。

    (D) According to a research, teens are at the highest accident risk of any age group.
        根據一項研究，青少年在任何年齡層都是發生意外最高的風險族群。

2. Smoking should be banned.
    抽菸應被禁止。

    (A) We should put smokers into rehabilitation to help them find other interests.
        我們應該把抽菸者送去勒戒以便幫助他們找到其他興趣。

    (B) Smoking causes both short-term and long-term health concerns.
        抽菸導致短期以及長期的健康隱憂。

(C) Cigarettes have toxins that promote cancer which will have both physical consequences on the user and impact on social welfare.

香菸具有會造成癌症的毒素，且會同時對抽菸者的生理健康以及社會福祉造成影響。

(D) The money spent on making and buying cigarettes could be used for something more important, such as social welfare or education.

花在製造以及購買香菸的費用可以被用在更重要的用途，例如社會福利或者教育。

3. The breathtaking scenery, fusion of culture, and diverse cuisine make Taiwan a place worth visiting.

美到令人震懾的風景，文化的融合，以及多樣化的料理使得臺灣是一個值得造訪的地方。

(A) Taiwan was once a colony of Japan from 1895 to 1945.

臺灣在 1895 年到 1945 年期間曾經是日本的殖民地。

(B) Because many different ethnic groups reside on this island, Taiwan is culturally diverse with all kinds of religion, languages, lifestyles, and especially, food.

因為很多不同族群的人居住在這塊土地上，臺灣具有文化多樣性，有著各式各樣的宗教、語言、生活型態，特別是食物。

(C) Taiwan's landscapes are quite diverse, and she has mountains, hills, plains, basins, islets, valleys, and shores.

臺灣的地形滿多元的，有山脈、山丘、平原、盆地、小島、山谷以及海岸。

(D) Different ethnic groups, such as indigenous tribes, Dutch, Spanish, Japanese, and Han Chinese, have successively populated Taiwan, creating a wide variety of culture and local customs.

各式各樣族群的人，例如原住民部落、荷蘭人、西班牙人、日本人以及漢人，都陸續居住於臺灣，並創造了各式各樣的文化以及當地的習俗。

參考答案

1. (B)　　2. (A)　　3. (A)

你提出的，是事實，還是個人意見？

　　我們這一輩子都在說服別人，從小拜託父母答應我們買玩具；求學時跟老師爭辯正課時間能否去打球，或分數可否多給幾分；長大之後在職場上要跟客戶提案或與他人達成協議等等。舉例說服別人這件事情，我們是不陌生的。

　　但很多人在寫段落時，經常碰到一個問題，就是批改的考官或是讀者常有疑問：「這明明就是你主觀的個人想法，怎麼會拿來當證據佐證呢？」而身為作者的你不明白的是「這明明就是事實，怎麼會是個人想法呢？」我們先來看看所謂的事實和個人意見究竟是什麼：

比較	事實	個人意見
定義	• 實際上有發生的事情。 • 能被證實的事件 • 有真假之分。 • 只會包含資訊，並不會讓讀者知道作者對於某件事的信念或是想法為何。 例如： 現在在下雨。 →只要看看外面就能知道是不是真的在下雨，能被證實真假。	• 表達你關於對某件事情的態度，可能是做出評價、闡述個人觀點或下結論。 • 無法被判斷真假的意見。 例如： 等等會下雨。 →這是你個人自己判斷會下雨，旁人無法分辨是不是真的會發生。
能否被證實	是	否
能否被辯論	否 （事實不須辯論，例如：地球是圓的）	是 （個人意見帶有主觀意識，常常因人而異，因此可被辯論。例如：麻辣鴨血比臭豆腐更好吃。）
是否會改變	否	是，因人而異
使用的文字	沒有疑義的文字	帶有個人色彩的文字
影響力	有，能說服並改變他人想法	沒辦法說服或改變他人想法

關鍵字	• The report <u>confirms</u>… 這份報告證實了…… • Scientists have recently <u>discovered</u>… 科學家近日發現…… • According to <u>the results of the study</u>… 根據研究結果顯示…… • The investigation <u>demonstrated</u>… 調查結果顯示……	• She <u>claimed</u> that… 她聲稱…… • It is <u>my view</u> that… 我個人認為…… • The report <u>argues</u> that… 這份報告表明…… • Many researchers <u>suspect</u> that… 很多研究者懷疑……

在舉例時，不能使用個人意見，一方面不客觀，一方面讀者也會覺得「你哪位呀？為什麼我要買你的帳呢？」但是有種情況是特例，那就是如果這個「個人意見」是出自於名人、知名的專家學者或機構。因為他們的話語是基於多年的研究成果或經驗累積，如果引用具有專業背景的人士所說過的話，就能大幅提升文章中舉例的可信度。

不過為了要能夠讓整個段落讀起來更流暢，引用這個知名人士的話語時，必須要和你的論點作出連結。以免寫了一句看似很厲害的名人話語，但卻要讓讀者花時間去找出和你觀點的連結在哪裡。例如在探討社群媒體對人類的影響時，突然沒頭沒腦地說「就如同賈伯斯說過的，求知若渴。」讀者即使很認可賈伯斯的這句話，也無法了解到底引用這句名人所說的話和你的主題有什麼關係。

如果還是不清楚舉例時，自己舉的例子是客觀的事實，或是個人意見，那麼可以這樣思考：帶有評斷字眼的句子就是個人意見，無論這句陳述的是否為科學研究或是可被證實真偽的事件。

> 例
> Many tasty vegetarian cuisines are available in Taiwan, even in the most remote areas.
> *許多好吃的素食料理在臺灣隨處可見，就算在最偏遠的地區也一樣。*

這句當中評斷的字眼就是「tasty」，雖然臺灣確實到處都可以找的到素食餐廳，但好不好吃是很主觀的感受。

如何避免在寫作時使用個人想法當作例子？

　　個人想法表達了作者本身的情感、對事情的態度或是個人信念，無法被評判真假或好壞，純粹只是對某個特定主題的情感抒發。也因為這是個人對某件事情或議題的觀點，因此不適合拿來當具有公信力的證據説服讀者。

　　我們該如何避免使用主觀的看法來當作舉例呢？首先要先能辨別主觀的句子長什麼樣子，通常含有個人意見的句子會是：

(1) 關於具有爭議性的問題發表你個人的感想或立場

 Death penalty should not be allowed in Taiwan because I think it is wrong to take other people's lives.
死刑在臺灣不該被允許，因為奪走別人的性命是錯的。

PLUS!
- 在這個句子中摻雜了個人意見「我認為是錯的」，因此不夠客觀。

(2) 預測關於未來可能會發生的事情

 People will most likely buy new houses in the next few months because banks have lower the mortgage interest rate.
因為銀行已經降低了房貸的利率，所以人們在接下來的幾個月可能會買新房子。

PLUS!
- 即使銀行降低了房貸的利率，人們也不一定會在接下來幾個月買新房子。

(3) 對於人、事、物的評價

 Red cars look more elegant than black cars.
紅色轎車看起來比黑色轎車更優雅。

PLUS!
- 青菜蘿蔔各有所好，每個人喜歡的顏色不同，因此是主觀意識。

　　在舉例時，除了避免以上主觀的看法之外，我們也要留意我們的用字遣詞過於絕對，除了讓人讀起來不夠有說服力，也會顯得過於武斷或自我。寫作時應該要避免的字詞如下：

有偏見的字眼	• bad 壞的 • worse 糟的 • worst 最糟 • good 好的	• better 較好 • best 最好 • worthwhile 值得的 • worthless 沒有價值的
限定詞	• a / an 一個 • the 這個 • this 這個 • that 那個 • these 這些 • those 那些 • all 所有 • both 兩者都 • half 一半 • either 也 • neither 也不 • each 每一 • every 每一 • my 我的 • your 你的 • his 他的 • her 她的 • its 它的 • our 我們的 • their 他們的 • a few 一些 • a little 一些 • much 許多	• many 許多 • a lot of 很多 • most 最 • some 一些 • any 任一 • enough 夠 • such 這樣的 • what 什麼 • rather 寧可 • quite 很 • always 總是 • likely 很可能 • never 從不 • might 可能 • seem 看起來 • possibly 可能地 • probably 可能地 • should 應該 • very 非常 • too 太 • really 很 • sort of ⋯⋯的

• 何謂限定詞？限定詞放在名詞前面，有修飾名詞的功能，限定詞可以用來表示它後面的名詞是否具有特定性，或是只是一般的名詞，也可以用來表示數量有多少。但是好的文章當中不會有太多的限定詞，試想一篇有很多 very、really、possibly 的文章，讀起來是不是過於廣泛又無聊呢？

（一）為什麼要區分事實與個人意見？有這麼重要嗎？

　　一篇好的作文裡如果能有事實佐證，除了說明了作者的寫作功力，也能展現作者本身的批判性思考能力以及分析的技巧，當然也就能說服讀者你的內容有可信度。但也因為事實和個人意見在寫作時很難分辨，所以身為作者的你在下筆前，必須仔細的思考什麼是你個人的價值觀，而什麼又是可以被分辨真假的事實。

　　以下我們來做個練習，下列的句子中，有些是事實，有些則是個人意見，請分別在相對應的欄位打勾。如果是個人意見的話，請圈選出句子中代表個人意見的部分。

作者舉的例子是事實或是個人意見？	Fact	Opinion
1.　Eating junk food is not so bad if you only eat it once a week. 如果一周只吃一次垃圾食物，其實也沒那麼糟。		
2.　Copying your classmate's assignments is wrong. 抄襲你同班同學的功課是錯誤的。		
3.　It was a great season for the Golden State Warriors. 對於金州勇士隊來說，這是一個絕佳的賽季。		
4.　Purchasing a brand new car is a terrible waste of money. 購買一部新車真的很浪費錢。		
5.　Larger animals tend to live longer than smaller ones, but for dogs, it works the other way around. 大型動物通常活得比小型動物久，但對於狗來說則是相反的。		

6. According to a survey, more and more Japanese men are deciding to take parental leave.
   根據一項調查，愈來愈多日本男性決定要放育嬰假。

7. Consuming food or drinks on the MRT train in Taiwan is against the law.
   在臺灣的捷運車廂內飲食是違法的。

8. *Animal Crossing: New Horizons*, a game developed by Nintendo, is the bestselling video game at present.
   《集合啦！動物森友會》是一款任天堂開發的遊戲，是目前為止販售的最好的電玩遊戲。

9. It is worth sacrificing some individual privacy to protect our country from terrorism.
   為了保護國家免於恐怖主義的威脅，犧牲一些個人隱私是值得的。

10. A hospital is not the best place for a cancer patient to end their life.
    對於癌症患者來說，醫院並不是一個結束他們生命的最佳場所。

11. Diabetes, stroke, and infection are three common reasons that older people get admitted to the hospital.
    糖尿病、中風以及感染是三個導致年紀較長的人住院的常見原因。

12. It is wrong to drive faster than the posted speed limit in a school zone when children are at school. 當學生在學校上學時，在校園附近開車的時速比規定的速限還快是不對的。		
13. J.K. Rowling, the author of Harry Potter, the best-written fantasy novel, gave a speech at Harvard University in 2014. J. K. 羅琳是哈利波特的作者，也是寫得最好的奇幻小說的作者，2014 年時在哈佛發表了一場演講。		
14. The yellow vest strike in France, now into its seventeenth month, has caused hardships on the small business owners, their families, and the rest of the nation. 法國的黃背心運動已進入到第 17 個月，造成小企業及其家人，還有整個國家的困境。		

參考答案

1. **Opinion**；吃垃圾食物這件事到底是好是壞是基於個人看法。
2. **Opinion**；抄襲作業是錯的這件事情並非每個人都認同，所以屬於個人意見。
3. **Opinion**；對某些球迷來說可能會覺得是最佳的打球季節，但有些人可能不認同。
4. **Opinion**；有些人不覺得買新車很浪費錢。
5. **Fact**；大型動物與狗的壽命是科學研究已證實的事情。
6. **Fact**；數據是經常被拿來佐證事實的典型例子。
7. **Fact**；這是一條明文規定的法律。
8. **Fact**；銷售數據是查的到的事實。
9. **Opinion**；並不是每個人都覺得犧牲個人隱私是值得的。
10. **Opinion**；好與不好屬於個人自由心證。
11. **Fact**；本句用了醫學研究佐證。
12. **Opinion**；雖然超速了，但是對與不對依然屬於個人意見。
13. **Opinion**；J. K. 羅琳雖然是作者，也的確於 2014 年時在哈佛發表了一場演講，但這本小說是不是寫得最好的奇幻小說則是見仁見智。
14. **Opinion**；有些人或許不認同這是困境。

牛刀小試 （二）利用事實寫出你的支持句

請在讀完主題句後，試寫出 3 句能夠佐證主題句的支持句。

1.

Topic Sentence:
Dogs are humans' best friends, and they are the best option for pets for three reasons.
狗是人類最好的朋友，牠們是寵物的最佳選擇是基於以下三點。

Supporting Sentence 1

_____

Supporting Sentence 2

_____

Supporting Sentence 3

_____

2.

Topic Sentence:
Regular exercise is critical in all age groups in maintaining good health.
規律運動對於所有年齡層的人維持健康來說都是非常重要的。

Supporting Sentence 1

_____

Supporting Sentence 2

_____

Supporting Sentence 3

1.
Supporting Sentence 1（支持句一）→
Dogs teach us what selflessness is. They give out pure love, asking nothing in return.
狗能教我們什麼是無私。牠們給予我們最純潔的愛，並且不要求任何回報。
Supporting Sentence 2（支持句二）→
Dogs mirror their owners' personalities, and human beings can use the information to better understand themselves.
狗能投射出主人的個性，而主人可以運用這些資訊來更了解自己。
Supporting Sentence 3（支持句三）→
As reported in different studies, there are many health benefits of living with a dog, such as a longer life span and lower risk of cardiovascular disease.
在多個不同的研究裡都有指出，與狗一起生活有許多健康的好處，例如更長的壽命與降低心血管疾病的風險。

2.
Supporting Sentence 1（支持句一）→
Exercise can help prevent excess weight gain and help maintain weight loss.
運動可以幫助預防體重過度增加，也可以幫助維持減輕體重。
Supporting Sentence 2（支持句二）→
Exercise stimulates brain chemicals that may leave us feeling happier, more relaxed, and less anxious.
運動可以刺激腦部產生的化學物質，這些物質可以讓我們感到更開心、更放鬆以及不那麼焦慮。
Supporting Sentence 3（支持句三）→
Physical activity can also help us connect with family and friends in a fun social setting, and we can even make new friends when exercising.
身體的活動也可以幫助我們與家人朋友在有趣的社會情境下產生連結，而我們更可以在運動時結交新朋友。

Section 10 | Conclusion（結論）：收筆勿草率！

多數人在文章開頭時絞盡腦汁，花很多心思鋪陳第一段，並加入了許多有利的證據在主體段落的支持句說明文章，但卻往往忽略了結論。也因為前面花太多時間與精力，導致寫到結論時，時間不夠而草草結束，有些人甚至還會寫出「Thank you very much.」這種令人摸不著頭緒的結論。一開始的開頭如大江大海般澎拜，讓讀者覺得滿心期待，但讀到最後卻感覺收尾像漏水般滴滴答答。

很多人說下筆難，從一開始就已經沒有靈感了，更何況要寫到最後一段。但也有一派人認為前面寫得洋洋灑灑不是問題，結論反而才是最難的，因為所有精力和想法都已經在前面陳述完畢了。不管是哪種情況，即使前面寫的再好，如果在結論的地方沒有辦法讓讀者有始終如一的感覺，還是會讓整體的觀點可信度下降。

正如同一段好的開頭可以讓讀者對這篇文章產生興趣，好的結論也能達到同樣的效果，不但能讓讀者讀完後覺得有始有終，還能讓讀者覺得讀完整篇文章受到啟發，或者產生新的思維。我們總不希望讀者看完整篇文章後覺得被浪費了時間，或者覺得「我看完了，然後呢？所以作者要表達什麼？」英文寫作不是連續劇，不能讓讀者期待下周同一時間還會出現續集。

結論的最終目標是回應到主題，也就是你提出的觀點。因此，在書寫各式文類結論時，可以依照以下的大方向來著手。

10-1 莫忘初衷：重申主旨句！

假如已經寫到了文章的尾段，你沒時間或考試就變金魚腦，請秒選以下這個常用方法：重申主旨句！

Step 1	Step 2	Step 3
重申主題	換句話說主旨句，接著提及主題句的內容，並總結先前說過的論點。	使用 therefore、thus、consequently 等轉折詞產生結論

來到文章的尾聲，結論的作用當然就是總結這整篇文章的核心概念。這個時候身為作者的你可能會想：「那不就跟第一段提出本篇的大意很雷同嗎？」沒錯，結論通常就是把第一段所說過的話換句話說，換湯不換藥，重新再包裝一次你第一段陳述過的論點。很多人會在結論狂塞前面忘記說的論點或例句，這都是不對的。

　　假設主題是「Should Animals Be Used for Commercial Testing?」（動物是否應被用於商業產品的試驗？），而我是持反對的立場，在第一段的主旨句說了反對的三個原因：

例 Animals should not be used for commercial testing because ① it is cruel and inhumane to conduct experiments on animals; in addition, ② new alternative testing methods now exist that can replace the need for animals, and that ③ animals are different from human beings in many ways that research on animals often makes no sense.
動物不應被用來做商業產品的實驗，因為在動物身上做實驗既殘忍又不人道。此外，目前已有新的替代方案存在，可替代對動物的需求，而且動物在許多方面都跟人不一樣，因此在動物身上做實驗是沒有道理的。

　　那麼在結論重新包裝的方式可以寫成：

例 ① The cruel and inhumane way of treating animals, ② new testing alternatives, and ③ the huge anatomic, metabolic, and cellular differences between animals and humans are three major reasons that people should not conduct commercial product testing on animals.
殘忍及不人道的對待、新的測試替代方案，以及動物與人之間在解剖、新陳代謝、細胞上的巨大差異，是人類不應在動物身上進行商業產品測試的三個主要原因。

　　注意到了嗎？其實這句改寫的方法只是把前後順序對調，以及稍微更換了字詞的使用。

　　結論的寫法還有很多種，通常會使用以下幾種方法讓讀者能再次聚焦整篇的重點：

(1) 為已提供的資訊或想法做總結：這種方法就像是在為讀者作重點整理，避免讀者讀到後面已經忘了前面你寫的東西，這個時候就是你把讀者思緒拉回來的最好時機。

> **例** Apparently, children and teenagers are not mature enough to handle the responsibility of a smart phone, and they should be strictly monitored to ensure their safety and mental health.
>
> *很明顯地，孩童和青少年還不夠成熟到足以應付使用手機的責任，而且他們應該被嚴格的監控以確保他們的安全及心理健康。*

(2) 學伊索寓言說一個小故事：大家都喜歡聽故事，就像伊索寓言的故事一樣，最後都會給個課題或是警世小提醒。如果是能夠以小故事達到傳達某個訊息的效果，卻又不希望太過嚴肅像在說教的話，不妨考慮用個吸引人又具有寓意的故事吧！

> **例** My attitudes have been greatly shaped after reading this study, as I have finally realized the practice of consuming meat has a negative impact on our health and Mother Nature. Going vegan has improved my health conditions, and this is a decision that I am grateful for making this year.
>
> *在讀完這個研究後，我的態度就大幅地被影響了，因為我終於了解到吃肉的作法對於我們的健康和大自然都有負面的影響。開始吃素這件事情改善了我的健康狀況，而我深深感激自己今年做了這個決定。*

(3) 使用名言佳句、提問或提供建議：有些文章可以在結論放一句名言佳句，或是提出問題，引起讀者反思和激盪想法，或是提供對未來有所助益的建議。例如：

> **例** As the saying goes, "Don't judge a book by its appearance." Judging people based on one's appearance is extremely shallow and lacks critical thinking ability.
>
> *俗話說：「不要以貌取人。」根據別人的外表評斷他人是極度膚淺而且缺乏批判性思考的事情。*

最後，寫結論的大忌就是絕對不要介紹或描述任何前面段落中未曾提過的論點，只要專注在總結已經講過的事情即可。

結論常用字		
• accordingly 因此 • after all 畢竟 • all in all 總之 • as a result 結果 • as a result of 因為 • as noted 如上所述 • as shown 如圖所示 • at last 最後 • briefly 簡而言之 • consequently 總之 • to summarize 總結 • ultimately 最後 • without a doubt 無疑	• finally 最後 • for this reason 　由於這個原因 • for these reasons 　因為這些理由 • hence 因此 • in a word 總之 • in a nutshell 　概括地說 • in short 簡言之 • in sum 總之 • in summary 總之 • in total 總之	• on the whole 　整體來說 • therefore 因此 • thus 因此 • to conclude 最後 • to sum up 總之 • in brief 簡言之 • in conclusion 總之 • in other words 　換句話說

■ 善用 Essay Checklist，寫作各要素都能兼顧

☑ 我寫作的語氣是否有配合主題？（故事可以用第一人稱，比較輕鬆；論述文則是需要使用第三人稱，需要公平客觀）

☑ 文章當中，我提出的例子是事實還是個人意見？這篇文章可以寫入個人經歷嗎？

☑ 我在文章當中是否有適時加入轉折詞讓句子讀起來更通順？

☑ 我有沒有加入太多不必要的細節，或是使用重複的例子來支持我的論點？

☑ 我有沒有使用引言？有的話，我有正確的引述嗎？

☑ 文章當中是否有錯字？使用錯的片語或單字？

　　前面提到可以在結論重申原有的主旨句或提及主題句，請參考範例，並根據以下題目的提示寫出結論。

範例

主題句：One factor that is said to contribute to global warming is deforestation.
據說其中一個導致全球暖化的因素是森林的砍伐。

結論：In a word, scientists warn that the massive clearing of trees around the world is just one factor that contributes to global warming.
簡言之，科學家警告全球各地大量砍伐樹木只是全球暖化的因素之一。

1.　主題句：Basic vocational training should be taught in school.
　　　　　學校應該教授基本職業訓練。

　　結論：_____

2.　主題句：Good stress can actually motivate us to reach our goals.
　　　　　好的壓力實際上可以激勵我們達成目標。

　　結論：_____

3.　主題句：Just as people have their own individual personalities, so do animals.
　　　　　就像人類也都有自己獨特的個性一樣，動物也不例外。

　　結論：_____

4.　主題句：The lack of affordable housing in major cities is just one of the factors to the increase in poverty.
　　　　　在大城市裡，缺乏可負擔的起的住宅的只是加劇貧困的其中一個因素。

　　結論：_____

5. 主題句：It is important that one listens to, and shows compassion, to be a good friend to someone.
要能成為別人的好朋友，傾聽與展現同理心是必要的。

結論：＿＿＿＿＿＿＿＿＿＿＿＿＿＿＿＿＿＿＿＿＿＿＿＿＿

6. 主題句：Schools should start later in the morning for K-12 students because there are several obvious benefits, such as better academic performance and improved sleeping schedules.
對於幼稚園到高三的學生來說，學校應該晚點上課，因為有一些顯而易見的好處，例如更好的學業成績以及改善的睡眠習慣。

結論：＿＿＿＿＿＿＿＿＿＿＿＿＿＿＿＿＿＿＿＿＿＿＿＿＿

參考答案

1. To get students prepared for the workplace, vocational training is a must-teach in schools.
要讓學生做好職場準備，學校就要把職業訓練作為必修。
2. If we make good use of stress, it can be beneficial to help us realize our dreams.
如果我們善用壓力，將有益於幫助我們實現夢想。
3. In order to understand animal behaviors, we need to keep in mind that they all have their unique traits, just like human beings.
為了理解動物行為，我們必須謹記，就像人類一樣，牠們也有獨一無二的特性。
4. Poverty rate increases because housing becomes far more expensive and less affordable to residents in major cities.
對於大城市的居民來說，貧窮率的增加源自於房子變得比以前還要更貴且更難負擔的起。
5. Friendship requires wholehearted listening and compassion.
友情需要全心全意的傾聽和同理心。
6. Although it seems a bit troublesome for working parents to take their children to school later on in the morning, it's far more important that students could achieve better academic performance than for the drop-off to be convenient for the parents on their way to work.
雖然對有上班的家長來說，早上晚一點送孩子去學校看起來有點麻煩，但比起家長上班途中順道送孩子下車的方便性來說，學生能達成更好的學業成績是更加重要的。

Section 11 善用PEEL及OREO公式，讓你寫作無往不利

寫作時儘管大家的想法可能大同小異，但是真正能讓你脫穎而出的是整齊有邏輯的架構。前面我們已經用人體圖教過了基本的段落結構，但是在主體段落部分，除了可以用中規中矩的架構之外，也可以使用國外非常流行的 PEEL 和 OREO 公式。

11-1 PEEL 剝皮公式

Peel 這個字本身是動詞，剝皮的意思，我們可以想成是把段落層層剝皮並拆解成四個部分：

我們以主題為「Should Driving Age Be Lowered from 18 to 16?」（駕駛年齡是否應由 18 歲降低至 16 歲？）為例，假使我反對這個論點，並在第一段的最後一句主旨句（Thesis Statement）提出這三個論點（詳見編號①、②、③）：

> 例 Driving age should not be lowered from 18 to 16 because ① emotional maturity increases as people age, and thus people are less likely to drive without giving in to peer pressure. In addition, ② removing the option to drive will decrease teenagers' obesity rate because teenagers are required to commute on foot or by public transportation. ③ Lastly, according to various studies, teenagers are involved in more fatal car crashes than any other age group.
>
> *駕駛的年齡不應該由 18 歲降低至 16 歲，因為隨著年紀增長，情緒的成熟度也會提高，也因此人們比較不可能因為屈服於同儕壓力而駕駛。除此之外，假如我們把駕駛這個選項剔除，青少年的肥胖率會降低，因為他們必須藉由走路或是搭乘大眾運輸工具通勤。最後，根據許多研究指出，相較於其他年齡層，青少年涉及更多的致命的車禍。*

利用 PEEL 寫作法，以第一個論點（情緒的成熟度）而言，我們可以在主體段落這樣寫作：

■ PEEL 寫作法

❶ Point 論點

① 論點就是先前提及的主題句，能讓讀者一眼看出本段核心重點。

② 每段論點只能有一個，而且是本段最核心、最需要被分享的概念。

③ 只能用精準的字，不讓讀者花心思猜你的想法。

④ 簡短扼要，只包含最重要的資訊，不要為了湊字數而塞一堆不相關的資訊。

論點句的起手式可以這樣寫：

- To begin with… 首先

- It is suggested that… 建議

- Many people believe that… 很多人相信

- One argument is that… 有一個論點是

 To begin with, driving age should not be lowered from 18 to 16 because teenagers' brains are not fully developed and matured, both in the neurological and psychological aspects.

首先，駕駛年紀不應從 18 歲降低至 16 歲，因為青少年的大腦在神經系統及心理層面都還沒有發育完全或成熟。

PLUS!
- 劃底線的第二句其實就只是換句話說並再次陳述主旨句已經提過的觀點。

❷ Evidence 證據

① 提出論點後，給予證據是為了支持你的觀點，讀者才能被說服。

② 證據可以是事實、數據、名人或是有公信力的機構所說過的話。引用時，如果沒有換句話說，就必須使用引號，才不會變成剽竊。

③ 必須和本段主題有直接關係，不要讓讀者還需要自行聯想這個證據和論點之間的連結。

提出證據的句子可以這樣開頭：

- ＿＿＿＿＿＿ said… 說過

- The text states / describes… 文中陳述／描述了

- For example / instance, … 舉例來說

- The evidence shows / demonstrates… 證據顯示／指出

- A study / paper / research shows that… 一項研究指出

- According to…, it shows that… 根據……指出

 Science has proved that the human brain tends to be underdeveloped during their teenage years. That is one of the reasons why teenagers tend to be impulsive, emotionally unstable, and find it hard to predict the consequences of their own actions.

科學已經證實了人類的大腦在青少年時期發育比較不完善，這也是為什麼青少年有衝動、情緒不穩定的傾向，並且覺得預測自己的行為是困難的。

 PLUS!
- 底線處的文字能讓讀者明白後面提出的內容為證據。

❸ Explain 解說

① 用自己的想法詳細解釋、分析、闡述、詮釋，或評估前面提供的證據如何證明論點是對的、有可信度的，以及為何你提供的證據與本段核心主題有關係。

② 提供解釋的目的是要把證據和論點串起來。

③ 提供讀者發人深省的資訊，拉攏讀者到你這一邊。

解說的句子可以這樣開頭：

- This shows / reveals / illustrates… 這顯示了

- This is because… 這是因為

- This means… 這意味著

- This highlights the difference between A and B.
  這凸顯了A和B之間的差異。

- This supports the argument by … 藉由……支持這個論點

- It appears / seems that… 看起來似乎

 <u>Because</u> all of these abovementioned factors play a vital role in the driving process, lowering the driving age would lead to more traffic accidents caused by teenage drivers.

也因為上述所提及的因素在開車的過程中扮演極為重要的腳色，降低駕駛的年齡將會導致年輕人造成更多的交通事故。

❹ Link 連結

① 加強自己的觀點，加深讀者的印象。寫這句時，可以仔細想想「我希望讀者讀完我這段時，記得我提出的什麼觀點？」

② 是連結到下一段的重要橋梁。

  解說的句子可以這樣寫：

- To sum up / In a nutshell,… 簡要地說／概括地說

- In summary, the evidence showed… 整體來看，證據顯示了

- Therefore / As a result / Consequently, it is evident / obvious that… 因此，很顯然是

- The most important evidence showed that… 最重要的證據顯示了

 <u>In a nutshell</u>, since teenagers' brains are still not fully developed, this can lead to a situation in which young drivers engage in risky driving. By giving teenagers more time to be fully matured, the chances that teenage drivers might take it too far and lose control over their cars decrease dramatically.

概括地說，因為青少年的頭腦還沒有發育完全，這件事可能會導致年輕的駕駛涉入風險駕駛的情況。藉由給予青少年更多時間充分成熟，會大幅降低青少年有時候開車太過頭或是失控的機率。

（一）利用 PEEL 拆解段落

　　請利用 PEEL 公式來解析以下的段落，在論點（Point）的部分寫上 P，證據（Evidence）寫上 Ev，解釋（Explain）的部分寫上 Ex，最後在連結（Link）的部分寫上 L。

（　）1. People need to think about all the responsibilities thoroughly before making the commitment.
在做出這個承諾前，人們必須要仔細想想所有需要負擔的責任。

（　）2. Keeping a pet requires commitment and investment of time and money, and hence it is not a decision which should be considered lightly.
養一隻寵物需要承諾，也需要投資時間和金錢，因此這不是一個應該輕易下的決定。

（　）3. Owners must provide their pets with proper and sufficient food and water, cages need to be cleaned out on a regular basis, and pets need annual checkups.
飼主必須提供他們寵物適當及足夠的食物和水，籠子必須要定期清理，而且寵物也需要年度健康檢查。

（　）4. Consequently, there are many factors which need to be taken into account before making such a decision.
因此，在做這樣的決定之前，有許多因素是需要被考慮的。

參考答案

1. **Ex**　　2. **P**　　3. **Ev**　　4. **L**

OREO 餅乾公式

OREO 這個好吃的餅乾從巧克力餅乾開始帶入整體味道,接著會吃到甜滋滋的內餡,我們可以想成段落的寫作法可以像是夾心的方式一樣:

前面第 85 頁練習 PEEL 時,我們以「Should Driving Age Be Lowered from 18 to 16?」(駕駛年齡是否應由 18 歲降低至 16 歲?)為主題,並在第一段的最後一句主旨句(Thesis Statement)提出了第二個論點:

> 例 In addition, ② removing the option to drive will decrease teenagers' obesity rate because teenagers are required to commute on foot or by public transportation.
>
> 除此之外,假如我們把駕駛這個選項剔除,青少年的肥胖率會降低,因為他們必須藉由走路或是搭乘大眾運輸工具通勤。

我們可以利用 OREO 公式這樣寫中間的主體段落:

■ OREO 寫作公式

❶ Opinion 意見

在段落一開頭告訴讀者對於主題你的意見或想法,或是對於題目所提出的問題給予答案。

> 例 If the driving age were lowered from its current limits, then it would discourage teenage drivers to be physically active when they commute.
>
> 假如駕駛年齡從現今的限制下降,那麼這將會使青少年駕駛無法在通勤時運動到。

❷ Reason 理由

用充分且有邏輯的理由來支持你所說的意見或想法。

> 例 Since the option to drive behind the wheels was not available, teenagers have no choice but to walk, cycle, and take public transportations.
>
> *既然開車的選項已不再可行，青少年們沒有其他選擇，只好走路、騎單車或是搭乘大眾交通運輸。*

❸ Evidence 證據

利用數據、引言、故事、研究等方法，依照適合論點的方式提供讀者能夠輔佐你的論點的例子。

> 例 According to different studies published in *The American Journal of Preventive Medicine*, active commuting, such as walking, cycling, or taking public transit to school, helps students lose body fat and weight.
>
> *根據刊登在美國預防醫學期刊的不同研究，活躍的通勤方式，例如走路、騎單車或搭乘大眾交通運輸去學校，可以幫助學生減脂及減重。*

❹ Opinion 論點

以換句話說的方式重申先前講過的意見，並為這段論點完成結論。

> 例 Being a car commuter can encourage obesity by eliminating physical activity. A teen's activity level plays an important role in determining his weight as many teenagers in the modern era spend a lot of time being physically inactive. As a result, teenagers should not be allowed to drive for the sake of their health and wellness.
>
> *成為以汽車代步者，而非以走路或騎腳踏車通勤的方式，將會因為減少體能活動而導致肥胖。一個青少年的活動程度，在決定其體重有多重之中扮演了重要的角色，因為很多現代的青少年大多的時間都是不活動筋骨的。因此，為了他們的健康，青少年不應被允許駕駛。*

（二）利用 OREO 拆解段落

請利用 OREO 公式來判斷以下的敘述哪句是 Opinion（放開頭）、Reason（理由）、Evidence（證據），以及 Opinion（放結論）。

（ ）1. Self-confidence is an important personal quality.
自信是一個很重要的人格特質。

（ ）2. For these reasons, it is crucial for parents and educators to assist our children to build self-confidence in their daily life and at school.
因為以上的原因，父母和教育人員必須要協助孩子們在日常生活和學校裡建立自信心。

（ ）3. In addition, self-confidence has been linked to success in the workplace, and happiness in people's personal lives.
除此之外，自信也與一個人在工作場合的成功與否，以及個人生活的幸福感有關。

（ ）4. When one fully believes in oneself, it will obviously impact a person's attitude towards life and the way he or she presents himself or herself to others.
當一個人全然的相信自己時，很明顯地會影響他的人生觀，也會影響到他如何在他人面前呈現自己。

（ ）5. Various psychological studies have shown that self-confidence makes people more attractive to others.
許多心理學的研究指出自信使人們在他人眼中更具吸引力。

（ ）6. When people are faced with uncertainties, a lack of self-confidence will hold us back.
當人們遇到不確定的事物時，缺乏自信會使我們退縮。

參考答案

1. **Opinion**（放開頭）　　2. **Opinion**（放結論）　　3. **Explain**
4. **Explain**　　5. **Evidence**　　6. **Explain**

讀者會因為我們的說服和佐證
而認可我們所提出的論點！

Chapter

02

論述文與
說明文

> "Don't raise your voice. Improve your argument." — Desmond Tutu, social rights activist
>
> 「不要只有提高音量,要改善你的論點。」——德斯蒙德‧杜圖(社運人士)

　　我們都有與人爭執或是想說服別人接受自己觀點的時候,寫論述文也是類似的情形:作者先選擇某一方的觀點,接著就是得使出渾身解數利用各種觀點與證據贏得讀者的芳心。讀者會因為我們的說服和佐證而認可我們所提出的論點,也因此在運用證據讓讀者買單時,要思考讀者會對什麼樣的證據感興趣,或是要加入什麼樣的例子才能打動讀者。

　　一篇好的論述文不會讓讀者覺得被迫接受觀點,而是無形中被作者說服而認同作者所言。作者若能在文章當中展現對讀者偏見的了解,並且能針對雙方論點精闢剖析解說,那麼不但能證明作者的論點是對的,更可以打臉對方的論點是比較弱的、不正確的。

　　說明文的目的主要是在教導或告知讀者某個主題,通常會用來解釋某件事情是如何進行、如何做某事、流程的步驟,或是為什麼某件事情的本質是如此。讀者最終會透過你的文章,對於你說明的主題有更進一步的認識。

Section
01 Persuasive Writing(論述文):
當溫良恭儉讓不再是美德

　　Persuasive Writing(論述文)需要作者提供論點說明他們支持或反對某件事情,並以此說服讀者他們的觀點。

對於華人來說,論述文相對而言是比較困難的文體,因為我們從小被教育要合群,沉默是金,最好是不要對事情發表太多看法,也因此在這方面的訓練比較少。在不習慣表達自己的情況下,若是碰到需要陳述自己意見時,我們可以運用一些技巧與策略來增加自己的說服力。

以下我們先討論寫作論述文的流程,接著來看看我們可以運用那些小撇步讓自己的論點更具有說服力。

1-1 論述文的樣貌

論述文可以細分成以下幾個段落:

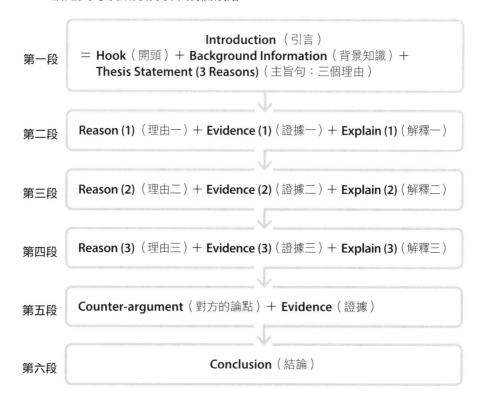

第一段　**Introduction**(引言)
＝ **Hook**(開頭)＋ **Background Information**(背景知識)＋
Thesis Statement (3 Reasons)(主旨句:三個理由)

第二段　**Reason (1)**(理由一)＋ **Evidence (1)**(證據一)＋ **Explain (1)**(解釋一)

第三段　**Reason (2)**(理由二)＋ **Evidence (2)**(證據二)＋ **Explain (2)**(解釋二)

第四段　**Reason (3)**(理由三)＋ **Evidence (3)**(證據三)＋ **Explain (3)**(解釋三)

第五段　**Counter-argument**(對方的論點)＋ **Evidence**(證據)

第六段　**Conclusion**(結論)

1-2 論點的構思步驟

論述文的段落結構一定要環環相扣不能彼此矛盾。以下說明上表這5個步驟的構思技巧。

(1) Step 1：選定主題

一般來說，考試都會給予論述文的題目，所以我們很少有選定題目的機會。但如果碰上國外大學申請，或是工作上需要寫一篇論述文，若是毫無頭緒該如何選定一個好下筆的題目，可以先從幾個比較具有爭議性的題目開始著手思考。大原則是挑出可以讓你想出至少兩至三個強烈且有衝突的觀點，當你能對某個主題產生愈多正反雙方的觀點，那麼在寫作時也更能與你的題目產生火花，同時也能展現批判性思考的能力來說服你的讀者。以下提供挑選題目的原則：

❶ 選擇你有興趣的題目，而不是討好批閱者的題目

在選擇題目時，學生會希望寫出教授「可能」會喜歡的題目，但如此一來題目的選擇變得很受限，而且在寫你沒有興趣的主題時，看起來就很沒創意又沒辦法展現你的優勢。

若你對於「Should Marijuana Be Legalized for Medicinal Purposes?（醫療用大麻製劑是否應合法化？）」很有興趣，即使這個主題看似會觸碰到禁忌，但在你對這個主題有熱情的情況下，是不是更能發揮你的想法呢？

❷ 選擇你能夠全面分析正反方論點的題目

　　很多人看到某個特定的主題，會因為自己的立場而想出很多支持或是反對的論點，但是沒有考慮到另一方的論點可能會有哪些。因此，如果選擇第一時間浮現的對自己有利的論點的主題，很有可能讓讀者覺得你避重就輕，對主題認識不夠透徹，只是為了支持而支持。

　　因此下筆前，不妨簡單畫出一張表格，分析利弊之後再動筆。特別是在這種給予時間思考後再書寫的文章，更是需要展現自己有分析事物一體兩面的功力。我們以這個主題「Should Marijuana Be Legalized for Medicinal Purposes?」（醫療用大麻製劑是否應合法化？）來分析其優缺點。

Pros（優點）	Cons（缺點）
① According to various studies, marijuana can relieve certain types of chronic pain. 根據許多研究，大麻可以緩解某些種類的慢性疼痛。 ② Marijuana has been used for centuries as a natural medicine. 大麻被用來當作天然的藥物已經有好幾個世紀了。 ③ Marijuana is safer than some other medications, such as opioids, prescribed to treat the same symptoms. 大麻相較於其他用來治療同樣症狀的處方藥物，例如鴉片，安全許多。	① Marijuana carries a risk of abuse and addiction. 大麻具有會讓人濫用和上癮的風險。 ② Frequent marijuana use can seriously affect your short-term memory and impair your cognitive ability. 經常性的使用大麻會嚴重影響短期記憶及傷害認知能力。 ③ Smoking marijuana can seriously damage the lung tissue. 吸大麻會嚴重傷害肺部組織。

　　可以從上表看出優缺點的數目平均，也就是不管你選擇哪一方辯護，都可以提出對方的論點攻擊。一方面可以顯得自己對主題有夠深入的了解，一方面也可以舉對自己最有利的論點出來論述。

❸ 選擇可以辯論的爭議性題目，不要寫答案不證自明的題目

　　爭議性的題目通常能引起讀者興趣，因為透過閱讀作者的論述，對比讀者心中的立場，可以產生激盪與火花。但是不證自明，答案就已經很清楚的題目，不適合成為可以寫的議題。例如「Should Children Be Left At Home Alone?」（是否應該讓孩童在沒有家長陪同下獨自在家？），或者是「Are Coal and Oil the Main Sources of Energy?」（煤炭和石油是主要的能源來源嗎？），前者不適合是因為法律已經有規定孩童不能獨自在家，後者是事實，這兩個都是不適合成為探討的議題。

　　我們來看幾個例子：

Alcohol（酒精）	
✔ 適合當題目	✘ 不適合當題目
Drinking is bad for our heath. 喝酒對我們的身體不好。 → bad是帶有個人意見的字，是可以拿出來辯論的題目。	Alcohol cannot be sold to people under the age of 20 in Taiwan. *在臺灣，不能販售酒精給20歲以下的人。* → 這是法律規定的事實，不需拿來辯論。
Public Transport（大眾交通）	
✔ 適合當題目	✘ 不適合當題目
Taking public transport is more environmentally friendly than commuting in our own personal vehicles. 搭乘大眾交通運輸比起用自己的交通工具通勤還要更加環保。 →「A比起B更加……」是帶有個人評價的字眼，因此可以做為探討的議題。	MRT, buses, and trains are different kinds of public transport. *捷運、公車和火車是不同種類的大眾交通。* → 這句話是事實，不需要辯論，不適合拿來做題目。

(2) Step 2：選邊站後，下好離手

　　就像在打電玩遊戲一樣，開始玩遊戲後就得選定角色，也就是選擇正方或反方，支持或反對這個論點。此時我們不能像是交朋友一樣的人人好，必須選定心目中要捍衛的論點，決定好後下好離手。

一旦選定題目後，無論你是支持或是反對，都要快速寫下關於這個主題的優缺點，或是正反雙方會提出的論點。所謂知己知彼，百戰百勝，你愈把反方意見清楚透徹地陳述，愈能把敵營拉攏到你這邊的陣營。

(3) Step 3：知己知彼，百戰百勝

當我們在形塑自己論點時，重點在於說服讀者為何我們的想法是合理且具有邏輯，而且比起反方的意見更為有理，我們必須把能支持我們想法的證據當作加分的武器，並同時淡化對方可以破壞我們論點的證據。也因此，除了花心思寫入能當我們靠山的證據之外，也需要好好思考如何打敗對方論點以證明我們的立場才是對的。

在強力推銷自己論點的同時，也別忘了把反方最強而有力的論點整理出來，當你攻擊對方最強的論點時，就愈能說服讀者你的觀點更有邏輯，以及更具可信度。提供證據支持你的論點時，專注在給予讀者數據以及清楚的例子，讓這些文字替你的立場發聲。

提出反方的論點是論述文當中非常重要的一環，寫這篇文章的目的雖然要大力推銷自己的論點，強調自己的證據最有可信度，但也須加入對方最強而有力的論點以及雙方各自可以取信於讀者的證據。

在文章當中寫進對方看似堅不可破的觀點，除了感覺我們很客觀，表現出一種體貼讀者也有可能比較喜歡另一方的論點之外，也可以避免整篇淪為老王賣瓜的感覺。在搭配證據清楚呈現對方的論點其實有瑕疵之後，讓讀者沉浸在我們很客觀的氛圍，這時候就是打擊對方論點可信度的好時機了。

在證據的使用上，並沒有哪一種是最能說服讀者的，可以依照主題混搭不同的證據來支持論點，例如可以從數據、研究開始，延伸到名言或是小故事等，以增加文章的層次感。（關於證據可以使用哪些，請參考第 64 頁「加點調味料，讓你的舉例更有風味：支持句的種類」）

(4) Step 4：依照邏輯排列論點與證據

為了讓文章讀起來更加有說服力，更容易被讀者吸收，有邏輯地組織想法與支持的證據是很重要的。我們可以利用兩種知名的論述方法來組織我們的論點：Toulmin Method（圖爾明論證模式）及 Rogerian Method（羅傑斯論證法）。以下分別以表格與範例說明：

❶ 圖爾明論證模式

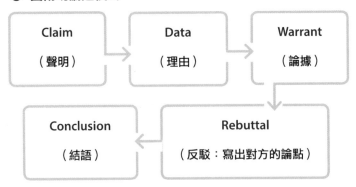

    Toulmin Method（圖爾明論證模式）在寫學術類的論述文時非常好用，因為可以逐步拆解我們要提出的論點。也因此，愈複雜的論點愈適合使用圖爾明論證，因為可以清楚地用細節呈現立場。

    我們以「Should Sugary Drinks Be Banned from School?」（學校是否應該禁止含糖飲料？）為題，示範如何以圖爾明論證法來寫這個題目，在本文中我採取支持禁止使用的立場。

    ① Claim（聲明）：描述主要的論點，也就是主題句。

> 例　School should ban sugary drinks from the campus.
> *學校應禁止含糖飲料。*

    ② Data（理由）：支持聲明的證據。

> 例　Banning sugary drinks would protect students from developing diseases.
> *禁止含糖飲料可以避免學生罹患疾病。*

    ③ Warrant（論據）：解釋為何你的理由足以支持聲明。

    先簡單的一句說明為何你的理由足以支持聲明。

例 A high sugar intake favors the development of health problems, such as weight gain, diabetes, cardiovascular disease, and metabolic syndrome.
攝取過多糖會助長健康問題的發展，例如增胖、糖尿病、心血管疾病以及代謝症候群。

接著用數據、研究、事實、引言等方法強化自己的論點。

例 Various studies show a high correlation between sugary drinks intake and obesity rates.
許多研究證實含糖飲料的攝取與肥胖率有著高度相關。

④ Rebuttal（反駁：寫出對方的論點）：提供反駁的目的是為了建立自己的可信度，讓讀者覺得自己是一個不帶有偏見的人。

例 However, some might argue that banning sugary drinks from school will not prevent students from drinking it. For instance, students might drink it at home or buy it from the convenience stores.
然而，有些人可能會爭論，禁止含糖飲料進入校園並不會讓孩子停止喝飲料。舉例來說，學生可能會在家喝，或是去便利商店購買。

⑤ Conclusion（結語）

開頭的地方要先認可與自己相反意見的一方說的有理，接著底線處要話鋒一轉證明自己的論點才是最好的。

例 Despite the fact that sugary drinks are available to students outside of school, <u>banning such drinks from school campus would greatly reduce the possibility of consumption, which is an important approach to protect students' health and growth.</u>
儘管含糖飲料在校外也是可以取得的，但是學校不販售這類飲料可以大幅降低消耗飲料的可能性，也是一個可以保護學生健康與成長的重要方法。

- 正規的圖爾明論證在這個區塊要使用 Qualifier（限定詞），例如使用 probably（或許）、possible（有可能）、impossible（不可能）、certainly（確定地）、presumably（據推測、大概地）、as far as the evidence goes（根據證據顯示）、還有 necessarily（必要地）等委婉的語氣來表達自己的論點尚有不足之處。但為了讓讀者更容易使用這個論證法，這個地方我改成 Conclusion（結語）。

❷ 羅傑斯論證法

| Introduction（簡介） | → | Opposing position（對方立場） | → | Your Position（你的立場） | → | Benefits（好處） |

羅傑斯論證法很適合用來探討具有爭議性的議題，因為這種論證法試圖在兩種論證中找到一個平衡點，也能讓讀者同時看到正反方的論點。但是在尋求平衡點的過程中，我們透過理性的探討兩方論點，讓讀者知道為何選擇作者所採去的立場是更好的。也因此，使用羅傑論證法可以達到兩個效果：一、你的論點看起來與對方有所妥協，找到了平衡點。二、你是一個包容心強，能夠理性接受對方立場的人。

我們以「Should Cell Phones Be Banned While Driving?」（手機是否應該在開車時被禁止使用？）為題，示範如何以羅傑斯論證法來寫這個題目，在本文中我採取支持禁止使用的立場。

簡單介紹一下問題點，並提出讀者和作者本身會如何被這個問題影響（例如對身體不好、造成經濟困難等等），讓讀者覺得這是個值得關注的問題。

① Introduction（簡介）

因為這個題目，我採取的立場是反對邊開車邊用手機，因此先提出智慧型手機的優點，接著營造轉折，再來則是本篇主題：邊開車使用手機是不好的，及其壞處。

例 Smartphones are ubiquitous, and they have seamlessly integrated into our everyday lives. Smartphones keep our loved ones in touch, help us to find easy ways to go anywhere, and we can carry out a wide range of tasks when on the go. However, there are some occasions and places where using smartphones are prohibited, for instance, driving and using cell phones. Drivers using mobile phones will put themselves and other people at risk.

智慧型手機的優點

營造轉折

本篇主題

智慧型手機無所不在，而且密切地與我們的日常生活結合。手機使我們與所愛的人保持聯繫，指引我們找到去任何地方的路，以及當我們人在外面時，能執行各式各樣的任務。然而，也有某些場合和地方是禁止使用手機的，例如邊開車邊使用手機。駕駛邊開車邊使用手機會讓自己和他人處於風險當中。

② Opposing Position（對方立場）：在這裡提出對方的論點，顯示你對另一方立場的了解夠深。

例 Some claim that a cell phone is only one of the distractions during the whole driving process, and its influence is no bigger than adjusting a radio, eating or drinking while driving, or talking to passengers.

有些人聲明手機在整個開車過程中只不過是其中一個會分心的因素，而它的影響不會比轉收音機、邊吃邊喝邊開車，或者是跟乘客講話還要嚴重。

③ Your Position（你的立場）：用中性的字眼呈現自己的立場，讓讀者知道你不批判對方，且能公平客觀的陳述自己的論點。

　　先簡單的認可對方的理由也有可取之處，接著再說明自己的論點，並舉例強化立場。

> 例　Although people have certain beliefs regarding the use of cell
> 　　　　　→認可對方
> phones while driving, many of them are doubtful. For instance,
> 　　　　　　　　　　　→説明自己的論點
> when it comes to distraction, people could actually choose not to
> use mobile phone when driving as such item is not necessary in
> the driving process. In addition, adjusting the radio or drinking
> will not place burden on the human brain; however, using a cell
> phone requires full attention and hence will increase the risk of a
> crash.
>
> *雖然人們對於開車使用手機有某些信念，但其實這些想法多數是有疑
> 慮的。舉例來説，一提到分心，人們事實上可以選擇不要在開車時使
> 用手機，因為手機不是在開車過程中需要使用到的物品。此外，調收
> 音機或喝東西不會對人的大腦造成負擔，但使用手機需要全心全意的
> 專注力，也因此會增加車禍的風險。*

④ Benefits（好處）：向跟自己持反對立場的觀眾精神喊話，讓
　讀者覺得如果改採取你的立場好處多多。

　　這裡要做的事情不是批判對方多差，而是讓讀者下意識的覺
得如果改成跟作者同樣立場，自己會獲得更多益處。

> 例　The dangers of cell phone use while driving cannot be
> overemphasized. Statistics have shown that with the technology
> advancement, crashes that included smartphone use have grown
> increasingly over the years. Using mobile phones while driving
> poses threats to drivers and all road users, in fact, it is as
> dangerous as drunk driving. Consequently, all drivers should
> avoid using mobile phones when they are on the road.
>
> *邊開車邊使用手機的危險無論如何強調都不為過。數據顯示隨著科技
> 進展，因為使用手機而造成的車禍這幾年逐漸增加。開車時使用手機
> 會造成所有駕駛與用路人的危險，事實上，邊開車邊使用手機的危險
> 性不亞於酒駕。因此，所有駕駛開車上路時都應該避免使用手機。*

(5) Step 5：攻擊完對方，也別忘了收尾

　　在先前的章節，我們提過要在最後一段聚焦，讓讀者回想整篇的

走向，反思或對這個議題未來的走向有所想法。也因此，在論述文中，一個好的結論能強化讀者的想法：「這個作者的立場是對的而且有道理的。」

如果有必要的話，可以把最強而有力的證據留在最後一段支持論點，讓讀者讀到文章最後一個字印象更深刻。如果真的沒有特別想提的內容，就使用先前章節中提到的，重申並換句話說我們的立場，也就是重新包裝主旨句。

1-3 說服別人買單的技巧

除了可以使用在先前的章節所提過的方式之外，不妨在文章中交錯使用以下的策略來撰寫你的論述文：

(1) 玩自問自答的遊戲

提出問題後再回答問題是吸引讀者閱讀的策略，特別是作者如果能提出一個讀者通常會有疑問的事情。例如：

> 例 You may ask: "How can people survive during their trip to the moon?" Indeed, this is a question that all rocket manufacturers are concerned about.
>
> *你有可能會問：「人類要怎麼在前往月球的旅程中生存下來呢？」確實，這也是所有火箭製造商所關心的事。*

透過提出一個大家都很有可能發問的題目，我們可以輕鬆提出自己的論點與說明，而不會像是在說教或賣弄學問。

(2) 說愛你千遍也不厭倦

重要的概念重複訴說可以讓讀者被洗腦：「這件事情是很有代表性的。」就像廣告或是大家朗朗上口的歌曲都有個特性：內容或歌詞重複出場的機率很高。假如讀者對於我們要表達的概念或立場不清楚時，重複出現的立場或想法可以讓讀者清楚了解整篇要陳述的概念。例如：

> 例 The kid made everyone angry when he was running around during dinner.
>
> *這個小孩在吃晚餐時亂跑，讓大家都很生氣。*

我們在別段可以改寫成：

> ⑩ The kid could not behave himself during the dinner, and his loud voice, impoliteness, and lack of respect infuriated every guest except his parents.
>
> *這個小孩沒辦法管束自己，而且他的大嗓門、無禮以及缺乏尊重激怒了除了他父母以外的所有人。*

同樣的一件事情，用不同的方法解釋更容易被讀者接受，也更能為讀者吸收。就跟表達愛意一樣，用不同的方法表達愛意總是比較容易獲得青睞的。

(3) 當一個說書人

大家都喜歡聽故事，也因此透過故事，我們更能把理念傳達出去。就像流傳已久的伊索寓言一樣，我們可以透過每一個故事所傳達的寓意學習到人生的哲學。也因此，透過名人故事或第三人的個人經驗與故事，我們所代表的立場和論點會變得比較生動、有親和力、帶有人性，也就能比較輕鬆地說服讀者站到我們這方。

舉例來說，當我們想要說明人權是很重要的，與其一直用論點說明或用冷冰冰的例子說明人權很重要：

> ⑩ Human rights are basic rights that belong to all of us because we are human. They represent key values in our society such as dignity, equality, and respect. They are important ways to protect us all, especially those who may face abuse, neglect, and isolation.
>
> *人權是屬於所有人的基本權利，因為我們身而為人。人權代表了我們社會中的核心價值觀，例如尊嚴、平等及尊重。人權是保護我們所有人的重要方法，特別是那些面臨霸凌、忽視或是隔離的人們。*

不如提出歷史上的事件，比如美國前總統林肯解放黑奴或是人權運動領袖金恩博士提倡非裔人士的權利，甚至到近年的「Black Lives Matter」（黑人的命也是命）運動，一個小故事更能貼近人心說服你的讀者。

> 例 George Floyd, a 46-year-old black man and father to five children, was killed in Minnesota on May 25, 2020, while being arrested for allegedly using a counterfeit bill to buy a packet of cigarettes. According to many witnesses, Floyd had complained about being unable to breathe before being restrained. He then became much more painful when the officer's knee on his neck, and after several minutes passed, Floyd stopped breathing and struggling. Floyd's death has triggered massive protests against brutality and racism.
>
> *2020 年的 5 月 25 日，喬治‧佛洛伊德，一位 46 歲的黑人男子，同時也是 5 個小孩的爸爸，被指控使用假鈔購買一包香菸，於逮捕期間被殺害。根據許多目擊者供稱，佛洛伊德在被限制行動前就已經抱怨說很難呼吸了。當警察的膝蓋壓在他的脖子上時，他變得更加痛苦，過了幾分鐘後，佛洛伊德停止了呼吸和掙扎。佛洛伊德之死觸發了大規模抗議，反對殘忍的暴行以及種族歧視。*

運用時事新聞或是小故事開頭，是不是更能讓讀者有感觸呢？

(4) Everybody 動起來！

　　想想金恩博士「I have a dream.」（我有一個夢想）慷慨激昂的演講、美國前總統歐巴馬在演講中溫暖卻又堅定地呼籲大家不要害怕新冠肺炎、賈伯斯生前在蘋果每場新產品的發表會中吸引顧客想要趕快下手購買新產品的介紹，又或是身邊那些非常具有演說魅力的朋友，是不是一聽到他們說話就很想起身執行他們所支持的理念呢？當我們在結論使用這種技巧時，我們可以鼓舞我們的讀者一起用行動支持我們所倡導的理念，比如減塑、關懷身旁弱勢，或是能夠針對公眾事務付諸行動。

　　舉例來說：

> 例 If you were waiting for the perfect time to seize an opportunity, the time is now.
> *假如你還在等待最完美的時機來抓住這個機會，現在就是那個時機了。*

> 例 There's no time like the present, take action and prevent the marine creatures from extinction.
> *不會有任何一刻會像現在一樣，起身行動並保護海洋生物免於滅絕。*

(5) 不要害怕挑戰主流

很多人，特別是學生，害怕如果提了一個跟主流相反的意見，是否會遭受批評或不受批閱者的喜愛。事實上，書寫作文時最好的方式是擁有自己的主張，並使用邏輯清晰的方式解釋或分析為何你會選擇這個立場。即使自己所同意的立場並不是主流或是一般人會提出的，也能透過舉例與客觀的分析說服讀者。

不管是 legalization of euthanasia（安樂死合法化）、legalization of abortion（墮胎合法化），或是 marijuana legalization（大麻合法化），只要心目中有清楚的論述與例子可以支持立場，而不是單純為了支持或反對而無條件同意某個論點，那麼都會有很好的發揮空間。

1-4　如何表現自己的支持或反對？

闡述論點的片語或轉折詞	• For instance, 例如…… • specifically, 特別是…… • namely, 也就是…… • like 像…… • to illustrate… 為了說明…… • Personally, 就我而言……	• For example, 例如…… • in particular, 尤其是…… • such as 像是…… • in other words 也就是說…… • In my opinion, 我認為……
提出例子的片語或轉折詞	• For example, 例如…… • For instance, 例如…… • Take … for example. 以……為例→這個片語的結尾是句點	
提出建議的片語或轉折詞	• To this end, 為此…… • for this purpose / reason 因為這個原因…… • therefore, 因此…… • As a result, 因此…… • Consequently, 因此……	
連接不同論點的片語或轉折詞	• Also, 並且…… • Additionally, 此外…… • besides that, 除此之外…… • likewise, 同樣地…… • otherwise, 否則…… • However, 然而……	• Furthermore, 再者…… • In addition, 此外…… • similarly, 同樣地…… • As a result, 因此…… • ; however, 然而……

提出雙方論點的片語或轉折詞	• Understanding the pros and cons of this topic is important. *理解這個主題的優缺點是很重要的。* • Let's take a look at the advantages and disadvantages of the topic. *讓我們看看這個主題的優點和缺點。* • The advantages outweigh the disadvantages. *優點遠大於缺點。* →*優點與缺點的位置可視文章情況互調。*
提出額外論點的片語或轉折詞	• What is more, 而且…… • In addition to…, 此外…… • Furthermore, 此外…… • Not only will…, but… will also… 不只……而且……
做出對比的片語或轉折詞	• On one hand, … On the other hand, 一方面……另一方面…… • nevertheless, 然而…… • despite +N / Ving 即使…… • Despite the fact that S + V 儘管…… • yet, 然而…… • instead 反而…… • instead of 而不是……
下結論的片語或轉折詞	• As a result of…, 由於……　• As a result, 因此…… • Because of this, 為此……　• for this reason, 為此…… • so 所以……　　　　　　• due to 由於…… • because of 由於……　　　• since 因為…… • finally, 最後，　　　　　• in short 總而言之／簡而言之…… • in conclusion 總之……　　• in a nutshell 概括而言……
下結論的句型	• What needs to be done / What we need to do is… 需要做的是／我們需要做的是…… • It is obvious that… 顯然是…… • Surely… 肯定…… • Regardless… 無論如何…… • This can be fixed by… 可以被……確定的是 • Although it may seem… 雖然看起來……

1-5　論述文的段落：PEE 寫作法

前面學過 PEEL 剝皮寫作法，論述文當中我們只需要用到 P (Point)、E (Evidence)、E (Explain)。跟 PEEL 的操作方法一樣，只是在論述文中，我們不需要為段與段之間搭起橋樑，只需要專心寫好要說服讀者的論點就好。

所以一篇以 PEE 寫作法構成的文章長相是這樣子的，我們一樣以「Is Social Media Good for Our Society?」（社群媒體對我們的社會是否有益處？），並在下面附上範例解說：

第一段 ▶ **Introduction（引言）**

Social media has grown tremendously in the last few years; for instance, Facebook and Twitter have captured millions of users in just a few years. Social media has changed people's lives, and it has brought a lot of advantages for the society, such as the spread of information. However, social media has also affected the society in the negative way, including **cyberbullying, addiction**, and **relationship issues**.

Hook（開頭）
Background Information（背景知識）
Thesis Statement（主旨句）
point 1　　point 2　　point 3

社群媒體在最近幾年發展快速。例如 Facebook 和 Twitter 在短短幾年內就吸引了數百萬用戶。社群媒體已經改變了人們的生活，並對社會帶來許多好處，像是資訊傳播。然而，社群媒體也已負面方式影響了社會，包括網路霸凌、上癮、人際關係問題。

第二段 ▶ **Body Paragraph 1（主體段落一）**

Social media has facilitated the rapid distribution of rumors and gossips because these comments are often posted anonymously that hide the true identity. According to the Pew Research Center, in the US., 75% of adults have seen cyberbullying happening around them, and 40% of these adults have personally experienced online harassment. Cyberbullying is a serious societal problem that will cause damage to children. In many cases, being bullied online leads to mental illness, such as anxiety and depression, which lowers an individual's self-esteem and confidence at work or school. In addition, cyberbullying also prevents people from trusting the internet and technology as a tool since unpleasant online experiences will decrease people's will to make good use of technology.

Point 1（論點一）
Evidence 1（證據一）
Explain 1（解釋一）

社群媒體促進了八卦和謠言的迅速傳播，因為這些評論通常是匿名發布以隱匿真實身分。根據美國皮尤研究中心，75% 的成人在周遭見過網路霸凌，這其中大約 40% 的成人親身經歷過網路性騷擾。網路霸凌是嚴重的社會問題，會對孩子造成傷害。在許多案例中，網路霸凌導致精神疾病，像是焦慮和憂鬱，會降低個人在職場或學校的自尊和自信。此外，網路霸凌也使人們不信任網路和將科技作為工具，因為不愉快的線上經驗會損害人們善用科技的意願。

第三段 ▶ Body Paragraph 2（主體段落二）

Many people have become deeply attached to social media, driven by an uncontrollable urge to use it, and wasting too much time and effort to social media that it affects other life areas. A research posted on *Psychology Today* showed that excessive use of social media has caused negative impacts on the health and wellbeing of users, such as depression and anxiety. In some cases, some users have developed "a fear of missing out" and become restless if they are unable to use social media. Although only a small proportion of people are truly addicted to social media, many people's social media use is habitual. However, it will gradually start to affect other aspects of lives and become problematic or hazardous, such as checking social media updates while driving. Other behaviors may simply be annoying, such as checking phones while eating with family or friends or constantly checking messages at work or in class.

Point 2（論點二）
Evidence 2（證據二）
Explain 2（解釋二）

許多人深深依賴社群媒體，因為無法控制的衝動而去使用它，並且浪費太多時間和精力在社群媒體上，影響了其他生活。《今日心理學》上的一個研究顯示，過度使用社群媒體影響了人們的健康和幸福，像是憂鬱和焦慮。在某些情況下，一些用戶產生了害怕錯過資訊恐懼症，如果他們不使用社群媒體就會焦躁不安。雖然只有一小部分人真正沉迷社群媒體，但很多人是習慣性使用社群媒體。然而，它會漸漸影響生活的其他面向，成為問題或是變成會危害生命的，像是開車時查看社群媒體的更新。其他行為可能只是令人討厭，像是和家人或朋友吃飯時一直查看手機，或是工作或上課時一直確認訊息。

People who spend too much time on social media have been proved to
→Point 3（論點三）
have lower satisfaction with their real life. Social media makes it easy to
→Evidence 3（證據三）
compare your relationship to someone else's. A study has shown that an
average of 80% of the teenagers, especially girls, has been upset about
the social image they present in front of the public. They feel inferior to
their peers and influencers, and they are not feeling comfortable with their
appearance. Furthermore, over 90% of teenage girls admitted that they
wanted to build a strong and positive image of social life. It's hard not to
be affected by social media, no matter how distant we may seem. We view
others' posts and photos to see their lives. Our natural reaction is to look at
our own life and compare it to others'.

在社交媒體上花費很多時間的人，經證實對現實生活的滿意度較低。社群媒體讓你
很容易比較自己與別人的關係。研究顯示，平均有 80% 的青少年，尤其是女生，會對自
己的公開形象感到不安，覺得自己不如同儕和其他有影響力的人，並且對自己的外表感到
不自在。再者，有超過 90% 的青少女承認，她們想要建立一個堅強且正向的社會生活形
象。不論我們看起來有多疏離，都很難不被社群媒體影響。我們經由別人的貼文和照片來
觀看他人生活，我們的自然反應是檢視自己的生活並與他人比較。

Social media can be very influential in society in both positive and
negative ways. It gives people a way to stay in touch with people they love
and allows for rapid communication. However, the downsides of social
media outweigh the advantages. Social media makes bullying easier and
will affect one's mental health. It is also reported that overusing social
media often leads to addiction and eventually leads to relationship issues.
Consequently, it's better to be safe than sorry when one uses social media.

社群媒體會對社會產生積極和消極的影響。它使人們可以和所愛的人保持聯繫並允許
即時溝通。然而，社群媒體的弊大於利，它使霸凌變得容易，並影響他人的心理健康。也
有報告指出過度使用社群媒體會導致上癮並最終引起關係問題。也因此，使用社群媒體時
最好是防範於未然。

1-6 論述文範文解析

我們以「Should Sugary Drinks Be Offered in Schools?」（學校是否應販售含糖飲料？）為題，來寫一篇論述文。

第一段 ▸ Introduction（引言）

Chocolate milk, soda, or juice. Do any of the above-mentioned sugary drinks sound like an essential item to you at work or in school? Sugary beverages fall at the bottom of the list when it comes to the ranking of healthy food options because they provide so many calories and literally no nutrients. Sugary drinks should not be allowed in schools, as they **cause weight gain**, **increase the risk of serious health problems**, and **lead to addiction.**

Hook（引言）
Background Information（背景知識）
Thesis Statement（主旨句）
Reason 1 ／ Reason 2 ／ Reason 3

巧克力牛奶、汽水或果汁，前述提到的含糖飲料聽起來是否是你工作或上課的必需品呢？當提到健康食品的排名時，含糖飲料絕對名落孫山，因為它們提供太多卡路里而根本沒有營養。學校不應該允許含糖飲料，因為會導致肥胖，增加罹患嚴重健康問題的風險，並導致上癮。

第二段 ▸ Body Paragraph 1（主體段落一）

According to nutritional experts, sugary beverages are loaded with empty calories and provide no essential nutrients. In addition, sugary beverages don't make people full, but it still increases calorie intake when one consumes liquid sugar. Not surprisingly, studies show that people who drink sugar drinks gain more weight than people who don't because the body doesn't compensate fully for beverage calories by reducing calorie intake from other foods.

Reason 1（理由一）
Explain 1（解釋一）
Evidence 1（證據一）

根據營養專家的說法，含糖飲料多為空熱量而沒有提供必要營養素。此外，含糖飲料不會讓人飽足，但當你食用液態糖時，仍會增加卡路里的攝取量。不意外地，研究顯示喝含糖飲料的人比不喝的人更容易變胖，因為身體不能透過減少其他食物的卡路里來補償飲料中的卡路里。

第三段 ▸ **Body Paragraph 2 （主體段落二）**

Sugar-sweetened drinks are linked not only to weight gain but also
——▸Reason 2（理由一）
to poor health. People consuming sugary drinks regularly, according
——▸Explain 2（解釋二）
to studies, have a greater risk of developing diabetes than people who
rarely consume such drinks. Furthermore, multiple studies have shown
——▸Evidence 2（證據二）
a strong link between sugary beverages and heart disease risk. Since
cancer is closely related to obesity, diabetes, and heart disease, for this
reason, sugary drinks are frequently associated with an increased risk of
cancer.

含糖飲料不只會影響健康還會使身體變差。根據研究顯示，經常飲用含糖飲料的
人比很少飲用的人罹患糖尿病的風險更大。再者，多項研究顯示了含糖飲料與心臟病
風險有極大的關聯。因為癌症與肥胖、糖尿病、心血管病息息相關，含糖飲料通常也
跟增加癌症風險有關聯。

第四段 ▸ **Body Paragraph 3 （主體段落三）**

The sugary drinks habit is one that frequently begins during childhood.
——▸Reason 3（理由三）
Sugar consumption can create a short-term high and spark energy,
——▸Explain 3（解釋三）
and hence some studies have suggested sugar is as addictive as
——▸Evidence 3（證據三）
cocaine. Although sugar brings pleasure, the addictive nature of sugar
——▸Explain 3（解釋三）
leads to health problems, like obesity and diabetes. It also brings about
low moods, anxiety, and stress. Additionally, once someone mentally
connects sugar with help providing energy, they may become dependent
on it and begin to crave sugar to balance emotional lows. Eventually,
people lose control over avoiding sugary foods, and a sugar addiction
has developed.

喝含糖飲料的習慣通常從童年就開始。糖的攝取會產生短暫的興奮感和激發能
量，也因此一些研究顯示糖就像古柯鹼一樣容易使人上癮。雖然糖帶來愉悅感，但是
糖的易成癮性會導致健康問題，像是肥胖和糖尿病，同時也帶來情緒低落、焦慮和壓
力。此外，一旦有人在心理上將糖和能量的來源連結，他們可能會更依賴它，並渴望
糖能平衡他們的低落情緒，最終，人們無法控制避免喝含糖飲料或食物，並產生對糖
上癮的現象。

第五段 ▶ Counter-argument（對方的論點）＋ Evidence（證據）

Some may argue that not everything in these drinks is harmful.
→ Counter-argument（對方的論點）
Indeed, the caffeine in some soft drinks can be good for you in small
→ Explain（解釋）
doses. Low levels of caffeine have been proved to boost brain function,
→ Evidence（證據）
help with focus and make work effective. A tiny caffeine intake may
→ Explain（解釋）
help people concentrate through the remaining hours at work or school
without getting tired. However, don't take sugary beverages as the
→ Argument（反駁）
ideal energy boosters. It may perk you up for a short while, but due to
its high sugar content, you'll experience an energy crash not long after
consumption.

有些人可能會說這些飲料中的內容物並不都是有害的。的確，一些軟性飲料中的少量咖啡因會對你有益。少量攝取咖啡因已被證實也許能幫助人們接下來在工作或學校內的幾小時集中注意力和促進工作效率而不感到疲勞。然而，我們不能把含糖飲料視為理想的能量飲料，它也許能使你振奮一小段時間，但由於其高含糖量，消耗完糖分後不久你就會經歷能量崩盤。

第六段 ▶ Conclusion（結論）

As weight gain and health problems seriously affect a person's
professional and personal life, it is important that we should not allow
→ Thesis Statement（主旨句）
sugary drinks in school. Furthermore, the consumption of sugar will
→ Evidence（證據）
eventually lead to a constant craving for sugar. Consequently, schools
Thesis Statement（主旨句） ◄
should offer healthier options to students.

由於體重增加和健康問題會嚴重影響一個人的職業和個人生活，因此不應該允許含糖飲料出現在校園中這件事是很重要的。再者，消耗糖分會導致持續渴望糖的攝取，因此，學校應該提供更健康的選擇給學生。

Section 02 | Expository Essay（説明文）：絕對理性中立

説明文，以字面上來説就是解釋某種東西的文體。「Expository」這個字來自「expose」暴露，也就是揭露某件事情的本質，讓讀者得以了解這個主題。也因此，説明文可以用來教導、澄清或告訴讀者關於某個主題的知識。

很多人經常會問：「那説明文跟論述文不是一樣的東西嗎？」這兩種文體最大的不同就在於説明文必須保持中立，而論述文必須選邊站，也就是針對議題的正方或反方提出辯護。

好的説明文可以讓讀者在文章當中得到對主題一定程度的知識，或是能夠透過清楚的解釋，消除讀者對主題原先有的誤解。也因此，一篇説明文能中立的給予主題詳盡的解説，並且不會涉及任何作者本身的觀點或立場。

2-1　説明文的樣貌

説明文可以細分成以下幾個段落：

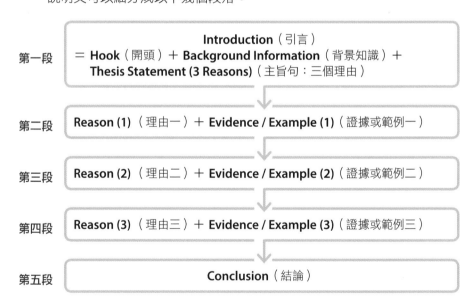

第一段
Introduction（引言）
＝ **Hook**（開頭）＋ **Background Information**（背景知識）＋
Thesis Statement (3 Reasons)（主旨句：三個理由）

第二段　**Reason (1)**（理由一）＋ **Evidence / Example (1)**（證據或範例一）

第三段　**Reason (2)**（理由二）＋ **Evidence / Example (2)**（證據或範例二）

第四段　**Reason (3)**（理由三）＋ **Evidence / Example (3)**（證據或範例三）

第五段　**Conclusion**（結論）

2-2　利用薯條寫作法（FRIES）來豐富你的說明文

因為說明文必須中立，因此在解釋主題時，可以添加薯條寫作法（FRIES）到文章當中，來客觀說明主題，並提供讀者關於主題最中立的知識和看法。

在前面的章節（詳見「你提出的，是事實，還是個人意見？」）我們說過要以事實而非個人意見來支持我們的論點，在寫說明文時也一樣，如果能善用薯條寫作法（FRIES）來增強我們論點的可信度，那麼在解釋主題時會更有根基，也就更能讓讀者獲得中立且豐富的資訊。

■ 薯條寫作法

F	R	I	E	S
Facts（事實）	Reasons（理由）	Incidents（事件）	Examples（範例）	Statistics（數據）

薯條寫作法	常用字句
Facts（事實：能被分辨真偽的事件）	• According to... 根據……
Reasons（理由：強而有力的論點）	• One reason... 一個理由是…… • Another reason... 另一理由是……
Incidents（事件：具體且有因果關係的事件）	• Once... 一旦…… • I remember when... 我記得當……
Examples（範例：數據、研究報告、名言佳句等。）	• For example, ... 例如…… • For instance, ... 例如……
Statistics（數據：可以從研究報告或專家學者的論述中取得。）	• many ... 很多…… • some ... 一些…… • a few / few 少數／些微…… • 35% of ... 35%的……

我們以「My Favorite Tourist Attraction」（我最喜歡的旅遊勝地）為題，來寫一篇說明文。

第一段 ▶ Introduction（引言）

Mountains, cliffs, beaches, and food – this amazing island – Taiwan, is
everything you desire. [Hook（開頭）] Taiwan is an island country in East Asia, offering
wondrous vistas, traditions and cultures, and a wide range of landscapes. [Background Information（背景知識）]
Grab your bag and get ready to embark on your trip to explore this
spectacular destination because the **variety of landscapes** and **a lifetime**
cycling experience will definitely blow your mind. [Thesis Statement（主旨句）] [Reason 1] [Reason 2]

山、崖、海灘及食物──這個令人驚喜的島嶼──臺灣，是你所想要的一切。臺灣是東亞的一個島國，擁有令人驚豔的美景、各式各樣的傳統及文化，以及不同種類的景色。拿起你的包包，準備好啟程去探索這個壯觀的目的地，因為多樣的景色和永生難忘的自行車體驗絕對會讓你大吃一驚。

▶ 第一段解說

依據著條寫作法分析第一段：

F（事實） → Taiwan is an island country in East Asia.
（臺灣是東亞的一個島國。）

R（理由） → ① Mountains, cliffs, beaches, and food – this amazing island
– Taiwan, is everything you desire.（山、崖、海灘及食物─
這個令人驚喜的島嶼─臺灣，是你所想要的一切。）

② offering wondrous vistas, traditions and cultures, and a
wide range of landscapes.（擁有令人驚豔的美景、各式各樣
的傳統及文化，以及不同種類的景色。）

③ the variety of landscapes and a lifetime cycling
experience（多樣的景色和永生難忘的自行車體驗）

第二段 ▶ **Body Paragraph 1（主體段落一）**

When it comes to mobility, the capital of Taiwan, Taipei, is a great
city for tourists because the local metro system is reliable and user-friendly. [→Reason 1（理由一）] The system has been highly praised for its safety, reliability, and
quality. According to a research conducted by Imperial College London,
the Taipei Metro has ranked number 1 in the world for four consecutive
years, from 2004 to 2007, when it comes to reliability, safety, and quality
standards. On the other hand, Taiwan is also incredibly green. No matter
where you are, there is always a park around the corner. [→Reason 1（理由一）] [Explain 1（解釋一）←] The landscape
changes dramatically across Taiwan, from sand to land, from beach to
cliffs. The island is also home to abundant flora and fauna, which makes
Taiwan a place with both urban and natural atmosphere. [→Evidence 1（證據一）] From rugged
mountains, gentle plains, to volcanos and forests, you will never get
bored with this mysterious land.

提到交通，臺灣的首都，臺北，對於遊客來說是很棒的城市，因為當地的捷運系統可靠並且對使用者來說很友善。這個系統經常被高度稱讚其安全性、可信賴度，以及品質。根據倫敦帝國學院所做的一項研究指出，臺北的捷運以可信賴度、安全性以及品質來說，連續四年，從 2004 到 2007，都是排名第一。另一方面，臺灣非常綠意盎然，無論你在哪裡，轉角處總是有公園。臺灣地景變化極大，從沙地到陸地，從沙灘到懸崖，島上也孕育了大量的原生動植物，使臺灣同時擁有都市和自然氣息。從崎嶇的山脈，平緩的平原，到火山和森林，你永遠不會對這塊神秘的土地感到厭倦。

▶ **第二段解說**

依據薯條寫作法分析第二段：

F（事實）→① The landscape changes dramatically across Taiwan.
（臺灣地景變化極大。）

② The island is also home to abundant flora and fauna.
（島上也孕育了大量的原生動植物。）

R（理由）→① mobility（交通）

② Taipei, is a great city for tourists.
（臺北，對於遊客來說是很棒的城市。）

③ The local metro system is reliable and user-friendly. The system has been highly praised for its safety, reliability, and quality.

（當地的捷運系統可靠並且對使用者來說很友善。這個系統經常被高度稱讚其安全性、可信賴度，以及品質。）

④ Taiwan is also incredibly green.（臺灣非常綠意盎然。）

⑤ makes Taiwan a place with both urban and natural atmosphere（使臺灣同時擁有都市和自然氣息）

E（範例）→ ① No matter where you are, there is always a park around the corner.（無論你在哪裡，轉角處總是有公園。）

② from sand to land, from beach to cliffs
（從沙地到陸地，從沙灘到懸崖）

③ from rugged mountains, gentle plains, to volcanos and forests（崎嶇的山脈，平緩的平原，到火山和森林）

S（數據）→ According to a research conducted by Imperial College London, the Taipei Metro has ranked number 1 in the world for four consecutive years, from 2004 to 2007, when it comes to reliability, safety, and quality standards.（根據倫敦帝國學院所做的一項研究指出，臺北的捷運以可信賴度、安全性以及品質來說，連續四年，從 2004 到 2007，都是排名第一。）

第三段 ▶ Body Paragraph 2（主體段落二）

Being a main exporter of bicycles, Taiwan is also a cyclers' paradise. → Reason 2（理由二） Cycling Taiwan is a must-do since the stunning nature along the ride → Explain 2（解釋二） is a once-in-a-lifetime experience. There are a wide range of cycling → Evidence 2（證據二） routes, from easy to challenging, in the island. There are many cycling lanes with beautiful scenery and wildlife as a companion. Furthermore, you will never be alone when cycling in Taiwan as there is many cycling communities around Taiwan. The locals and police are also known for their hospitality; you can always depend on them along the journey.

作為自行車的主要出口國，臺灣也是自行車騎士的天堂。騎自行車環島臺灣是一輩子一定要做的一件事，因為沿途的迷人景色是一生一次的經驗。臺灣有許多自行車路線，從簡單的到有挑戰性的。除此之外，騎單車時，自行車道沿路的美景和野生動物會是你的旅伴。再者，在臺灣騎自行車永遠不會孤單，因為臺灣有很多自行車社團，當地人和警察也以熱情好客聞名，一路上你都可以依靠他們。

▶　**第三段解說**

依據箸條寫作法分析第三段：

F（事實） → being a main exporter of bicycles
（作為自行車的主要出口國）

R（理由） →① Taiwan is also a cyclers' paradise.
（臺灣也是自行車騎士的天堂。）

② the stunning nature along the ride is a once-in-a-lifetime experience（沿途的迷人景色是一生一次的經驗）

E（範例） →① There are a wide range of cycling routes, from easy to challenging.（有許多自行車路線，從簡單的到有挑戰性的。）

② There are also many cycling lanes with beautiful scenery and wildlife as a companion.
（騎單車時，自行車道沿路的美景和野生動物會是你的旅伴。）

③ many cycling communities（很多自行車社團）

④ The locals and police are also known for their hospitality.
（當地人和警察也以熱情好客聞名。）

第四段 ▶ **Conclusion（結論）**

Taiwan is an island of unexpected beauty with various natural scenic
　　　→Thesis Statement（主旨句）
spots and fun activities. It is an ideal destination for those who love to spend their vacation exploring both indoor and outdoor activities. Once you have visited Taiwan, you will definitely get addicted to Taiwanese's

hospitality, breathtaking views, and amazing biking routes. If you are still thinking about where to go for a getaway, why not book a ticket to Taiwan and **enjoy the beauty of nature** and **a fun cycling ride**?

    → Reason 1   → Reason 2

臺灣是一個意想不到的美麗之島，且有各種景色和有趣的活動。對於喜歡在假期探索室內和戶外活動的人而言，臺灣是理想的目的地。一旦你造訪了臺灣，你絕對會對臺灣人的好客、美到令人屏息的美景，以及驚為天人的自行車道上癮。如果你還在考慮去哪裡小小度假一番，為何不訂張票去臺灣，享受自然景觀和有趣的自行車之行呢？

▶ **第四段解説**

依據著條寫作法分析第四段：

R（理由）→① Taiwan is an island of unexpected beauty with various natural scenic spots and fun activities.（臺灣是一個意想不到的美麗之島，且有各種景色和有趣的活動。）

② It is an ideal destination for those who love to spend their vacation exploring both indoor and outdoor activities.（對於喜歡在假期探索室內和戶外活動的人而言，臺灣是理想的目的地。）

③ enjoy the beauty of nature（享受自然景觀）

④ a fun cycling ride（有趣的自行車之行）

I（事件）→ Once you have visited Taiwan, you will definitely get addicted to Taiwanese's hospitality, breathtaking views, and amazing biking routes.（一旦你造訪了臺灣，你絕對會對臺灣人的好客、美到令人屏息的美景，以及驚為天人的自行車道上癮。）

Section 03 那些細微卻又顯著的不同

看到這裡，你是否開始思考論述文和說明文有何不同呢？以下用表格的方式讓你一目了然。

文體	論述文	說明文
目的	辯論某個觀點的正反兩面	解釋或說明某事
作用	提出證據佐證的目的是為了驗證自己的論點是最有可信度，或是自己的立場是對的。	提出證據佐證的目的是為了解釋主題，讓讀者能透過例子了解核心概念及其包含的內容。
切入角度	不是正方就是反方，只能擇一	從各個角度切入並探討主題
寫作人稱	主觀，可以是第一人稱	客觀，通常是第三人稱
主旨句	呈現作者的論點	呈現主題
舉例	以第二次世界大戰為例，一篇論述文會提出德國應該全權為這場戰事負責。	以第二次世界大戰為例，一篇說明文會探討第二次世界大戰對世界情勢的影響。

　　我們以「Should Animal Testing Be Allowed?」（我們是否應該允許動物測試？）為題，來比較論說文和說明文的不同。

(1) 論述文

Throughout the history, animal testing has played an important
　　　　　　→說明動物測試淵源已久，也確實為人類帶來好處。
role in leading to scientific and medical discoveries, not to mention
the benefits humans have received from such experimental method.
However, people ignore the fact that countless animals are treated
inhumanely or even killed during the painful experimental process.
Many of us are not familiar with the laboratory procedures and
techniques that are executed on the animals. The cruel procedures
are not reliable because animals are essentially different from human
beings. Animal testing is an awful way to treat other living creatures,
　　　　　　→標示了作者反對在動物身上做實驗此事。
and it should not be allowed in our modern society.

　　綜觀歷史，動物測試在科學和醫學發現中都扮演了重要的角色，更不用提人類從這種實驗方法中受益了。然而，人們忽視了一個事實，無數的動物在這個痛苦的實驗過程中受到不人道的對待，甚至被殺死。多數的我們並不熟悉在動物身上施行的實驗過程和技術。這個殘忍的過程並不可信，因為動物和人類在本質上並不相同。動物測試是一種對待其他生物的可怕方式，不應該被允許在現代社會發生。

(2) 説明文

Animal testing is the use of animals in scientific researches or
commercial products for developing medicine or product safety
説明了何謂在動物身上做實驗
testing. The method has been practiced for hundreds of years and has
rapidly improved the quality of our lives. On the other hand, animal
testing also violates animal rights and causes pain to animals during
the process. Supporters believe that the existence of animal testing
contributes to advances in treating health conditions, while opponents
show concerns for the cruelty and violation against animal rights. This
controversial issue is still in debate.

不帶任何評價地說明了正反雙方對於在動物身上做實驗的看法，整段
文字只有說明主題，並沒有呈現自己支持或是反對。

　　動物測試是為了開發藥物或測試產品安全，利用動物進行科學研究或研發商業
產品。這個方法施行幾百年之有，並且快速提升我們的生活品質。另一方面，動物
測試也侵犯了動物權利，並且在過程中給動物帶來痛苦。支持者相信動物測試的存
在有助於改善健康狀況，而反對者則關注對動物權利的虐待和侵犯。這項爭議仍在
討論當中。

文字必須要具體，
讓讀者覺得親臨現場！

Chapter

03

敘述文與
故事寫作

> "Don't use adjectives which merely tell us how you want us to feel about the things you are describing. I mean, instead of telling us a thing was 'terrible,' describe it so that we'll be terrified."— C. S. Lewis, British writer
>
> 「使用形容詞時,不要只是為了告訴我們你希望我們如何能感受到你正在描述的事物。我的意思是,與其告訴我們某件事情是『很可怕的』,不如描述到讓我們感到很害怕。」──英國作家 C·S·路易斯

　　國內外都有研究顯示,母語非英文的學生或嘗試用英文寫作的人認為敘述文和故事是非常難寫的文體。一來是因為描述場景、人物或事件時,需要大量的形容詞來讓讀者想像文字要呈現的場景、人物特色與激起讀者個人感受,對於英文非母語者來說是一大挑戰。二來是書寫陳述自己意見的論說文或解釋某個主題的說明文時,我們只需要提供事實來支持我們的論點即可,但敘述文是作者主觀的描寫場景,而使用感官類的文字需要讀者抽象的思考,相較之下較難讓讀者馬上買單。

Section 01 Descriptive Essay（敘述文）：從乏人問津到趣味橫生

　　敘述文可以用來描述某個人,通常是作者,所經歷過的事情,或者是某個事件,或是一連串的事件。當我們在描述事情時,描寫的文句通常與五種感官有關（視覺、聽覺、嗅覺、觸覺和味覺）,比如說:

> 例 My bowl exploded into tiny shards of glass, catching the attention of everyone in the classroom.
> 我的碗炸裂成一片片碎片,抓住了教室裡的人的目光。

　　我們的大腦在接受到沒有任何感官描述的文字時,就只會讀到內文而已。但是一篇有著感官描述的文章,可以讓文章鍍金,發出吸引大腦的光芒。例如我們讀到「有著糖霜與巧克力脆片的杯子蛋糕。」這個時候我們的大腦會感受到甜甜的滋味,嘴巴會分泌唾液,彷彿真的就在吃這個蛋糕一樣。想像一下廣

告公司常用的策略，營造消費者擁有那份商品的快樂，提高購買慾。

因此，著墨於感官的描寫能造就一篇好的敘述文，運用五感描繪出一個整體的意象就能使讀者更能體會你要陳述的意境。最後，敘述文雖然需要描述感官方面的感受，但是描寫也需要目的。敘述文的宗旨可以是你從某個人生經驗中學到的課題，某個事件如何啟發了你，某樣物品對你的意義等等。也因此，連結事件與你所得到的啟發，可以使敘述文更容易被讀者所接受。

例如我們會用 gloomy（黑暗的）、dazzling（耀眼的）、bright（明亮的）、foggy（多霧的）、gigantic（巨大的）來形容跟顏色、形狀或外表有關的單字；或是用 gritty（多沙的）、creepy（詭異的）、slimy（泥濘的）、fluffy（毛茸茸的）、sticky（黏的）來表示質地或抽象的概念。

與聽覺有關的可能會使用 crashing（東西掉落時發出的巨大聲響）、thumping（巨大的、極大的）、piercing（刺耳的）、tingling（令人刺痛的）、squeaky（吱吱響）這類的狀聲詞。描述食物時最苦惱的是都只會使用 good（好的）、nice（好的）、bad（壞的）、terrible（糟的），但其實可以用 zesty（美味的）、tantalizing（誘人的）、stale（腐壞的）來形容口感。

形容動作的詞更是需要生動活潑，在描述動作或事件時，如果能使用 soaring（飆升的）、skyrocketing（急遽攀升）、mind-blowing（令人印象深刻的）、staggering（令人震驚的）、bumpy（崎嶇的）等詞，能讓讀者更身歷其境，以下就來說明可以使用那些詞讓寫作更加生動有趣。

1-1　給讀者活跳跳的海鮮：讓句子活起來的感官敘述

在文章當中，我們必須讓讀者在看到我們描述的文字時，腦袋就浮現作者希望呈現出來的畫面。如果缺少了感官類的細節，讀者很難真正投入情感，也很難憑藉著文字去模擬你想要表達的場景或氛圍。

感官類的文字必須要具體，讓讀者覺得親臨現場。就像到海產店吃現煮的海鮮一樣，可以在現場看到新鮮的海產，想像要如何料理它，最後品嘗可口的菜餚。使用空洞或籠統的文字會讓讀者無法用腦袋意象化情境。

感官類的敘述泛指可以修飾視覺、聽覺、嗅覺、觸覺的文字，也包含了顏色的敘述、故事主角的特徵與人物間互動的情景。感官類的細節可以避免文章淪為空泛的描述，使得文章讀起來更生動。講到這裡，可能還是不清楚要如何操作，那麼我們可以利用一個大原則來示範如何寫好的敘述文。

■ 要 show 不要 tell

「Telling」的句子通常是充滿了空洞、抽象或是會產生歧義的句子；「Showing」的句子則是以精準又符合情境的形容詞來描述句子。

空洞的 Tell 句	生動的 Show 句
• The food was really delicious. 食物很好吃。	• The roasted bulk meat was floating gently in a pool of fat and grilled vegetables, making all the guests mouth-watering. 大塊的烤肉輕輕地漂浮在一池脂肪與烤蔬菜中，使得所有賓客口水直流。
• The water was cold. 水很冷。	• The cool refreshing water from the drinking fountain sprayed our chapped lips. 飲水機裡冰涼清爽的水，撒在我們乾裂的嘴唇上。
• The traffic was terrible. 交通很糟。	• During the rush hour, it seems like we would never pull out of the hectic traffic. Besides, our car was overheated because it was bumper-to-bumper for almost two hours. 在尖峰時刻，看起來我們似乎擺脫不了繁忙的街道了。此外，我們的汽車因為路上大塞車將近兩個小時而過熱。

• bumper-to-bumper 形容汽車保險桿彼此緊貼，有大塞車之意。

1-2 活力十足的形容詞

　　如果仔細觀察生動的句子，可以發現多了許多形容詞來描述名詞的特色。與其只有說「食物很好吃。」不如增添一些感官方面的描述。以下整理了一些詞，大家可以選出一些正面與負面的詞，在寫作時斟酌使用，可以讓文章更加生動有趣。

(1) 形容詞的使用順序

在文章中使用形容詞時，一樣東西會具有多種特質，這時就需要很多不同的形容詞才能讓讀者閱讀時宛如親臨現場的感覺，此時則需要依照規則來排列組合我們所使用的形容詞。

形容詞的使用順序為：<u>前置限定詞、數字、代名詞＋冠詞＋帶有評價的形容詞＋尺寸＋形狀＋顏色＋來源＋材質名詞、非材質名詞＋名詞</u>。

 such a disgusting huge brown cockroach
如此一隻巨大噁心的棕色蟑螂

- such（前置限定詞）＋ a（冠詞）＋ disgusting（帶有評價的形容詞）＋ huge（尺寸）＋ brown（顏色）＋ cockroach（名詞）

 the specially designed gigantic local garbage truck
這輛經過特殊設計巨大的當地垃圾車

- the（前置限定詞）＋ specially designed（帶有評價的形容詞）＋ gigantic（尺寸）＋ local（來源）＋ garbage（非材質名詞）＋ truck（名詞）

 a neatly woven round Atayal bamboo basket
一個精細編織的圓形泰雅族竹籃

- a（冠詞）＋ neatly woven（帶有評價的形容詞）＋ round（形狀）＋ Atayal（來源）＋ bamboo（材質名詞）＋ basket（名詞）

 her innocent big blue eyes
她那無辜的藍色大眼睛

- her（代名詞）＋ innocent（帶有評價的形容詞）＋ big（尺寸）＋ blue（顏色）＋ eyes（名詞）
- 中文是藍色的大眼睛，但英文要說「大藍色眼睛」。

■ 認識限定詞

前置限定詞	倍數	• twice 兩倍	• three times 三倍
	分數	• half (1/2) 一半 • one third (1/3) 三分之一 • two-thirds (2/3) 三分之二 • three-fourths (3/4) 四分之三	
	強調	• what 這樣的 • rather 相當、稍微	• such 如此的 • quite 相當、很、頗
	其他	• both 兩者都 • all 全都 • any 任一 • some 一些	
中置限定詞	冠詞	• a 一個 • the 這個	• an 一個
	指示代名詞	• this 這個 • these 這些	• that 那個 • those 那些
	人稱代名詞	• my 我的 • his 他的 • its 它的、牠的 • their 他們的、它們的、牠們的	• your 你的、你們的 • her 她的 • our 我們的
後置限定詞	基數詞	• one 一個 • three 三個	• two 兩個
	序數詞	• first 第一 • third 第三	• second 第二
	量詞	• much 很多 • few 些微 • several 一些 • a piece of 一片	• many 很多 • little 些微 • a cup of 一杯

(2) 基礎形容詞

形容狀態	• slowly 慢地 • quickly 快地 • fast 快地 • silently 靜默地 • loudly 大聲地 • softly 溫柔地 • nervously 緊張地 • quietly 安靜地	• awfully 糟地 • happily 快樂地 • sadly 悲傷地 • aloud 大聲地 • noisily 吵地 • wildly 野生地 • joyfully 愉悅地 • proudly 自豪地	• gently 溫柔地 • protectively 保護地 • generously 慷慨地 • angrily 生氣地 • politely 禮貌地 • rudely 粗魯地 • nicely 好地 • kindly 好地
形容頻率	• rarely 少地 • never 不曾 • sometimes 有時 • often 時常	• daily 每天 • a lot 常常 • again 再一次 • weekly 每週	• monthly 每月 • yearly 每年 • once in a while 偶爾
形容地點	• under 之下 • over 之上 • inside 裡面 • outside 外面 • up 上	• down 下 • beside 旁 • next 下一個 • nearby 附近 • close 靠近	• far 遠 • here 這裡 • away ……遠 • out 外 • in 內
形容時間	• soon 快 • later 之後 • early 早 • finally 終於 • daily 每日 • today 今天 • tomorrow 明天	• yesterday 昨天 • now 現在 • suddenly 突然 • first 首先 • second 第二 • third 第三 • last week 上週	• last month 上個月 • last year 去年 • the next day 隔天 • next month 下個月 • next year 明年 • the same day 同一天

形容人的態度或個性

- absent-minded
心不在焉的
- adventurous
冒險的
- affectionate
深情的、充滿愛的
- agreeable
欣然同意的
- alert 機警的
- ambitious
雄心勃勃的
- amiable
和藹可親的
- assertive
堅定自信的
- attentive
認真傾聽的
- awful 惡劣的
- beneficent
行善的
- blunt 直率的
- boisterous
喧鬧的
- brave 勇敢的
- bright 聰明的
- brilliant 聰明的
- callous 冷酷無情的
- candid 率直的
- cantankerous
愛爭吵抱怨的
- careful 小心的
- careless
粗心的
- caustic 刻薄的
- cautious 小心翼翼
- childish
幼稚的

- cheerful
高興的
- circumspect
小心的
- civil 有禮貌的
- cold 冷漠的
- composed
鎮靜沉著的
- conceited
自以為是的
- condescending
表現出高人一等的
- confident
有自信的
- confused 困惑的
- conscientious
盡心盡責的
- considerate
體貼的
- content
滿足的
- cool
冷靜的、冷漠的
- cool-headed
沉著的
- cooperative
樂於合作的
- courageous
勇敢的
- cowardly
膽小懦弱的
- crafty 狡猾的
- cranky 易怒的
- critical 批判的
- cruel 殘忍的
- curious 好奇的
- cynical
憤世嫉俗的

- decisive 果斷的
- deferential
尊重的
- deft 巧妙的
- dependent
依賴的
- delightful
吸引人的、有趣的
- demure
端莊文靜的（特指女性）
- depressed
沮喪的
- devoted
忠誠的
- diligent
勤奮的
- direct
直率的
- disagreeable
令人討厭的
- disruptive
搗亂的
- distant 冷漠的
- distrustful
無法相信人的
- dramatic
戲劇性的
- dutiful 盡責的
- eager
認真、有決心的
- easy-going
脾氣隨和的
- egotistical
自負的
- emotional
感情激動的
- energetic
精力充沛的

形容人的態度或個性

- enterprising
  有進取心的
- enthusiastic 熱衷的
- even-tempered
  性情平和穩重的
- exacting
  要求嚴格的
- excitable
  易興奮激動的
- experienced
  熟練的
- judgmental
  愛批評人的
- keen 渴望的
- kind
  善良友好的
- lame
  （藉口或論據）站
  不住腳的、無說服
  力的
- lazy 懶惰的
- leery 防備的
- lethargic
  懶散倦怠的
- level-headed
  冷靜沈穩的
- listless
  無精打采的
- lively
  精力充沛的
- lovable
  惹人喜歡的
- maternal
  母性的
- mature 成熟的
- mean 惡劣的
- meddlesome
  愛管閒事的
- mercurial
  反覆無常的

- methodical
  做事有條理的
- meticulous
  嚴謹的
- mild 溫和的
- modest 謙虛的
- morose 陰鬱的
- motivated
  積極的
- naïve
  天真的（負面意
  思）
- nasty
  讓人討厭的
- natural 自然的
- negative 負面的
- nervous 緊張的
- noisy 吵的
- nosy
  愛管閒事的
- obliging
  樂於助人的
- obnoxious
  可憎的
- one-sided
  不公正的
- ostentatious
  很招搖的
- outgoing
  外向的
- outspoken
  坦率的
- passionate
  熱情的
- passive
  被動消極的
- patient
  有耐心的
- paternal
  父親般的

- peaceful 和平的
- peevish 易怒的
- passionate
  熱情的
- patient 耐心的
- peaceful
  和平的
- peevish
  易怒的
- pensive
  憂鬱的
- persevering
  堅忍的
- persnickety
  吹毛求疵的
- petulant
  脾氣暴躁的
- picky
  挑剔的
- plain
  直截了當的
- plain-speaking
  直率的
- playful
  開玩笑的
- pleasant
  令人愉快的
- plucky
  大膽的
- polite
  有禮貌的
- popular
  受歡迎的
- positive 正向的
- powerful
  強而有力的
- practical
  實際的

- prejudiced 有偏見的
- pretty 美麗的
- proficient 熟練的
- proud 自豪的
- provocative 挑撥的
- prudent 謹慎的
- punctual 準時的
- quarrelsome 好爭論的
- querulous 愛抱怨的
- quick-tempered 易怒的
- quiet 安靜的
- realistic 現實的
- reassuring 使人安心的
- reclusive 隱居的
- reliable 可靠的
- reluctant 不情願的
- resentful 憎惡的
- reserved 拘謹矜持的
- resigned 無可奈何的
- resourceful 足智多謀的
- respected 受尊敬的
- respectful 恭敬的
- responsible 負責的
- restless 焦躁不安的
- ridiculous 可笑的
- sad 悲傷的
- self-assured 有自信的
- selfish 自私的

- sensible 明智的
- sensitive 敏感的
- sentimental 傷感的
- serene 平靜的
- serious 嚴肅的
- sharp 敏捷的
- short-tempered 易怒的
- shrewd 精明的
- shy 害羞的
- silly 愚蠢的
- sincere 真誠的
- slight 脆弱的
- sloppy 草率的
- slothful 怠惰的
- slovenly 懶散的
- smart 聰明的
- sneering 輕蔑的
- snobby 勢利的
- somber 憂鬱的
- sober 冷靜的
- sophisticated 世故的
- soulful 深情的
- soulless 沒有靈魂的
- spirited 精神飽滿的
- spiteful 懷恨的
- stable 沉穩的
- staid 沉靜的
- steady 穩定的
- stern 嚴厲的
- stoic 堅忍的
- striking 突出的
- strong 堅強的
- stupid 愚笨的
- sturdy 堅定的

- sullen 悶悶不樂的
- sulky 生氣的
- supercilious 傲慢的
- superficial 膚淺的
- superstitious 迷信的
- surly 粗魯無禮的
- suspicious 多疑的
- tactful 機智的
- tactless 不得體的
- talented 有才能的
- testy 易怒的
- thoughtful 體貼的
- thoughtless 輕率的
- timid 膽小的
- tolerant 寬容的
- touchy 易生氣的
- unaffected 不矯揉造作的
- uncertain 不確定的
- uncooperative 不合作的
- undependable 不可信賴的
- unemotional 無動於衷的
- unfriendly 不友善的
- unguarded 不謹慎的
- unhelpful 不願幫忙的
- unimaginative 缺乏想像力的
- unmotivated （對工作或學習）沒興趣的、沒熱情的

形容人的態度或個性		
• unpleasant 不愉快的	• unwilling 勉強的	• well-behaved 有禮貌的
• unpopular 不受歡迎的	• venal 腐敗的、貪贓的	• well-intentioned 出於好心的
• unreliable 不可靠的	• versatile 多才多藝的	• well-respected 受尊敬的
• unsophisticated 不懂世故的	• vigilant 警戒的	• well-rounded 面面俱到的
• unstable 反覆無常的	• warm 溫暖的	• willing 樂意的
• unsure 不確定的	• warmhearted 熱心的	• volcanic 易怒的
• unthinking 考慮不周的	• wary 謹慎的	• vulnerable 易受傷害的
	• watchful 警惕的	• zealous 熱心的
	• weak 弱的	

形容顏色或光線		
• blazing 閃耀的	• faint 微弱的（光）	• mellow 柔和的（陽光）
• ashen 灰色的、蒼白的	• fiery 火紅的	• milky 乳白色的
• ashy 像灰燼的	• flashy 華麗的	• mingled 混合的
• beaming 光亮的	• flecked 有斑點的	• mixed 混合的
• bi-color 雙色	• fluorescent 螢光的	• monochromatic 單色的
• blazing 耀眼的	• glistening 閃耀的	• mottled 斑駁的
• bleached 變白的	• glittering 閃閃發光的	• multicolored 多彩的
• bright 明亮的	• glowing 熾熱的	• murky 黑暗的
• checkered 方格的	• hazy 朦朧的（天色）	• neutral 中性的
• chromatic 彩色的	• illuminated 發光的	• opalescent 乳白色的
• colored 有色的	• incandescent 熾熱的	• opaque 不透明的
• colorful 多彩的	• iridescent 色彩斑斕的	• pale 蒼白的
• colorless 無色的	• kaleidoscopic 萬花筒似	• pastel 顏色柔和的
• contrasting 鮮明對比的	• lambent 光線柔和的	• patchy 顏色不均的
• dappled 斑紋的	• light 明亮的、淡的	• patterned 有圖案的
• dark 深色的	• luminous（在黑暗中）發亮、發光的	• plain 樸素的
• deep 深色的		• prismatic 彩虹色的
• delicate 精緻的	• lustrous 閃亮的	• radiant 光芒四射的
• dim 黯淡的		• ruddy 紅色的
• dotted 有斑點的		
• dusty 有灰塵的		
• faded 褪色的		

形容顏色或光線	• saturated 飽和的 • shiny 閃亮的 • sooty 炭黑色的 • sparkling 閃閃發光的 • speckled 有斑點的 • stained 有污漬的	• tinted 有色的（玻璃） • translucent 透明的 • transparent 透明的 • two-tone 兩種色調的 • undiluted 未稀釋的	• uneven 不均勻的 • vibrant 醒目的 • vivid 生動的 • warm 溫暖的 • washed-out 褪色的 • waxen 蒼白的

(3) 描述感官方面的詞

跟視覺有關的單字	• bulky 龐大的 • crooked 彎曲的 • drab 單調的 • dull 無趣的 • gigantic 巨大的 • glitter 閃閃發光的 • gloomy 黑暗的 • glowing 發光的 • hazy 朦朧的	• knotty 有結的 • murky 黑暗的 • shadowy 昏暗的 • shimmering 閃爍的 • shiny 閃亮的 • sparkling 閃閃發光的 • teeny-tiny 極小的 • vibrant 鮮豔的
跟觸覺有關的單字	• chilled 放鬆的 • creepy 讓人起雞皮疙瘩的、毛骨悚然的 • crisp 脆的 • fluffy 毛茸茸的、蓬鬆的 • hairy 多毛髮的	• itchy 使人發癢的 • rough 粗糙的 • slimy 黏糊糊的 • smooth 光滑的 • sticky 黏的
跟聽覺有關的單字	• boom 隆隆聲 • buzz 嗡嗡聲 • crunchy 口感脆的 • deafening 震耳欲聾的、刺耳的 • earsplitting 震耳欲聾的、刺耳的 • faint 微弱的（聲音）	• humming 嗡嗡作響的 • roaring 喧囂的、轟轟作響的 • squeaky 吱吱作響的、發出尖銳聲的 • hiss 嘶嘶聲 • sizzle （油炸物）滋滋作響

跟味覺、嗅覺有關的單字	• bland 平淡的、沒有滋味的 • rotten 爛掉的 • fragrant 芳香的 • stale 不新鮮的、走味的 • juicy 多汁的 • stinky 臭的 • gooey 軟黏的 • bitter 苦的 • yummy 好吃的 • sweet 甜的 • sour 酸的	• spicy 辣的 • fishy 魚腥味的 • fresh 新鮮的 • fruity 水果味的 • minty 薄荷味的 • mouth-watering 令人垂涎的 • salty 鹹的 • perfumed 芳香的 • scented 有香味的 • stinky 臭的 • sweaty 有汗味的

(4) 寫敘述文時只有形容詞可以用嗎？

除了形容詞之外，我們還有其他方法為文章描述增添趣味與變化。

❶ 添加地方副詞

描述事情時，如果能把地點交代清楚，讀者更能馬上意象化整個故事的場景，因此使用地方副詞是必要的。

• on the first floor 在一樓 • straight ahead 直直向前 • underneath the bed 在床下 • on your right-hand side 在你的右手邊 • adjacent to the fences 緊鄰圍欄	• behind the door 在門後 • against the wall 面對牆壁 • above the head 高於頭頂 • to the left 朝左

❷ 倒裝的地方副詞：地方副詞＋ V ＋ S

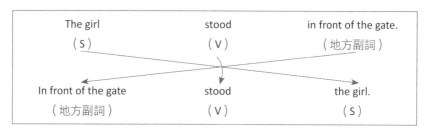

The girl　　　　　stood　　　　　in front of the gate.
（S）　　　　　　（V）　　　　　　（地方副詞）

In front of the gate　　　　stood　　　　　the girl.
（地方副詞）　　　　　　　（V）　　　　　　（S）

把地方副詞提前之後，有強調這個地方正在發生這件事情的功能。但是以下幾種情形不適用此種方式。

① 代名詞如果是主詞，就不能使用這個句型

> 例
> Here comes the bus.
> 公車來了。→不能改寫成「Here comes it.」

> 例
> There you are!
> 你在這裡呀！→不能改寫成「There are you.」

② 原句裡如果有助動詞，也不能使用這個句型

> 例
> The passengers <u>should</u> wait behind the white line.
> 乘客應該在白線後等候。
> →不能改寫成「Behind the white line should wait the passengers.」

③ 遇到Ving進行式時，改寫方法有所不同

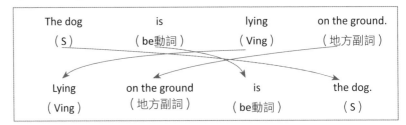

❸ 形容詞子句／關係子句

國中學過的文法概念，用到敘述文裡就可以變成修飾名詞的好朋友。只要使用了 who、whom、whose、that、which 的句子都是形容詞子句／關係子句，用來形容句子當中的名詞具有何種特質。

> 例
> It is an elegant dress <u>that looks delicate and feminine</u>.
> 這是一件看起來精細且女性化的優雅洋裝。

 PLUS!
- that 後面的 delicate（精細的）和 feminine（女性化的）可以修飾前面的 an elegant dress（一件優雅的洋裝），並且添加細節讓讀者知道這件洋裝除了「優雅」之外，還有何種特質。

As I walked into the restaurant, I was stunned by the luxury interior design, <u>which is rarely seen in this part of the area.</u>

當我走進餐廳時，我被這奢華的室內設計震懾住了，因為在這個地區很少見到。

PLUS!
- which 後面的句子修飾了這樣的室內設計是如何的特別。

 Taipei 101, <u>which is the tallest building in Taiwan</u>, rises 508 meters in the air.

臺北 101 是臺灣最高的建築物，高度 508 公尺。

PLUS!
- which 後面的句子修飾了臺北 101 是怎樣的建築物。

使用形容詞子句的好處在於可以串聯起所有跟主題有關的資訊，並提供一個組織過後的敘述，讓讀者閱讀時閱讀更流暢自然。假如讀者在讀文章時，沒辦法得到整理過後的一系列資訊，而是被很多短句或句號所打斷閱讀的過程，那麼讀文章這件事會變的非常吃力。

❹ 能讓句子長得更好看的分詞

看起來像是動詞的 Ving ／ Vpp，其實是具有形容詞作用的分詞。主動的時候用 Ving，被動則用 Vpp 的型態。

型態	Ving（主動）	Vpp（被動）
放在前面修飾的分詞	• a <u>screaming</u> kid 　正在尖叫的孩子 • <u>boiling</u> water 　正在沸騰的水	• a <u>stolen</u> car 　一輛被偷的車 • a <u>hidden</u> truth 　一個被隱瞞的事實
放在後面修飾的分詞	• Anyone <u>who majors</u> in foreign literature should see this movie. →Anyone <u>majoring</u> in foreign literature should see this movie. *任何主修外國文學的人都應該看這部電影。*	• The products <u>which are made</u> in this company are good. →The products <u>made</u> in this company are good. *任何在這間公司生產的產品都很好。*

分詞 當主詞補語	• The little boy ran away <u>screaming</u>. 這個小男孩跑邊跑邊尖叫。 →這裡的Ving修飾主詞小男孩的狀態。	• I stood there <u>amazed</u> by the scenery. 我站在那，被景色所震懾住了。 →這裡的Vpp修飾主詞「I」的狀態。
分詞當 受詞補語	• Don't leave the water <u>running</u> if you are not using it. 如果你沒有要用水，就別讓它一直開著。 →這裡的running修飾受詞 the water的狀態。	• The student heard his name <u>called</u>. 學生聽到他的名字被叫到。 →這裡的called是用來修飾受詞the name。
分詞用來 描述情緒	• a <u>boring</u> lecture 一堂無聊的課	• a pair of <u>terrified</u> eyes 一對驚恐的雙眼

(5) 如何描述人

　　描述人時，可以從外表開始，並逐漸延伸到其行為。以外表來說，我們可以從幾個方面著手：臉部表情、頭髮及五官的樣子、說話的方式、衣著的樣式、身形、走路的樣子。

　　以下面這段文字來說，文字當中陳述了 Christine 的美貌，從頭髮、嘴巴、嘴唇再到笑容。

例 Christine is as elegant as any celebrity you can see on the TV. Her long, curly brown hair falls down to her waist and always glistens like a diamond wherever she walks. She has a delicate small mouth, and her lips are always covered with rose pink lipstick. When she smiles, her straight white teeth lighten up her face. Her beauty is beyond description, and there is nothing but a stunning beauty in her face.

克莉絲汀就像你在電視上會看到的明星一樣的優雅。她一頭長捲棕髮垂墜至腰部，無論何時，當她在走路時，這頭長髮總是像鑽石般閃爍著光澤。她有著一個精緻小巧的嘴巴，而她的嘴唇總是覆蓋著玫瑰粉的口紅。當她笑的時候，她的一口整齊白牙總是讓她的臉亮了起來。她的美難以言喻，在她臉上什麼都看不見，就只有驚為天人的美麗而已。

但如果你想描述的對象真的沒有太多可以陳述之處，寫敘述文其實也沒有硬性規定一定要寫幾個細節。有時候，挑出一到兩個特別有趣或是明顯的特徵專注寫好，也能達到很好的效果。

> (例) When it comes to Leonardo da Vinci's most famous painting, Mona Lisa is definitely second to none. The oil painting, famous for the smile of the lady, has attracted millions of visitors to visit the museum to decipher her mysterious smile. Her smile is up to the imagination: at first, she seems like gazing at you, then the smile disappeared when you move. After staring at her for a while, it seems like she has always been fixing her eyes on you.
>
> 一提到達文西最有名的畫像，蒙娜麗莎絕對是第一名。這幅油畫以這名女士的微笑著名，已經吸引了數百萬遊客造訪博物館來解密她那神秘的笑容。她的笑容給大家留下許多遐想空間，一開始看起來好像在看你，接著隨著你移動，笑容消失了。再繼續盯著她一陣子後，看起來似乎她從頭到尾都在看著你。

在這段文字中，雖然都是繞著蒙娜麗莎的笑容打轉，但是光是仔細的描述清楚笑容這一件事情，就已經可以達到吸引讀者的效果了，這個時候描述蒙娜麗莎的其他五官或是樣貌反而會分散讀者注意力，並沒有太大的幫助。

1-3 選擇時態的小撇步

(1) 現在簡單式

不會因為文章當中所採取的時態而改變的事實或真理。

> (例) The Great Wall is in China.
> 萬里長城在中國。

> (例) Light travels faster than sound.
> 光比聲音傳遞的速度還快。

(2) 過去簡單式

當遇上一系列接續發生的事件時，就可以使用簡單過去式來描述一個接著一個的事件。

Nate got up late and rushed to the bus stop. When he arrived at the bus stop, he realized that he was not the only one who slept over.

內特晚起並衝去公車站。當他抵達公車站，他明白他不是唯一一個睡過頭的人。

(3) 未來簡單式

講述未來才會完成的事情。

例 The director will shoot a movie next year.

這位導演明年將會開拍新電影。

(4) 現在進行式

用來形容目前正在進行中（通常是短期、暫時的）事件。

例 I am making dinner for my family.

我正在為家人作晚餐。

(5) 過去進行式

為了要表達故事發生當中出現了中斷事件發展的小插曲，我們會使用過去進行式來描述被中斷的當下發生了什麼狀況。

例 As we were discussing the homework, one of my friends let out a scream. We stopped talking immediately because everyone was shocked by her scream and the big cockroach crawling on her face.

當我們在討論作業時，一個朋友發出尖叫，我們立刻停止討論，因為每個人都被她的尖叫和一隻爬行在她臉上的大蟑螂嚇到了。

(6) 未來進行式

用來形容未來預期會持續發生一段時間的事件。

例 The whistleblower will keep breaking the news to several TV programs for the next few weeks.

這位告發者將會在接下來幾周內持續爆料給幾個電視節目。

(7) 現在完成式

描述在過去開啟的事件，而且預期還會持續下去，也可以用來強調過去事件與現在的關聯。

> 例 She has finished most of her projects, but she still has some documents left to revise.
>
> *她已經完成她大部分的專案，但她仍然有一些剩下的文件需要修改。*

(8) 過去完成式

當我們想要強調某件事情在過去時比另外一件事情早結束，可以使用過去完成式。使用這個時態時有個好處，那就是當我們需要強調先前所發生的事情時，可以採取這個時態，並讓事件的發展更加清楚。

> 例 We decided to go out and celebrate because we had just finished remodeling our home.
>
> *我們決定出去慶祝，因為我們剛剛完成裝修我們的家。*

> 例 Janet didn't join us for dinner as she had already eaten.
>
> *珍妮特不和我們一起吃晚餐，因為她已經吃過了。*

(9) 未來完成式

當我們想描述介於現在和未來某個特定的時間點會完成的事情時，就必須使用未來完成式。

> 例 The company will have launched more than a hundred products by the end of the first quarter.
>
> *這間公司在第一季結束前，將會發行超過一千種產品。*

(10) 現在完成進行式

用來描述在過去某件在過去開始的事件，但持續發生到現在，或是很快就會結束的事件。透過這個時態，可以強調過去發生的事情與現在這個當下的連結。

The students have been burning the midnight oil, and now they need to get some sleep.

這些學生已經熬了一整個晚上，現在他們需要去睡一下。

(11) 過去完成進行式

當我們想要陳述在過去的某個時間點裡，一個動作延續了多長的時間時，可以採用過去完成進行式。

例 The kid had been begging his mother for months to get him a PS5 when he finally got one.

這個小孩幾個月以來一直吵著要他的媽媽買一台 PS5 給他，直到他終於拿到一台了。

例 She had been nagging him for months to get a better job when he finally was hired.

她幾個月以來一直嘮叨著要他找一份更好的工作，直到他終於被雇用。

(12) 未來完成進行式

未來完成進行式通常會有時間副詞，例如 for several weeks、since last year，且會使用「will have been Ving」或「be going to have been Ving」來表示時態，這兩種寫法通常可互換，可用來表示未來某個時間之前持續的動作，或預估動作還會持續下去。

例 The author will have been writing this book for three years when she gets her book published.

到了出版她的書那天，這位作者將會花三年的時間寫這本書。

■ **現在簡單式、現在進行式的對比**

現在簡單式	現在進行式
• 用來表示長期的習慣，因此句子當中常有always（總是）、usually（通常）、often（經常）、sometimes（有時候）、seldom（很少）、never（從不）。	• 描述在寫作或說話的這個當下，一連串動作中的某一個特定動作

• 描述不變的真理或是科學已證實是真的事情。	• 描述在不久的將來會發生的一個安排或計畫,通常在句子中會包含時間,例如tonight(今晚)、tomorrow(明天)、this week(這周)、this year(今年)、this century(本世紀)。

例句:
• He goes to work by bus every morning.
  每天早上他都搭公車去上班。
• The Sun rises in the east.
  太陽從東邊升起。
	例句:
	• They are writing their homework.
	  他們正在寫功課。
	• I am leaving for Taipei tomorrow.
	  我明天就要上臺北了。

■ 過去簡單式、過去進行式、過去完成式的對比

過去簡單式	• 用來表達發生在過去的動作或事件。 • 句型中常會看到before(以前)、yesterday(昨天)、yesterday morning / afternoon / evening(昨天早上/下午/晚上)、last night(昨晚)、few hours ago(幾小時前)。

	例句:
	• Everything seemed normal that evening.
	  那個傍晚,一切看起來跟往常一樣。
	• It was pretty dark when my wife and I finally found our way to the nearest eatery.
	  當我和我的太太終於找到最近的小餐館時,天色滿晚了。

過去進行式	• 句型為was / were+Ving,句型中常會看到while(當)或是as(當)。 • 用來表達過去某一特定時間內開始且正在持續或進行的動作。 • 也可以在文章中使用此句型來特別標示就是在過去的這個時間點發生了某件事。

	例句:
	• <u>While</u> I was waiting patiently in line, I noticed that a guy cut in line.
	  當我正耐心排隊等候時,我發現有個男的插隊。
	  →用while表達事件同時發生。
	• It was pouring rain <u>as</u> we hiked up the mountain.
	  我們爬山的時候正在下大雨。
	  →用as代表兩件事情同時發生。

145

過去完成式	• 句型為had＋Vpp。 • 這個句型用來表示表達過去事件中，某件事情比另一件事情還早發生。先發生的事件用had＋Vpp，而後發生的事件用過去簡單式來表示。 • 大考常用的倒裝句型「no sooner... than」（一……就）以及「Hardly... when」（一……就）必須使用hap＋Vpp。
	例句： • When I arrived at the station home, the rain had stopped. *當我抵達車站時，雨已經停了。* →雨停之後，我才到車站。 • I had no sooner turned off the air-conditioner than I started to sweat like a pig. *我一關冷氣就汗流浹背。* • The cyber celebrity had hardly started to take a selfie when it began to rain heavily. *這個網紅一開始自拍就開始下大雨。*

搞懂時態，避免亡者死而復生

請看以下的敘述，並回答問題。

1. 請問誰現在不一定在講電話？
   (A) My mom talks on the phone.
   (B) My dad has been talking on the phone for an hour.
   (C) My girlfriend is talking on the phone.

2. 請問誰已經離開了？
   (A) My grandparents never left Taiwan.
   (B) My dad has never left Taiwan.

3. 請問誰的行為最有可能被班上討厭？
   (A) The guy sitting in front of me is talking loudly in class.
   (B) Chris always talks loudly in class.
   (C) Our class leader is always talking loudly in class.

4. 請問這五個選項裡的人，誰沒有和 Bob 碰到面？
   (A) Celine left when Bob arrived.
   (B) Lyndsey left when Bob had arrived.
   (C) When Bob arrived, Maddie was leaving.
   (D) Peter had left when Bob arrived.
   (E) After Bob arrived, Joseph left.

5. 請在現在簡單式的句子底下畫線，現在進行式的句子用螢光筆畫底色。

> Justin wants to be a veterinarian, so he is attending a university in Taichung during the daytime and is majoring in Veterinary Medicine. In addition, he also volunteers at an animal shelter at night, and he is responsible for giving the homeless animals baths. This semester, he is taking a course in animal nursing, and he is giving a presentation on his experience of working in the animal shelter next week. Justin is extremely anxious about speaking in front of the public, and he worries about the presentation all the time. He practices hard every day, and he speaks to the animals when he is taking care of them.

參考答案

1. **(A)**：「My mom talks on the phone.」這句話用的是簡單式，通常代表事實，所以這件事可能常發生，但不代表現在這個當下媽媽就在講電話。
2. **(A)**：(B) 的「My dad has never left Taiwan.」用的是現在完成式，表示這件事情在過去開啟，而且預期還會持續下去，但 (A) 的「My grandparents」用的是過去式，可以推測祖父母已離開。
3. **(C)**：「is always talking」代表總是在講話，一直持續的行為，因此會被班上討厭。
4. **(D)**：句中描述 Peter 的動作時，使用了 had left（過去完成式），而 Bob 的抵達則是使用過去式，代表 Peter 早在 Bob 到之前就已經離開這個地方了，所以不可能碰到面。
5.

> Justin wants to be a veterinarian, so he is attending a university in Taichung during the daytime and is majoring in Veterinary Medicine. In addition, he also volunteers at an animal shelter at night, and he is responsible for giving the homeless animals baths. This semester, he is taking a course in animal nursing, and he is giving a presentation on his experience of working in the animal shelter next week. Justin is extremely anxious about speaking in front of the public, and he worries about the presentation all the time. He practices hard every day, and he speaks to the animals when he is taking care of them.
>
> 賈斯汀想成為一名獸醫，所以他白天在台中念大學並主修獸醫學。此外，他晚上在動物收容所當志工，負責幫無家可歸的動物洗澡。這學期，他修一門動物護理課程，下周他要報告他在動物收容所工作的經歷。賈斯汀對於在大眾面前講話非常焦慮，他一直在擔心報告。他每天都認真練習，並且在照顧動物時和他們說話。

1-4 常見的敘述文題型以及攻破法

敘述文的題型很多元，以下提供兩種常見題型及寫作技巧給大家參考。

(1) 描述個人經驗

通常這類型的題目會請你描述你個人經驗，例如：第一次嘗試做不擅長的事情的感受，描述你最喜歡的電影以及它如何影響了你，又或是請你描述一個至今難忘的經驗等等。

你需要做的就是使用個人的感受以及當下的反應來引發讀者的同理心，讓他們也想起自己的經驗，引發好奇與認同感。雖然每個人未必會歷經同樣的事，但是能讓讀者想像你當下的情境，並激發他們的理解。但是通常描述個人經驗時，往往會過於冗長或用詞不精準，而導致整篇文章讀起來抽象又空洞。這個時候只要記得三個要點：

一、 只選擇最能表達你當下感受的經驗來陳述，其他不相關或是與主題不那麼有直接連結的經驗就不須書寫而占用段落。

二、 只使用生動且精準的文字，例如你要形容是一個非常糟的回憶，比起 a bad memory 你可以說 a bitter（苦澀的）memory、a painful（痛苦的）memory、an unpleasant（令人不快的）memory。

三、 因為是要你描寫個人經驗，可以用主觀的口吻陳述事情，因此通常都是用第一人稱。

(2) 客觀描述所見所聞

這類文章跟論述文有點類似，主要是透過詳細陳述某事，或是提出核心概念，客觀提供你所陳述的事情的全貌，而不是依照個人過去經驗或自身想法。這類型的題目通可能會是請你介紹臺灣、解釋氣候變遷是怎麼發生的，或是陳述某個歷史事件。

與前面主觀描述自己的經驗不同，如果要請你介紹臺灣，就必須如實陳述臺灣的地形、氣候、都市或是可以進行的文化活動等，內容就不能是：

> 例 Kaohsiung is a city located in southern Taiwan, and it is my favorite city.
> 高雄是位於臺灣南部的一個城市，也是我最喜歡的城市。

1-5 敘述文範文解析

我們以「The Person I Admire the Most and The Reasons」（最崇拜的對象以及原因）為題，來寫一篇敘述文。

第一段 ▶ Introduction（引言）

During the COVID-19 pandemic, keeping our hands clean has become not only an effective way of preventing disease but also an obsession _{Hook（開頭）} for all. To prevent the spread of germs, people are advised to wash their hands with soap and water thoroughly. However, this practice may seem quite common today, but that has not always been the case. You might _{主題} want to know who was the first person proposing such a brilliant idea. _{引起讀者興趣}

在新冠肺炎肆虐期間，保持手部的乾淨不但是一個有效防止疾病的方法，也變成大家瘋狂著迷的事情。為了要避免細菌傳播，人們被建議要用肥皂和清水徹底洗手。洗手在現代是很常見的做法，但在以前並不是如此的。你也許會想知道是誰先提出這麼聰明的建議。

▶ 第一段解說

第一段要寫出崇拜的對象是誰，以及簡單介紹這位主角的事蹟。不需要寫出太多細節，否則後面就沒有內容可寫了。

第二段 ▶ Body Paragraph 2（主體段落二）

A bald man with a mustache, appearing on the homepage of Google on March 20th, 2020, was honored by Google Doodle for promoting the practice of handwashing. Ignaz Semmelweis, a 19th-century

Hungarian doctor, was known as the first to promote handwashing. When Semmelweis was working for a hospital in Vienna, he discovered that childbed fever, a life-threatening disease that was killing mothers in maternity wards across Europe at the time, was related to a sort of infectious substance being transmitted on the hands of doctors who had performed autopsies. However, his revolutionary discovery was rejected by the medical community. What's worse, years of controversy gradually undermined his spirit, and he ended up dying from an infection in a mental hospital.

一個禿頭又有鬍子的男人，在 2020 年 3 月 20 日出現在 Google 的首頁上，Google Doodle 向其致敬推廣洗手的做法。伊格納茲‧塞麥爾維斯，一位 19 世紀的匈牙利醫師，以首先推廣洗手聞名。當塞麥爾維斯在維也納的一間醫院工作時，他發現產褥熱，一種在當時的歐洲奪走許多在產房母親們性命的致命疾病，是與一種有傳染力的物質有關連，而這是由執行過解剖的醫師之手所傳染的。然而，他具有開創性的發現被醫界所否定。更糟的是，多年來的爭議逐漸削弱的他的意志，而他最終在精神病院死於感染。

第三段 ▸ **Body Paragraph 3（主體段落三）**

Although people at the time did not appreciate the significance of his findings, thanks to Semmelweis, modern people have benefited greatly from this now-basic hygienic practice as a way to stop the spread of COVID-19. He has achieved a crucial medical breakthrough, and his valuable contribution to modern medicine cannot be overemphasized.

雖然當時的人們並不感謝他的發現，但正因為塞麥爾維斯，現在的人們大大地從他的現在看起來很基本的衛生習慣獲得好處，並作為一種預防 COVID-19 散播的方法。他在醫學的突破取得了極其重要的成就，而他對現代醫學極具價值的貢獻無論如何強調也不為過。

▸ **第二、三段解說**

　　第二、三段中的底線字都是形容詞，在描述一個人或事情時，適時的加入形容詞可以讓讀者更覺得身歷其境。

在中間段落的開頭，先描述了塞麥爾維斯的外型：禿頭以及鬍子，接著描述他的出身與職業，再來強調他在醫學方面的貢獻，最後提到不被理解、抑鬱而終，慢慢鋪陳這位悲劇性人物的一生。從文章當中的形容詞可以形塑出這個人值得被尊敬的形象，並同時以各種歷史上發生的事件說明原因。

<table><tr><td>第四段</td></tr></table> ▶ Conclusion（結論）

Semmelweis' advice on handwashing was probably more <u>influential</u> than he imagined. If Semmelweis were alive today, he could be <u>amazed</u> to find that billions of people around the globe were now acting on his advice to weather the storm. Semmelweis <u>paid a heavy price</u> as he devoted his life to pushing the boundaries of medical knowledge, and it seems <u>fitting</u> that we pay grand tribute to this <u>pioneering</u> doctor's brilliance, originality, and dedication to <u>countless</u> lives.

塞麥爾維斯對於他建議要洗手這件事的影響力可能超乎他的想像。假如他現在還在世的話，他可能會很驚奇地發現全球數百萬的人正奉行他的建議來度過難關。塞麥爾維斯以他的性命付出了沉重的代價來挑戰醫學知識的極限，也因此，我們理所當然的要向這位先驅醫師的聰穎、原創性，以及對無數性命的奉獻致敬。

▶ **第四段解說**

末段的部分，底線字是形容詞，此段進一步強調了我們應當感謝塞麥爾維斯對於現代人的貢獻，並且藉由新冠肺炎，這個影響全球人類生活的疾病，強化了當時與現在的對比。藉由提出作者與讀者都曾經歷過的類似事件，更能讓讀者感受到這位醫師真的是值得我們敬仰的對象。

Story（故事寫作）：很久很久以前……

故事發展流程表 ▶

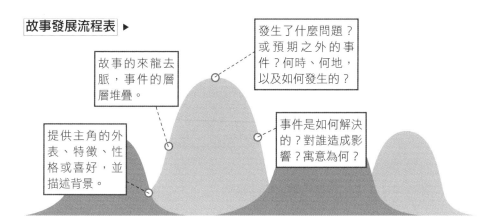

發生了什麼問題？或預期之外的事件？何時、何地，以及如何發生的？

故事的來龍去脈，事件的層層堆疊。

提供主角的外表、特徵、性格或喜好，並描述背景。

事件是如何解決的？對誰造成影響？寓意為何？

國外的英文課在教故事寫作時，經常會用到「Story Mountain」來構思，從故事的背景開始，隨著山勢的變化，逐漸發展出故事的重點，最後再帶到結尾，也許是故事所要教導的寓意，也許是皆大歡喜或是意想不到的結局。下次寫故事時，不妨使用這個「Story Mountain」來構思，能更有邏輯的鋪陳故事的時間軸與書寫細節喔！

另外，我們也可以利用表格化的方式來提醒自己在寫故事時，各段需要注意帶入何種細節，才能讓故事讀起來更有趣生動。

在故事的開頭……	可以使用以下幾種開頭的方式： **(1) 使用狀聲詞** Shhhhh! The baby is sleeping! *噓！寶寶在睡覺！* **(2) 創造懸疑感** An expected event happened on my 21st birthday, and my life has been changed ever since. *我 21 歲生日那天發生了一個意料中的事，從此我的生活就改變了。* **(3) 使用帶有情緒的單詞** Relieved. My eyes were filled with relief as I know my dad would come back home from the battlefield. *鬆了口氣。當我知道父親將從戰場回家時，我的眼睛充滿了寬慰。*

	(4) 對話
	"What on Earth were you thinking?" my teacher scolded me loudly in front of the class.
	「你到底在想什麼？」我的老師在全班面前責罵我。
	(5) 描繪意象
	My heart leaped up, and I could hear my heartbeats clearly. My hands were covered with sweat, and my mouth was like sandpaper.
	我的心快跳出來了，我都能聽到我的心跳聲。我的手都是汗，而我的嘴像沙紙。
描述各個事件	**(1) 多使用精準的形容詞**
	例如：delighted（高興的）、marvelous（令人驚豔的）、sloppy（粗心的）、awkward（尷尬的）、clumsy（笨拙的）等。（請參考敘述文的章節）
	(2) 使用轉折詞連接各個事件
	例如：first（首先）、next（下一個）、and then（然後）、afterward（之後）、in the end（最後）、meanwhile（同時）等等。（請參考轉折詞的章節。）
	(3) 在各個事件當中可以穿插對話、預告、提及過去的事情，以及提供解決故事主角所遭遇的困境的方法。
終於來到 結尾……	**(1) 提供令人意想不到的結局**
	讓讀者在讀完結局後感到驚喜。
	(2) 提供有寓意的結局
	就像伊索寓言一樣，在讀完這個故事之後讀者可以從故事主角的經驗學到一課。
	(3) 使用對話的結局
	通常這類對話帶有震撼效果，可以讓讀者透過對話得到反思，也可以在對話中安插名言佳句，更具說服力。
	(4) 帶有懸念的結局
	有些開放式的結局可以留給讀者自己去解讀，這類的結局會帶給讀者很多想像空間。

2-1　不只是好人、壞人與結局：寫故事的眉眉角角

常看到寫故事有 5W1H，實際上要如何運用呢？

Where & When（場景）	場景包含的不只是實際的環境描述，也包含事件發生的時間，故事發生的時間與地點都包含在場景描述中。
Who（主角）	可以考慮故事的本質來決定主角是人、東西或是動物，而故事的主角主導的對話或動作則是故事情節發展的重點。
What（情節）	情節與故事當中發生的事件有關，大致上可分為：開頭、劇情鋪陳、高潮、故事收尾以及結局，情節都常都圍繞在故事主人翁所遭遇的困難與問題，以及這個難題是如何被解決的。
Why（衝突）	每一個精彩的故事都會穿插一些動人心弦的小故事，不管是奮發向上的主人翁或是復仇的王子，在在都刻劃了充滿戲劇性情節的轉折。故事當中的主角所面臨的挑戰或是難題都能夠讓整個故事更具可看性，也會吸引讀者跟著主角一起闖關打怪。假如能在故事當中加入因果關係的事件，能讓讀者讀起來更有同理心與參與感。
Theme（主題）	主題跟情節不太相同，情節偏向陳述發生的事情與經過，主題則是本篇故事要傳達的宗旨、課題、道理或是道德方面的反思，也就是故事所要呈現給讀者的訊息。

2-2　如何排列組合故事

　　透過轉折詞以及跟時間標記有關的單字，可以讓事件發展讀起來更流暢有邏輯，以下整理了從故事開始到結束可以使用的字詞。

(1) 故事的開頭

- Once upon a time, … 很久很久以前……
- First of all, 首先……
- To start off with, 以……開始

- Initially, 首先……

- To begin with, 首先……

- In the beginning, 首先……

> 例 <u>Once upon a time</u>, a farmer lived in a shabby house.
> 很久很久以前，有一個農夫住在一間殘破不堪的房子裡。

> 例 <u>To begin with</u>, I lined up patiently in order to buy my favorite drink.
> 首先，為了買我最喜歡的飲料，我很有耐性地排隊。

> 例 <u>To start off with</u>, they decided our destination was Tainan. <u>Initially</u>, I thought it was a great idea.
> 一開始，他們決定了我們的目的地是臺南，事實上我一開始也覺得是個好主意。

(2) 各個情節間的連結

- as soon as ─ ……就……

- after 在 ……之後

- Then, 接著，

- After that, 在之後，

- Next, 接著，

- As soon as / When + S+V 當……就……

- …but then 但是接著……

- Immediately, 瞬間……

- Shortly after, 不久之後……

> 例 <u>Then</u>, I started to get worried.
> 接著，我開始感到很擔心。

> 例 <u>After that</u>, we knew that we could never trust him anymore.
> 在那之後，我們知道我們再也無法相信他了。

> 例 <u>Next</u>, he painted the wall with the color red.
>
> *接著，他用紅色漆滿了整面牆。*

> 例 <u>As soon as</u> the tourists arrived, they changed their clothes and unpacked their luggage.
>
> *遊客一抵達，他們馬上換衣服並打開行李箱。*

> 例 I was absolutely sure everything was packed before I got on the train, <u>but then</u> something happened unexpectedly.
>
> *在我上火車前，我確信所有東西都有打包好，但之後一件毫無預警的事情發生了。*

> 例 <u>Immediately</u>, he hopped on the bus.
>
> *他馬上跳上公車。*

(3) 營造故事的轉折

- Suddenly, 突然……
- All of a sudden, 突然……
- Unexpectedly, 出乎意料地，……

> 例 <u>Suddenly</u>, she burst into tears and started to cry like a baby.
>
> *她突然間像個嬰兒一樣大哭了起來。*

> 例 <u>Unexpectedly</u>, all the students in the room disagreed with the chief of the Students' Union.
>
> *毫無預警的，房間裡的學生們反對學生會的會長所言。*

(4) 為故事畫下結局

- Finally, 最後，……
- In the end, 最後，……
- Eventually, 最終，……
- When things came to an end, 結束的時候，……

> 例 <u>Finally</u>, I have made the decision and will take a year off.
> 最後，我下定決心要請假一年。

> 例 <u>In the end</u>, he decided to postpone the family reunion.
> 最後，他決定推遲家庭聚會。

> 例 <u>Eventually</u>, the two family feud made peace and became best friends.
> 最終，這兩個家庭世仇也和解了，並成為最好的朋友。

(5) 描述同時發生的事件

- While / As ＋ S ＋ V ＋從屬子句
- 獨立子句＋ while / as ＋ S ＋ V
- During ＋ N / 名詞片語或子句

> 例 <u>While</u> the singer was giving a performance, a fan rushed to the stage and grabbed her by the arm.
> 當這個歌手正在表演的時候，一個粉絲衝上台抓住她的手臂。

> 例 I shared the story <u>as</u> my parents prepared dinner.
> 我父母在準備晚餐的時候，我邊分享這個故事。

> 例 <u>During</u> the conversation, our boss showed no interest in solving the problem.
> 在對談中，我們的老闆毫無解決問題的意思。

> 例 We conducted a variety of experiments <u>during</u> the process.
> 我們在過程中做了一些實驗。

2-3　描述人物特徵的字

　　寫故事時，要能夠強化主角的人格特質，也因此需要使用不同的形容詞來描述故事的主角性格，在前面說明文的地方有許多形容詞可以使用，這裡則是提供描繪正反面的人格特質形容詞給大家參考。

正面的人格特質		
	• active 活潑的	• fair 公平的
	• adventurous 愛冒險的	• friendly 友善的
	• affectionate 充滿感情的	• generous 慷慨的
	• ambitious 有野心的	• gentle 溫和的
	• brave 勇敢的	• hopeful 有希望的
	• brilliant 傑出的	• humorous 幽默的
	• capable 有能力的	• independent 獨立的
	• careful 仔細的	• intelligent 聰明的
	• caring 關心他人的	• insistent 堅持的
	• charismatic 領袖魅力的	• logical 邏輯的
	• charming 迷人的	• lovable 可愛的
	• clever 聰明的	• loving 親愛的
	• compassionate 有同情心的	• loyal 忠誠的
	• concerned 關心的	• optimistic 正向的
	• confident 有自信的	• peaceful 和平的
	• conscientious 認真的	• persistent 堅持的
	• considerate 體貼的	• polite 有禮貌的
	• cooperative 合作的	• reliable 可靠的
	• courageous 勇敢的	• respectful 恭敬的
	• courteous 禮貌的	• responsible 負責的
	• dependable 可靠的	• sincere 真誠的
	• determined 堅決的	• smart 聰明的
	• efficient 有效率的	• thoughtful 深思熟慮的
	• energetic 精力充沛的	• trustworthy 可信賴的
	• enthusiastic 熱情的	

負面的人格特質	• afraid 害怕的	• irresponsible 不負責任的
	• anxious 焦慮的	• jealous 嫉妒的
	• argumentative 好辯的	• lonely 孤單的
	• bossy 專橫的	• mean 刻薄的
	• bully 霸凌	• moody 易怒的
	• boring 無趣的	• obnoxious 討厭的
	• childish 幼稚的	• pessimistic 負面的
	• clumsy 笨拙的	• picky 挑剔的
	• cranky 暴躁的	• restless 焦躁的
	• cold-hearted 冷血的	• rowdy 吵鬧的
	• competitive 好勝的	• rude 粗魯的
	• conceited 自負的	• sarcastic 諷刺的
	• cowardly 膽小的	• secretive 秘密的
	• critical 愛挑剔的	• selfish 自私的
	• cruel 殘忍的	• sensitive 敏感的
	• dishonest 不誠實的	• sly 狡猾的
	• eager 渴望的	• sneaky 鬼祟的
	• foolish 愚蠢的	• snobbish 勢利的
	• gloomy 沮喪的	• stingy 吝嗇的
	• greedy 貪婪的	• strict 嚴格的
	• grouchy 不滿的	• stubborn 頑固的
	• hateful 可恨的	• thoughtless 輕率的
	• hopeless 絕望的	• timid 膽小的
	• ignorant 無知的	• unfriendly 不友善的
	• immature 不成熟的	• unruly 不守規矩的
	• impolite 無禮的	• unsure 不確定的
		• withdrawn 沉默寡言的

2-4　經常被誤用的形容詞與副詞

　　以下是 15 個容易被誤用的形容詞與副詞，請先看單字，想想詞性再讀例句。

(1) bad、badly：bad 是形容詞，表示壞的、不好的、令人不悅的或是卑劣的人格。badly 是副詞，表示嚴重地。

> 例 Our weekend was spoiled by bad weather.
> *我們的周末被壞天氣給毀了。*

> 例 Miraculously, none of the passengers was badly injured in the crash.
> *奇蹟似地，沒有任何一個乘客在車禍中受重傷。*

(2) good、well：good 是形容詞，表示令人滿意、愉快的。well 是副詞，表示非常、充分地、很好地，令人滿意地（well 也可以當形容詞使用，表示健康的，例如「My grandfather hasn't been very well lately.」我的祖父最近身體不太好。）

> 例 This xiaolongbao was as good as the ones Ding Tai Fung sells.
> *這個小籠包跟鼎泰豐賣的一樣好吃。*

> 例 I can't do it as well as you can.
> *我沒辦法做得像你一樣好。*

(3) everyday、every day：everyday 是形容詞，表示日常的、通常的、普通的。every day 是副詞。

> 例 Going to cram school is the everyday life of many ordinary Taiwanese students.
> *去補習班這件事是許多一般臺灣學生的日常生活。*

> 例 Many Taiwanese students go to cram school every day.
> *很多臺灣學生每天都去補習班。*

(4) real、really：real 是形容詞，表示現實的、真實的。really 為副詞，表示事實上、實際上、真正地、確實地、的確。

> 例 Parents who are too protective of their children could not equip these children to deal with the real world.
> *太保護自己小孩的父母沒辦法讓這些小孩具有面對真實世界的能力。*

> 例　Can you help me with my homework?
> 你可以協助我寫功課嗎？

> 例　I'm really sorry, but I can't this time. I've got to finish my report now.
> 我很抱歉，但這次真的不行。我現在必須要完成我的報告。

(5) sure、surely：sure 是形容詞，表示確定的、肯定的。surely 是副詞，表示肯定地、無疑地。

> 例　I was quite sure that I left my cell phone on the bus.
> 我還滿確定我把手機留在公車上了。

> 例　Without food and emergency supplies, these refugees will surely not survive.
> 沒有這些食物和救援物資的話，這些難民們肯定無法存活。

(6) hard、hardly：hard 是形容詞，表示困難的、費力的、堅硬的、堅固的。hardly 是副詞，表示幾乎不……。

> 例　It's hard to say which options suit your needs better.
> 很難說哪一個選項比較適合你。

> 例　The words are printed so small that I can hardly read them.
> 這些字印得太小了，我幾乎無法看清楚。

(7) high、highly：high 是形容詞，指高的。（high 也可以當副詞使用，表示很高地，例如「The baseball player batted the ball high into the air.」，這位棒球選手將球高高地打到天空中。）highly 是副詞，意思是非常、極度。

> 例　The dining table is 1 meter high and two meters wide.
> 這張餐桌一公尺高，兩公尺寬。

> 例 For our company to remain highly competitive, we need experienced and highly-educated employees.
> 為了讓我們的公司維持高度的競爭力，我們需要有經驗且受過高等教育的員工們。

(8) short、shortly：short 是形容詞，表示短的、矮的。shortly 是副詞，表示不久、很快。

> 例 It's only a short walk to the destination.
> 走一小段路就會到我們的目的地了。

> 例 We arrived at the party shortly before it ended, so we did not get to meet everyone.
> 我們在派對結束前不久才抵達，所以我們沒能見到所有人。

(9) near、nearly：near 是形容詞，表示近的、接近的。nearly 是副詞，表示幾乎、差不多、將近。（near 也可以當副詞，表示「離……不遠、靠近」。例如「Is there an eatery near here?」這附近有小餐館嗎？）

> 例 Where's the nearest eatery?
> 最近的一間小餐館在哪？

> 例 It has been nearly a year since my last trip to Taitung.
> 距離我上次去臺東玩已經將近一年了。

(10) wrong、wrongfully：wrong 是形容詞，意指錯誤的、不正確的。wrongfully 是副詞，表示不正當地、不法地。

> 例 Some of the facts in this historical drama are questionable, while the others are completely wrong.
> 這部歷史劇裡的事實有些是值得懷疑的，而其他的則是完全錯的。

> 例 The ex-con sued the court for being wrongfully convicted for killing a victim.
> 這名前科犯控告法庭誤判殺人罪。

(11) deep、deeply：deep 是形容詞，表示深的。deeply 是副詞，表示深深地、極其、非常。

> 例 Take a deep breath and calm down. Everything will be just fine.
> *深呼吸，冷靜一下。一切都會很好的。*

> 例 After 30 years of marriage, the couple are still deeply in love.
> *經過三十年的婚姻，這對夫妻依然深深愛著彼此。*

(12) dead、deadly：dead 是形容詞，表示死亡的、去世的。deadly 是形容詞，指致命的。

> 例 The patient was dead on arrival at the hospital.
> *病人在到院前已死亡。*

> 例 Stroke is one of the deadly diseases of long-term disabilities.
> *中風是其中一種會造成長期殘疾的致命疾病。*

(13) late、lately：late 是形容詞，表示遲的、晚的。（late 也可以當副詞使用，表示很晚地，例如「We talked late into the night.」，我們聊天聊到很晚。）lately 是副詞，意指最近、近來。

> 例 You'll be late for school if you don't hurry up.
> *你再不動作快一點，上學就要遲到了。*

> 例 Have you been reading any books lately?
> *你最近有讀什麼書嗎？*

(14) wide/widely：wide 是形容詞，表示多少寬的、寬的、寬廣的。widely 是副詞，意指範圍廣地、廣泛地。

> 例 The yard is three meters wide.
> *這個院子三公尺寬。*

例　The new COVID-19 vaccination was starting to be more widely accepted by people around the globe.

新的新冠肺炎疫苗開始廣泛地被全球人民接受。

(15) all together、altogether：all together 是形容詞片語，表示一起。altogether 是副詞，意指總共、一共。

例　Put your assignments all together in one pile, and I will grade them later.

把你們的作業堆成一疊，我等等再改。

例　That'll be $3120 altogether. Cash or plastic?

一共 3120 元，現金或信用卡付費？

2-5　故事寫作範文解析

　　請仔細觀察以下三幅連環圖片的內容，並想像第四幅圖片可能的發展，然後寫出一篇涵蓋每張圖片內容且結局完整的故事，文長至少 120 個單字。

運用故事山構思：

故事發展流程表 ▶

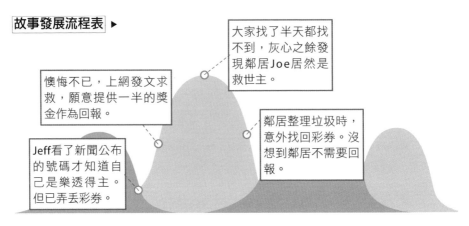

大家找了半天都找不到，灰心之餘發現鄰居Joe居然是救世主。

懊悔不已，上網發文求救，願意提供一半的獎金作為回報。

鄰居整理垃圾時，意外找回彩券。沒想到鄰居不需要回報。

Jeff看了新聞公布的號碼才知道自己是樂透得主。但已弄丟彩券。

整理故事山的重點並寫成完整文章。

第一段 ▶

As the proverb goes, "One man's trash is another man's treasure," and the same is true of Jeff's experience. Before heading to work, Jeff was having a cup of coffee leisurely, and meanwhile, he was checking the news on his social media website. Seeing the headline "LOTTERY WINNING NUMBERS," Jeff was in extreme shock to discover that he hit the jackpot. He could not believe what he had read on the news, so he kept checking the numbers repeatedly. Recovering from the shock, Jeff was filled with excitement and joy.

俗話說：「某人無用之物，可能是他人的寶貝。」傑夫的經歷也是如此。上班前，傑夫悠閒地喝著咖啡，同時查看他的社群媒體網站上的新聞。看到標題「樂透中獎號碼」，傑夫極度吃驚地發現自己中了大獎。他無法相信他在新聞上看到的消息，所以他不斷地核對數字。傑夫從震驚中回神，心裡充滿了興奮和喜悅。

Unfortunately, the thrill did not last very long — Jeff realized he had mistakenly thrown away the lottery ticket. Yelling and screaming, he could not believe he was so careless that he missed this once-in-a-lifetime opportunity. What's worse, the garbage truck had already taken the garbage to the dump early in the morning. Jeff raced to the dump in hopes that he could retrieve the million-dollar worth of ticket — but no such luck. He searched high and low for the ticket, turning the dump upside down and still could not find it.

不幸的是，這種興奮並沒有持續多久——傑夫意識到他誤把樂透丟了。他大吼大叫，不敢相信自己竟然如此粗心，導致錯過了這個千載難逢的機會。更糟的是，垃圾車一大早就已經把垃圾送到垃圾場了。傑夫跑到垃圾場，希望能拿回價值百萬元的樂透，但沒有這種好運。他把垃圾翻遍了，也沒找到那張樂透。

▶ **第一、二段解說**

先利用俗語：「某人無用之物，可能是他人的寶貝。」來引起讀者的好奇心，接著逐步鋪陳傑夫從上班前悠哉地喝咖啡、看新聞，接著吃驚地發現自己得了大獎（hit the jackpot）。但不幸地是，他的喜悅並沒有維持太久，因為他發現自己不小心把彩券丟了。他不敢相信自己居然把一生就這麼一次的機會給弄丟了，更慘的是，他想起垃圾車早上就已經運走垃圾了。他只好拔腿跑向垃圾場並努力翻找這張價值百萬元的彩券。

整個故事必須循序漸進，並營造懸疑感，同時讓讀者感同身受傑夫懊悔自己的粗心大意、努力想要補救，甚至是感受到在垃圾場翻找的臭味。

With despair, Jeff decided to post on social media for help. He stated clearly in the post that anyone who could rescue his ticket from the trash could split the prize in half. Before long, numerous enthusiastic prize hunters went to the dump, digging through trash. However, the ticket remained missing despite everyone's exhaustive search. Sitting in his living room, Jeff cast a regretful glance at his post on social media, wondering what kind of fool would toss the winning ticket away. Suddenly, the doorbell rang. He answered the door listlessly only to discover it was his neighbor, Joe.

絕望之下，傑夫決定在社群媒體上發文求助。他在文中明確表示，任何人只要能把他的樂透從垃圾桶裡救出來，就可以平分獎金。不久，無數的賞金獵人來到垃圾場，在垃圾堆裡翻找。然而，儘管大家竭盡全力地尋找，那張樂透還是不見。傑夫坐在客廳裡，遺憾地看了一眼他在社群媒體上發的文，想知道什麼樣的笨蛋會把中獎的樂透扔掉。突然，門鈴響了。他無精打采地開門，原來是他的鄰居，喬。

第四段 ▶

Inside Joe's hand was a wrinkled paper – it was Jeff's lottery ticket! Seeing the question in Jeff's eyes, Joe explained that someone in the community placed the wrong item in the recycling bin, and thus the sanitation worker refused to empty the bins and take the garbage away unless the residents in the community recycle properly. Joe volunteered to do the recycling for all the residents, and that was why he recovered the ticket from the trash. He handed the ticket to Jeff, requesting nothing but a donation to the local charity. Jeff pondered on Joe's selfless decision about the prize he deserved to split, then he claimed the prize the next day. With happiness, Jeff announced the good news in a press conference "Thanks to Joe, I managed to recover the ticket from the trash. The odds of winning the prize are extremely low, but the odds are probably lower if the winner has a kind-hearted neighbor to dig through the dumpster to find the ticket. One man's treasure is everyone's treasure, and that's why I have decided to donate my prize to the local schools and charity."

喬手裡拿著一張皺巴巴的紙 —— 那是傑夫的樂透！喬看到傑夫眼中的疑問，解釋說社區裡有人把錯誤的東西放在回收箱裡，因此清潔工拒絕清空回收箱並把垃圾帶走，除非社區裡的居民適當地回收。喬自願為所有的居民回收垃圾，所以他從垃圾堆裡找到了那張樂透。他把樂透遞給傑夫，只要求傑夫捐助給當地的慈善機構就好。傑

夫思考著喬無私的決定，決定給他應得的獎金，接著第二天他取得獎金。傑夫高興地在記者會上宣佈了這個好消息：「多虧了喬，我才從垃圾裡找回了樂透。中獎的機率非常低，但如果中獎的人有一個好心的、會翻遍垃圾桶尋找樂透的鄰居，這個機率可能更低。一個人的寶藏，就是所有人的寶藏，這就是為什麼我決定把獎金捐給當地的學校和慈善機構。」

▶ **第三、四段解說**

　　傑夫決定上網求助，任何可以找到彩券的人將可以和他平分獎金。消息一出果然吸引大批人到垃圾場翻找，但仍然沒有彩券的蹤跡。這裡鋪陳了故事的高潮：原來彩券自始自終都在社區的垃圾桶內。傑夫的鄰居喬因為知道社區內有人回收沒有做好，導致清潔隊拒收垃圾，熱心的喬幫忙大家整理垃圾時找到了彩券。善良的喬不求回報，只要求傑夫必須把要平分的那一份獎金捐出去給當地的慈善機構。

　　故事的寓意鋪陳在開頭句子，而在結尾時利用傑夫的這番話呼應：「得到大獎的機率很低，但是能遇到這麼善良的鄰居機率更低。一個人的寶藏，應該要是所有人的寶藏才對。」

　　利用改寫開頭第一句，將善良以及分享的精神發揮出來，並透過劇情的轉折「原來彩券離傑夫這麼近」讓讀者有驚喜的感受。

Section 03　老是John, John, John，別再醬寫了！

　　寫故事或看圖寫作時，很容易碰上一個尷尬的狀況，那就是無止境的用代名詞開頭。以下經原作者同意，分享一篇看圖寫作的作品：

> 例 It was a sunny day outside, so John decided to go picnicking with his friends. <u>John</u> invited all his friends, and asked them to prepare some food and drinks. <u>When John</u> was heading to the park, he bumped into a car. <u>John</u> stood up and found that everything he had prepared was on the floor. <u>He</u> started to cry, and the police came. <u>John</u> had to walk home because his bike was broken. <u>When he</u> got home, he saw the posts and photos of his friends picnicking happily in the park. <u>John</u> was very upset, and he couldn't help but burst into tears again.

> 這是一個陽光普照的日子。所以約翰決定和朋友去野餐。約翰邀請所有朋友，並請他們準備食物和飲料。當約翰前往公園時，他撞上一輛車，約翰站起來並發現所有準備的東西都掉在地板，他開始哭，警察來了。約翰必須走回家，因為自行車壞了。當他回家時，他看到他朋友在公園愉快野餐的貼文和照片，約翰很難過，他忍不住又哭了出來。

仔細數一數，並觀察底線字的部分，在只有 8 句的短段落裡，用 John 或是代名詞開頭的句子居然高達 7 句。有沒有覺得這樣一直重複 John 或是 he，讓句子讀起來很死板無聊，沒有任何變化呢？

正是因為這樣，所以一篇好的文章需要不同句型，才能讓讀者覺得你描述的事件是有趣的，讀者閱讀起來也才不會覺得很吃力，感覺一直鬼打牆在讀同樣的主題。

要能夠增添句型的變化，以大方向來說，使用長句可以把多種資訊融合在一起，短句則可以強調重要資訊，句型穿插使用可增添閱讀的樂趣。以下我們先來看如何改善一直 John 的窘境，接著我們會複習基本的句型有哪些，最後我們會進入如何結合句型並營造句型的變化。

3-1　整篇都是你我他她它，你，累了嗎？

其實要改善句子一直 I、I、I 或是 John 和 Mary 開頭的窘境，最簡單的方式就是在每一句開頭營造不同驚喜，讓讀者去找出彩蛋。不妨試試每種句型都使用 2 ～ 3 句，如此一來就可以營造句型的層次感。

如何開頭	例句
使用副詞開頭	• <u>Slowly</u>, the rain began to fall. 慢慢地，雨開始下。
使用形容詞開頭	• <u>Smart</u> though he is, he has been scammed for millions of dollars. 雖然他很聰明，但他被騙了數百萬美元。 • <u>Speechless</u>, I couldn't believe what I have just heard. 無言以對，我無法相信我剛聽到的。
使用地點開頭	• <u>From the rooftop</u>, you can see the magnificent view of the city. 你可以從屋頂上看到這城市宏偉的景觀。

使用時間開頭	• <u>At midnight,</u> the snow had already piled up against the walls. 雪在半夜時已經堆積在牆角。
使用分詞開頭 (-ing/-ed)	• <u>Feeling</u> intense pain, the patient cried like a baby. 病人感到劇烈疼痛,哭得像個孩子。 • <u>Stunned</u> by the breathtaking view, all the tourists let out a scream with joy. 被這令人驚嘆的景象震懾,所有遊客開心地尖叫。
使用比喻開頭	• <u>As white as a ghost</u>, her face turned pale. 她的臉色蒼白地像鬼一樣。 • <u>Like a streak of lightning</u>, the burglar grabbed the money and ran out of the shop. 竊賊快如閃電,抓了錢跑出了商店。
使用連接詞開頭	• <u>Although</u> Philip burned the midnight oil, he failed to finish his assignment before class. 雖然菲利浦熬了夜,他還是未能在上課前完成作業。
使用當下的狀況開頭	• <u>Out of fear,</u> the thief ran out of the house and broke his leg. 小偷出於恐懼跑出了屋子,並摔斷了腿。 • <u>Not caring at all,</u> the visitors broke into the National Park and stole the precious plants. 遊客毫不在乎地闖入國家公園並偷走珍貴植物。

黯淡的原句	妙筆生花後的句子
The dog lies in the sun.	1. 以 -ing 的字開頭
	_____
	_____
	2. 以 -ly 的字開頭
	_____
	_____
	3. 以介係詞片語開頭
	_____
	_____
	4. 以形容詞開頭
	_____
	_____
The man was waiting.	5. 以地點開頭
	_____
	_____
	6. 以時間開頭
	_____
	_____
	7. 以比喻開頭
	_____
	_____

8. 以連接詞開頭

_____

_____

9. 以當下的狀況開頭

_____

_____

參考答案

1. **以 -ing 的字開頭**
   Lying in the sun, the dog was doing his daily sunbathing.
   躺在陽光下，狗狗正在做牠的每日日光浴。

2. **以 -ly 的字開頭**
   Happily, the dog lies in the sun. 狗狗快樂地躺在陽光下。

3. **以介係詞片語開頭**
   On the meadow, the dog lies in the sun. 狗躺在陽光下的草地上。

4. **以形容詞開頭**
   Feeling laid-back, the dog lies in the sun. 狗懶洋洋地躺在陽光下。

5. **以地點開頭**
   Outside the department store, the man was waiting in the line.
   那個男人在百貨外面排隊等著。

6. **以時間開頭**
   At midnight, the man was waiting in line, hoping to the be the first to win the prize.
   那個男人在半夜排隊等著，希望他是第一位獲獎的人。

7. **以比喻開頭**
   As patient as Job, the man was waiting in the line.
   那個男人像約伯一樣超有耐心地等在隊伍裡。

8. **以連接詞開頭**
   Because the department store was having an annual sale, the man was waiting patiently outside the store.
   因為百貨公司在舉行年度特賣，那個男人很有耐心地在店外等著。

9. **以當下的狀況開頭**
   With patience, the man was waiting in the line.
   那個男人耐心地排隊等候。

粉絲男孩們指的是七個寫作常用的連接詞：

FANBOYS（粉絲男孩們）	
F	For：用來解釋原因
A	And：用來添加理由，或是接續下一個動作
N	Nor：用來表示既非A也非B
B	But：用來比較，或是表達發生了沒有在預期當中的事情
O	Or：表達選項或是當下的狀況
Y	Yet：用來比較，或是表達發生了沒有在預期當中的事情
S	So：表達因為前面發生了某件事，所以才有so之後的事件

對等連接詞是連接詞當中最小的單位，可以用來連接字和字、片語和片語以及句子和句子，也因為長度通常很短，所以通常不需在 FANBOYS 後方再加逗號。

但也正因為如此，所以經常有以下被忽略的情況：

假如有兩句主要子句（兩個主詞和兩個動詞）時，一定得加上逗號才能符合文法規則。舉例來說：

 You have a keen mind, but you don't have execution.
你有敏銳的頭腦，但你沒有執行力。

這個句子必須在 FANBOYS 的前方加上逗點，因為有兩個主詞（you）和兩個動詞（have）。

又像是：

 My dog likes to play fetch, so I bought her a frisbee.
我的狗喜歡玩接球，所以我買了一個飛盤給她。

這個句子必須在 FANBOYS 的前方加上逗點，因為有兩個主詞（my dog 還

有 I）和兩個動詞（likes、bought）。

但如果改寫成：

> (例) You have a keen mind but lack execution.
> *你有敏銳的頭腦但缺少執行力。*

> (例) My dog loves to play fetch and eat meatballs.
> *我的狗喜歡玩接球和吃肉丸。*

這樣的句子只有一個主詞，因此不須加上逗號。

除此之外，要表達一系列的事物時，例如 A, B, and / or C，雖然不加逗號是可以接受的，但是還是建議一律都在 and / or 的前面加個逗點；特別是如果前面列舉的東西文字長度都很長時，一定要加上逗點。

> (例) You can try cycling around the island, going mountain-climbing, and surfing Taiwan.
> *你可以試著在這座島上騎自行車，去爬山，並在臺灣衝浪。*

> (例) You can try cycling around the island, going mountain-climbing and surfing Taiwan.
> *你可以試著在這座島上騎自行車，去爬山，並在臺灣衝浪。*

> (例) A good listener pays attention to others without interrupting, asks questions once in a while, and provides full support during the whole conversation.
> *一個好的傾聽者會全神貫注而不打斷，偶爾問問題，並在整段對話中傾全力支持。*

接著，假如有兩個，或多於兩個形容詞在句中，而且沒有使用連接詞 and / or 連接的話，務必在形容詞之間使用逗號。

> (例) He was an ambitious, powerful, determined runner.
> *他是一個有野心的、有力量的、有決心的跑者。*

> (例) The timid, anxious student handed in the wrinkled, thick report.
> *那個膽小焦慮的學生交了一份又皺又厚的報告。*

(1) 簡單句＝ S ＋ V ＝一句獨立子句。

例　The cell phone rang during the exam.
　　手機在考試中響起。

例　We will help you.
　　我們會幫你。

例　The restaurant serves delicious burgers.
　　這家餐廳提供美味的漢堡。

(2) 合句＝包含兩句完整句（獨立子句），並且由粉絲男孩們（FANBOYS：for、and、nor、but、or、yet、so）所組成。

例　The students complained that they have studied many hours for the test, but they failed to pass it.
　　學生抱怨他們已為考試讀了好幾小時，但是沒有及格。

例　Tim arrived at school early, so he decided to clean up the class.
　　湯姆很早到校，所以他決定打掃教室。

(3) 複句＝包含了一句獨立子句，中間會用連接詞結合一句或多句從屬子句。

例　The girl turned away her face <u>because</u> she didn't feel like talking.
　　那個女生轉過臉去，因為她不想談話。

(4) 複合句＝由合句以及複句所組成。

例　Because the teacher wanted to keep her students' attention focused exclusively on studies, she asked the students to put away their cell phones, and she asked them to meditate for a while.
　　因為老師想讓學生只專注在學習上，她要求學生把手機拿走，並讓他們沉思一會兒。

你必須在短時間內讀懂
多種數據要呈現的意義、
所佔的比例或是比較的訊息。

Chapter

04

圖表寫作

　　透過上面的引言，我們可以知道，能讀懂圖表的人，就掌握了數字。也因為圖表讓讀者能在短時間內讀懂數字要呈現的意義、所佔的比例或是想要比較的訊息，寫作時若能善用這種視覺元素，或是能夠清楚的表達出數句本身的意義，對於呈現資料會有很大的助益。

Section 01　圓餅圖？長條圖？各種圖表怎麼説？

以下就以考試最常見的四種圖表來做説明：

	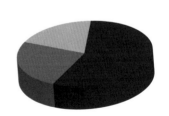
bar chart 長條圖	**pie chart 圓餅圖**
用來比較概念、比例，以及用來比較在某個特定的時間軸所發生的事情，長條圖可以拿來解説比例、趨勢、對比和比較。	圓餅圖很適合用來解説各種資料之間的比例，也可以清楚看出各種資料分布的狀況，特別是在需要分類的資料時，更能看出資料之間的關係與所佔的比重。

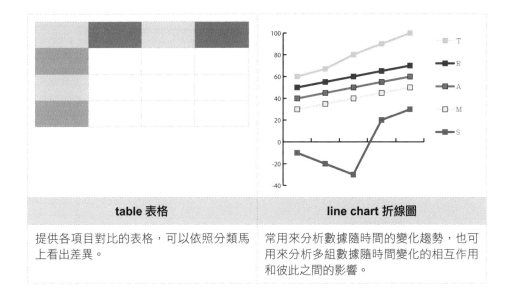

table 表格	line chart 折線圖
提供各項目對比的表格，可以依照分類馬上看出差異。	常用來分析數據隨時間的變化趨勢，也可用來分析多組數據隨時間變化的相互作用和彼此之間的影響。

Section 02 萬用圖表寫作句，讓你考試不用一直show, show, show

　　圖表寫作因為牽涉到數字、比例，以及需要呈現資料之間的關係，因此腦袋中建立起一些常用的字句是必要的。以下透過表格整理出三種常見句型給大家。

(1) 這個圖表描述了……

這個	圖表探討的內容	圖表「描述」了……
The +	• figure 數字 • statistic 數據 • number(s) 數字／據 • percentage 百分比 • proportion 比率	+	• shows 顯示 • describes 描述 • illustrates 闡述 • reveals 顯示 • demonstrates 顯示 • suggests 顯示

(2) 從圖表可以看出……

從	圖表	可以	看出	什麼……
From the	• table, 表格， • figures, 數據， • data, 資料， • results, 結果， • information above, 上述資訊中，	it can / may be	• seen 看出 • concluded 總結 • shown 顯示 • estimated 預測 • calculated 計算出 • inferred 推論出	that...

(3) 如圖所示……

所示	如圖
• As can be seen from / in 可以看到…… • As is shown in the 從表格可以看到……	• the chart / table /graph / figures / statistics, 表格／表格／圖表／數據／數據
• It has been	• shown / revealed / illustrated in the chart that... 從表格可以看到……

2-1 形容趨勢的變化：動詞篇

圖表中最重要的就是要能精準的描述趨勢，而趨勢的變化往往與動詞息息相關。

(1) 形容趨勢上升

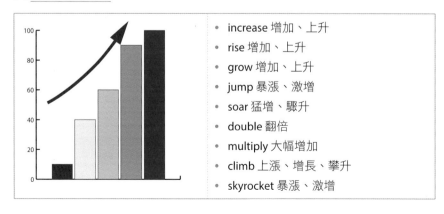

- increase 增加、上升
- rise 增加、上升
- grow 增加、上升
- jump 暴漲、激增
- soar 猛增、驟升
- double 翻倍
- multiply 大幅增加
- climb 上漲、增長、攀升
- skyrocket 暴漲、激增

> **例** The number of college students in Taiwan <u>increased</u> significantly between 2000 and 2012.
> 臺灣的大學生數量在 *2000* 年和 *2012* 年大幅地增加。

> **例** Production of rice <u>rose</u> from 800 tons in 2017 to 3000 tons in 2019.
> *米的生產量從 2017 年的 800 噸增加到 2019 年的 3000 噸。*

(2) 形容趨勢下降

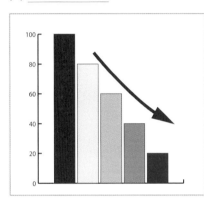

- decrease 減少、降低
- drop 減少、降低
- fall 減少、降低
- decline 減少、降低
- go down 下跌
- plummet 暴跌、急遽下降
- plunge 暴跌、急遽下降

> **例** Prices of product A <u>dropped</u> significantly once product B became available on the market.
> 一旦 *B* 產品在市場可以買得到時，*A* 產品的價格開始顯著的下降。

> **例** Company profits <u>decreased</u> in 2020 by 15%.
> *公司的利潤在 2020 年減少了 15%。*

(3) 描述圖表波動

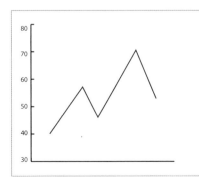

- fluctuate 波動、起伏
- undulated 波動、起伏

圖表寫作

Chapter 4

> 例 The price of Bitcoin started to <u>fluctuate</u> at this level for a few hours before the eventual new high.
>
> 比特幣的價格到了這個階段開始持續波動數小時，直到最後的高點。

(4) 保持穩定的狀態

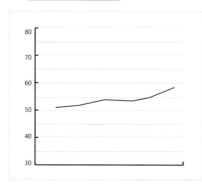

- maintain / remain / stay 保持
- stable / steady / constant / unchanged 穩定的
- level off 回穩

> Prices have <u>leveled off</u> gradually and are no longer increasing.
>
> 價格逐漸地回穩，而且不再漲價。

(5) 到頂點

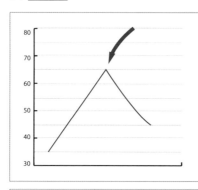

- reaches a peak 到達頂點
- peak 抵達巔峰
- reaches its highest level 抵達最高點

> 例 The euro <u>has reached its peak</u> since 2018.
>
> 自從 2018 年，歐元已經到達它的高峰。

(6) 降到最低

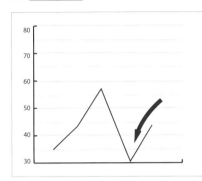

- hit a low 達低點
- bottoms out 達最低點
- sank to a trough 降至低谷
- sank to the lowest level 降至最低點

例 Oil prices have <u>hit a low</u> in 2020 by the COVID-19 pandemic.
油價在 *2020* 年因為新冠肺炎大流行而降至最低點。

2-2 形容趨勢的變化：副詞篇

　　善用副詞可以讓我們在形容趨勢時更能傳遞圖中的數字變化的情形，也能讓讀者透過文字判讀圖表。

(1) sharply / steeply 急遽地

例 The coronavirus cases have risen <u>sharply</u> in the past few days.
新冠肺炎的病例在過去幾天急遽增加。

例 The infection rate of such disease decreases <u>steeply</u>.
該種疾病的感染率急遽減少。

(2) rapidly / quickly 快速地

例 With the investment from top leading companies, eyedrops for the cataract market will grow <u>rapidly</u> in the forthcoming years.
有了頂尖公司的投資，治療白內障的眼藥水市場將會在來年快速成長。

例 One way to lose weight <u>quickly</u> is to cut back on sugars and starches, or carbohydrates.
一個能快速減重的方法就是減少攝取糖、澱粉或碳水化合物。

(3) considerably / substantially 可觀地

> 例 The figure provides a valuable indication of trends in the local area, which can fluctuate <u>considerably</u> from day to day.
> 這個數據提供了有用的跡象說明當地的趨勢，每天通常都會波動很大。

> 例 House prices in some of the country's holiday hotspots have skyrocketed <u>substantially</u> this year.
> 房價在某些國家的旅遊勝地大幅地暴增。

(4) dramatically 大幅地

> 例 The price of raw materials has increased <u>dramatically</u>.
> 原物料價格大幅地增長。

(5) noticeably / significantly 明顯地、顯著地

> 例 The cost of the product increased <u>noticeably</u>.
> 該項產品的價格明顯地增加了。

> 例 Airfares have dropped <u>significantly</u>, down to a minimum of $50 one way.
> 飛機的票價顯著地降低了，低至單趟 50 元。

(6) steadily 穩定地 / moderately 適度地

> 例 The cost of living has been increasing <u>steadily</u>.
> 生活費穩定增加。

> 例 The start-up remains <u>moderately</u> profitable, but it is not making as much money as the investors have expected.
> 這間新創公司維持適度地獲利，但它並沒有像投資人預期的一樣賺錢。

(7) slightly / slowly 微幅地、緩慢地

 Temperatures <u>slowly</u> fall this evening.
溫度在傍晚慢慢地下降。

(8) gradually 逐漸地

 Our production is improving <u>gradually</u>.
我們的生產逐步地改善。

2-3 形容趨勢的變化：介係詞篇

我們可以根據以下的圖來描述一段趨勢，請仔細觀察動詞所搭配的介係詞。

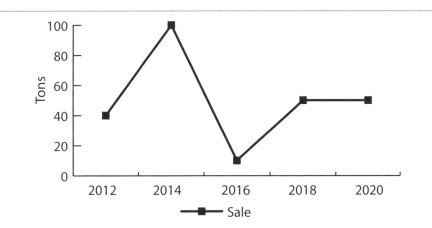

The graph started <u>at</u> 40 tons <u>in</u> 2012, and it peaked <u>at</u> 100 tons <u>in</u> 2014. <u>From</u> 2014 <u>to</u> 2016, the sales dropped significantly, and it sank <u>to</u> the lowest level <u>at</u> 10 tons <u>in</u> 2016. Then the sales rose <u>to</u> 50 tons <u>in</u> 2018, and it remained stable <u>between</u> 2018 <u>and</u> 2020.

此圖從 2012 年的 40 噸開始，在 2014 年的 100 噸到達高峰。在 2014 年到 2016 年之間，銷售大幅跌落，並在 2016 年抵達最低點 10 噸。接著在 2018 年銷售上漲至 50 噸，並在 2018 年到 2020 年間保持穩定。

● 從……年到……年有兩種寫法，第二種比較容易寫錯，要多留意喔！
① from XXXX 年 to XXXX 年（例如：from 2010 to 2015）
② between XXXX 年 and XXXX 年（例如：between 1900 and 1920）

看完前面的範例之後，我們可以快速地用以下這個表格檢核，寫作的時候可隨時翻閱，加深自己的熟練度和記憶力喔！

詞組	動詞＋介係詞	名詞＋（介係詞）
增加	rise to	a rise
	increase (to)	an increase
	go up to	
	grow to	growth
	climb to	a climb
	boom	a boom
	peak at	reach a peak at
減少	fall (to)	a fall of
	decline (to)	a decline of
	decrease (to)	a decrease of
	dip (to)	a dip of
	drop (to)	a drop of
	go down (to)	
	reduce (to)	a reduction of
		a slump
保持不變	level out	
	remain stable / steady at	
	stay at	
	stay constant at	
	maintain the same level	

2-4 形容趨勢的變化：形容詞篇＋名詞篇

這個圖表／表／表格顯示了	形容詞＋名詞		在……方面
The graph / chart / table shows / reveals that there has been a / an ＋	• slight 些微的 • steep 急遽的 • sharp 急遽的 • steady 穩定的 • gradual 逐漸的 • marked 顯著的 • significant 顯著的 • considerable 可觀的 • dramatic 大幅度的 • dramatically 大幅度地	• rise 增加 • growth 增加 • increase 增加 • fall 減少 • decline 減少 • decrease 減少 • dip 暫時性或小幅度的下降 • drop 下降 • slump 大跌 ＋	in…

2-5 形容趨勢的變化：倍數篇

描述趨勢時，常常會需要用到跟倍數有關的詞。

(1) S ＋ V ＋倍數＋形容詞／副詞比較級＋ than

例 The birth rate of native English speakers is three times higher than the rate for non-English speakers.
母語為英文者的出生率是母語非英文者的三倍。

• 使用此句型時，不能使用 half，另外「兩倍」不能寫 twice，需寫 two times。

(2) S ＋ V ＋倍數＋ as ＋形容詞原級／副詞＋ as

例 The gear is twice / two times as heavy as that one.
這個裝備是那個裝備的兩倍重。

例 The new machine produces four times as efficiently as the old one.
新的機器生產效率是舊的四倍。

(3) S ＋ V ＋倍數＋ the ＋ size（尺寸、大小）／ length（長度）／ height（高度）／ weight（重量）／ number（數字）／ price（價錢）＋ of ＋某物

> 例 Taipei 101 is nearly <u>twice the height of</u> the Eiffel Tower.
> 臺北 101 大概是接近艾菲爾鐵塔的兩倍高。

(4) 倍數＋ as ＋ many ＋可數名詞＋ as ...

倍數＋ as ＋ much ＋不可數名詞＋ as ...

> 例 He has half <u>as many</u> hoodies <u>as</u> his best friend does.
> 他的帽 T 數量是他摯友的一半。

> 例 Humans sleep five times <u>as much as</u> large land mammals do.
> 人類睡眠的時間是大型陸上哺乳類的四倍。

PLUS!

- 兩倍用 twice / two times 皆可，超過兩倍一律都是數字加 times。

請將以下的單字填入段落中。

particularly	high	up	with	reached
compared	estimated	number	increase	in

The ① _____ of people leaving Taiwan for 12 months or more ② _____ a record ③ _____ in 2008, ④ _____ an estimated 100,000 people emigrating. This was ⑤ _____ from 80,000 in 2019.

There has been a large ⑥ _____ ⑦ _____ the number of people emigrating for working abroad, ⑧_____ those with specialties. In 2019 a(n) ⑨ _____ 30,000 people emigrated from Taiwan to take up a definite job, ⑩_____ with 20,000 in 2018.

圖表寫作

Chapter 4

參考答案

The ① <u>number</u> of people leaving Taiwan for 12 months or more ② <u>reached</u> a record ③ <u>high</u> in 2008, ④ <u>with</u> an estimated 100,000 people emigrating. This was ⑤ <u>up</u> from 80,000 in 2019. There has been a large ⑥ <u>increase</u> ⑦ <u>in</u> the number of people emigrating for working abroad, ⑧ <u>particularly</u> those with specialties. In 2019 a(n) ⑨ <u>estimated</u> 30,000 people emigrated from Taiwan to take up a definite job, ⑩ <u>compared</u> with 20,000 in 2018.

長達 12 個月或 12 個月以上離開臺灣的人數，在 2008 年到達歷史新高，計有 10 萬人移出，此數字高於 2019 年的 8 萬。移往國外工作的人數大幅增加，特別是那些有專業技能的人。2019 年計有 3 萬人移往國外從事特定工作，而 2018 年則為 2 萬人。

以下為兩種常見圖表類型的範文，留意文中畫底線處，考試時善用這些句型，就可以輕鬆寫出一篇清楚明瞭又富有句型變化的圖表分析。

3-1 圓餅圖寫作

看到圓餅圖時，請先找出占比或變化最多，和占比或變化最少的類別。假如題目給了兩張圓餅圖，請一定要寫出對比；假如題目給的兩個圓餅圖是不同時間發生的事情，那就一定要強調關鍵變化或趨勢。

關於 proportion（份額、比例）和 percentage（百分比）的使用小技巧：proportion 可以用百分比或分數呈現；percentage 則只能以百分比呈現。

下方圓餅圖為臺灣人每日糖的消耗總量，請根據下圖，試說明表中陳述的情況。

2020 DAILY SUGAR INTAKE, TAIWAN

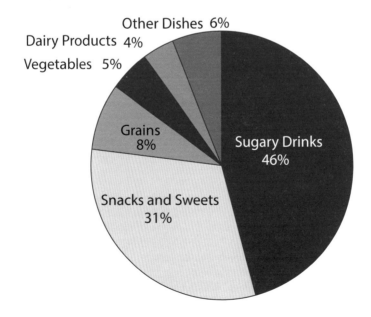

第一段 ▶ **簡單寫個開頭**

The pie chart shows the amount of sugar people consume on a daily basis in Taiwan, held by each of six different food categories in 2020.

這張圓餅圖顯示了 2020 年臺灣人每日消耗的糖總量，共有六種不同的食物種類。

- 文章中有顏色字為書寫圖表題時常用的字詞，底線處為變化較大、較顯著，或是特別值得讀者留意之處。
- 題目有時候會給予描述，這時候可以透過改寫的方式直接轉換題目的提示，就不怕臨時擠不出東西了。例如題目如果用了「show」，那麼我們可以改寫成「reveal」（顯示）、「illustrate」（顯示））。如果題目說「across the span of three decades」（橫跨了 30 年），我 們 可 以 寫 成「at different points in history」（歷史上不同的時間點）。

▶ **第一段解說**

　　就跟寫論述文一樣，圖表類的作文也需要開頭，簡短扼要的描述讓讀者知道圖表的主題。這個時候只需描述概況，不要提到任何特定的數字。

第二段 ▶ **強調重點或關鍵字**

Sugary drinks are consumed the most, at 46 percent. Snacks and sweets have the second highest consumption levels, at 31 percent. Grains consumption represents 8 percent of the total. Other dishes share of consumption is 6 percent, and then followed closely by vegetables at 5 percent. The smallest food category in terms of sugar consumption is dairy products, at 4 percent.

含糖飲料被消耗的最多，占了 46%。零食和糖果則是第二高消耗量，共 31%。穀物的消耗則代表了整體的 8%。其他菜餚的部分為 6%，緊接著是蔬菜的 5%。在糖的消耗中占比最小的食物種類是乳製品，只有 4%。

- 看到圖表時必須馬上找出關鍵的趨勢，變化最大的區間，或是圖表之間的差異。

　　圖表當中可以由最顯著或是占比最多的種類開始寫起，也可以從數字變化最大的開始，接著逐漸依照數字遞減描述圖表狀況。

第三段 ▶ **下結論**

The chart illustrates that the overall sugar consumption in Taiwan is widely spread across food types. However, sugary drinks have a majority share. Snacks and sweets account for second largest proportion of sugar intake. Grains, other dishes, and vegetables make up one-fifth of sugar consumption when added together, followed by dairy products representing the lowest.

　　這張圖表闡述了臺灣消耗糖分的食物種類廣泛分布的整體情況。然而，含糖飲料占了大部分。零食和糖果則占了糖類攝取的第二大部份。假如加總起來的話，穀物、其他菜餚和蔬菜占了糖類攝取的 1 / 5，接著是占比最低的乳製品。

● 一定要搞懂題目的要求才能拿到高分，題目如果有要求個人想法或預測，則在最後一兩句簡單針對圖表發表看法即可，若無，則只需要把圖表的概況扼要呈現。

▶ **第三段解說**

　　結論不需多說，若題目沒有特別要求加入個人想法或預測，則只需要陳述圖表整體的概況即可。因為前面已經詳細描述的數字，在結論的地方則只需要簡短做個總結，讓讀者再次回顧圖表的大致意義即可。

下表為亞太地區 2018 與 2019 年的青年（18 ～ 25 歲）失業率，請就下表描述整體趨勢與變化。

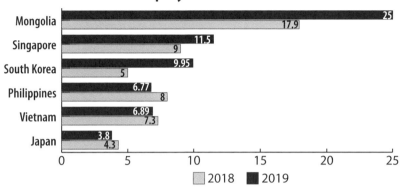

Youth Unemployment Rate APAC 2018/2019

（圖表內容：
Mongolia　2018: 17.9　2019: 25
Singapore　2018: 9　2019: 11.5
South Korea　2018: 5　2019: 9.95
Philippines　2018: 8　2019: 6.77
Vietnam　2018: 7.3　2019: 6.89
Japan　2018: 4.3　2019: 3.8
2018　2019）

第一段 ▶ **簡單寫個開頭**

The bar chart above compares youth unemployment rates <u>for two years - 2018 and 2019 -</u> in six countries in the Asia Pacific region. The countries compared are Mongolia, Singapore, South Korea, the Philippines, Vietnam, and Japan.

上圖比較了 2018 至 19 年在亞太區六國的青年失業率。比較的國家分別為：蒙古、新加坡、南韓、菲律賓、越南以及日本。

- 文章中有顏色字為書寫圖表題時常用的字詞，底線處為變化較大、較顯著，或是特別值得讀者留意之處。
- 開頭不需要很瑣碎的細節，所有的解釋都留到接下來的趨勢說明裡。

▶ **第一段解說**

把圖表名稱 bar chart（長條圖）先寫出來，接著點出圖片中的主題「youth unemployment rate（青年失業率）」，再把比較的年分和國家點出來，讓讀者可以秒懂圖片概況。

In these two years, youth unemployment was highest in Mongolia. The unemployment rate in Mongolia reached 25 percent in 2019, and 18 percent in 2018. Unemployment was second highest in Singapore for both 2018 and 2019. Third came youth unemployment in South Korea (2019), while the Philippines came in third in 2018. One significant difference is that the youth unemployment rate in South Korea has doubled within twelve months. Vietnam had the second to lowest youth unemployment rates for both years, and the rate was very close to the Philippines's youth unemployment rate in both years with approximately 8 percent in 2018, and 7 percent in 2019. Among all the countries, Japan had the lowest unemployment rates, around 3 to 4 percent in both years.

在這兩年中，青年失業率在蒙古最高。2019 年，蒙古的青年失業率到達了 25%，在 2018 年則是 18%。青年失業率第二高的則是新加坡，連續 2018 及 2019 年都是。青年失業率第三名則是南韓（2019），而菲律賓則是 2018 年的第三名。其中一個顯著的不同就是南韓的青年失業率在 12 個月內翻倍。越南則是這兩年倒數第二高的青年失業率國家，而失業率則跟菲律賓非常相近，2018 年大約是 8%，2019 年是 7%。在所有國家當中，日本的青年失業率最低，大概這兩年都是 3 ～ 4%。

▸ **第二、三段解說**

因為是對比的圖，因此需要把圖中兩年的趨勢分別說明清楚。

In all countries observed, when compared with the previous year's statistics, for Mongolia, Singapore, and South Korea, the youth unemployment rate was higher in 2019. Mongolia has particularly increased by 8 percent. On the other hand, for the Philippines, Vietnam, and Japan, unemployment was lower in 2019.

在所有觀察到的國家中，當與前一年的數據相比，對於蒙古、新加坡以及南韓來說，2019 年的青年失業率是比較高的。特別是蒙古增加了百分之 8。另一方面，對於菲律賓、越南以及日本來說，青年失業率在 2019 年是較低的。

PEEL
OREO
FRIES
Story Mountain
Expository Essay
Argumentative Essay
Narrative Essay
Table Chart Essay

一篇好的比較和對比的文章
不只是單純指出兩者可以拿來比較的地方，
而是藉著提出有意義的論點
來彰顯被比較的事物。

Chapter

05

比較和對比

05 比較和對比

> "Comparing and contrasting is a valuable human skill - and not just during high school English exams. Our ability to rank-order things is invaluable in making choices and setting priorities."
> — Martha Beck, American writer

「比較與對比是人類所擁有的一個很有價值的技能，而且不是只有高中英文考試會用到而已。當我們需要作出抉擇以及列出優先事項時，我們排序事情的這種能力是非常有價值的。」──美國作家瑪莎‧貝克

　　英文當中，比較與對比的文體叫做 Compare（比較事物的相同之處）and Contrast（對比事物的相反之處）。有時候文章的要求會需要作者同時進行對比與比較，有時則只要比較相同之處，或對比相異之處。一篇好的比較和對比的文章不只是單純指出兩者可以拿來比較的地方，而是藉著提出有意義的論點來彰顯被比較的事物。

Section 01 比較和對比文章的樣貌

　　比較與對比的文章，以五段式文章來說，可以分成兩種寫作方式。

(1) 方式一

第一段
Introduction（引言）
= **Hook**（開頭）+ **Background Information**（背景知識）+ **Thesis Statement**（主旨句）

第二段
Subject 1（要比較的東西一：使用論點或證據支持）+ **Transition Paragraph / Sentence**（簡短利用幾句話從第一項要比較的東西轉折到第二項東西。）

第三段　Subject 2（要比較的東西二：使用論點或證據支持）＋
Transition Paragraph / Sentence（簡短利用幾句話從第一項要比較
的東西轉折到第二項東西。）

第四段　Conclusion（結論）

(2) 方式二

第一段　Introduction（引言）
＝ Hook（開頭）＋ Background Information（背景知識）＋
Thesis Statement（主旨句）

第二段　Subject 1（要比較的東西一）＋ Point 1（論點一）＋
説明＋證據 ＋ Point 1（重申論點一）

第三段　Subject 2（要比較的東西二）＋ Point 2（論點二）＋
説明＋證據 ＋ Point 2（重申論點二）

第四段　Subject 3（要比較的東西三）＋ Point 3（論點三）＋
説明＋證據 ＋ Point 3（重申論點三）

第五段　Conclusion（結論）

1-1　三步驟讓你搞定比較與對比的文章

　　寫比較與對比的文章時，可以利用以下的流程來構思與書寫，如此一
來不但能有邏輯的比較兩件事物，也能確保自己在寫作的過程中沒有漏掉
任何環節。

(1) Step 1：想到什麼列什麼

在寫比較與對比的文章時，先快速利用幾分鐘的時間寫出要比較或對比的事物的特質，會比較清楚自己要提出的論點是什麼，也才能佐以更有利的證據説明兩者間相同與相異之處為何。

我們可以利用簡單的表格或是文氏圖（Venn Diagram）來快速分類要呈現的論點。舉例來説，我們可以在擬大綱時，快速地用表格寫出寫同與相似之處，以便安排接下來的各段落需要有什麼論點。

❶ **表格**

Topic：Dogs and Cats （主題：狗與貓）	
Similarities（相似）	**Differences**（相異）
They are both animals. 他們都是動物。	Dogs bark, howl, or growl, whereas cats meow or snarl. *狗是吠、嚎叫或咆哮，但是貓是喵喵叫或咆哮。*

❷ **Venn Diagram（文氏圖）**

文氏圖可以用來顯示某件事情的關係，特別是顯示這件事情的相似或相異之處。把所有需要比較的東西視覺化呈現出來之後，就更能了解接下來文章內容的走向、要提出的論點及證據。使用文氏圖時，在相異之處寫出不同之處或是特別可以提出來的論點，把兩者共通的點列在兩個圓有交集的區域。

Topic : Dogs and Cats

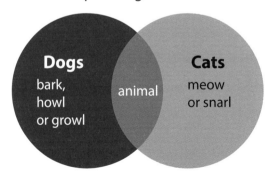

隨著我們快速書寫出要比較或對比的東西各有什麼特質，我們可能會發現自己對於某個主題是比較偏心的，此時要特別注意寫作時須保持客觀，不能特別著墨於某個點而看起來不專業。列點的方式會是比較能平衡寫作的技巧，非常推薦使用。假如列點之後發現相同或是相似之處遠多於另一部份，那麼可以專注於書寫這一個部分，提供強而有力的論點以及適切的證據說明。

(2) Step 2：妥善安排論點的位置

關於整篇的格式，可以參考第 196 頁的「比較和對比文章的樣貌」。在排列重點的部分可以使用兩種方式：Parallel Structure（平行結構）以及 Point-by-Point Method（逐點法）。Parallel Structure（平行結構）會在一段中陳述 A 論點的所有相關內容，下一個段落陳述 B 論點的所有相關內容。Point-by-Point Method（逐點法）則相反，在一個段落中集中討論 A、B 兩者在第一個主題的相同與相異之處，而另一個段落同時討論兩者在第二個主題的相同與相異之處。

假設我們要比較線上學習跟傳統教室的差別，而相同與相異之處各有 A、B、C 三個論點：

❶ 使用 Parallel Structure（平行結構）

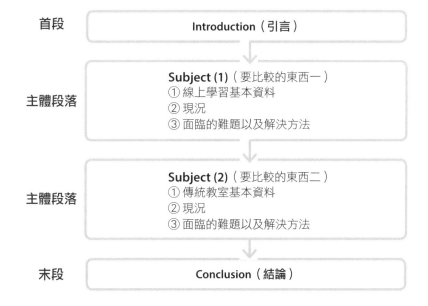

❷ 使用 Point-by-Point Method（逐點法）

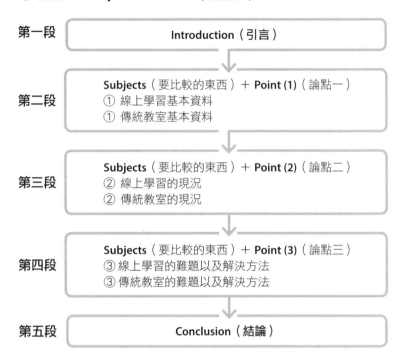

第一段　Introduction（引言）

第二段
Subjects（要比較的東西）＋ Point (1)（論點一）
① 線上學習基本資料
① 傳統教室基本資料

第三段
Subjects（要比較的東西）＋ Point (2)（論點二）
② 線上學習的現況
② 傳統教室的現況

第四段
Subjects（要比較的東西）＋ Point (3)（論點三）
③ 線上學習的難題以及解決方法
③ 傳統教室的難題以及解決方法

第五段　Conclusion（結論）

(3) Step 3：加上轉折詞

　　轉折詞可以讓讀者了解文章發展的來龍去脈，也可以讓讀者快速抓到文章的重點。特別是在比較與對比的文章當中，因為有大量的資訊需要讀者吸收，在文章當中如果能有個像是警示鈴的詞語讓讀者能隨時抓到我們要表達的論點，那麼讀起來就不會讓大腦的負擔太重。

用來比較的字詞	用來對比的字詞
• both 兩者都	• although 雖然
• too 也	• differ 異於
• Similarly, 同樣地，……	• unlike 不像是
• like 像是	• even though 即使
• as well as 和……一樣	• yet 然而
• Likewise, 同樣地，……	• but 但是
• also 也	• differ from 異於
• both... and... 都……	• conversely 相反地

- not only… but also…
  不只……而且……
- neither… nor… 不……也不……
- in common with 和……一樣
- the same as 和……一樣
- in the same way 同樣
- just like + N 就像……
- similar to + N 和……類似
- to be similar to 和……類似
- to be the same as 和……一樣
- beV / V alike 像是
- to compare to / with 和……相比

- instead 反而
- however, 然而,
- in contrast 與此相反
- in comparison 相比之下
- otherwise 否則
- by comparison 相較之下
- On the other hand 另一方面
- On the contrary 相反
- while 然而
- whereas 然而
- but / yet / still 但是／然而／仍然
- to differ from 異於
- to be different (from) 不同於
- to be dissimilar to 不同於
- unlike N 不像是

例句:

- Laptops can be used to contact others easily, like using emails. Similarly, the cell phone is a convenient tool for communication.
  筆記型電腦可被用來更易於與他人聯絡,像是使用電郵。同樣地,手機也是溝通的方便工具。

- Both laptops and cell phones can be used to contact people with ease.
  筆記型電腦和手機都被用來更易於與他人聯絡。

例句:

- Laptops, although small, are not always easy to carry from one place to another. However, the cell phones can be carried easily.
  筆記型電腦雖然小,卻不總是易於攜帶。但是手機易於攜帶。

- Laptops are usually not very portable, while cell phones are.
  筆記型電腦並不總是便攜式的,但是手機可以。

- Laptops differ rom cell phones because of their lack of portability.
  筆記型電腦不同於手機,因為缺乏便攜性。

(1) 比較相同之處

❶ A and B are ＋ similar / the same / alike ＋ because…

例 Apple and Microsoft <u>are similar / alike because</u> they both focus on computer manufacturing and the consumer electronics industry.
蘋果和微軟很相似，因為他們都專注於製造電腦與消費電子產業。

❷ A and B both…
Both A and B…

例 <u>Cats and dogs both</u> rely on body language to communicate.
貓和狗都用肢體語言溝通。

例 <u>Both mammals and reptiles</u> breathe through lungs.
哺乳類和爬蟲類都用肺呼吸。

❸ A is ＋ like / similar to ＋ B because…

例 Energy drink <u>is like / similar to</u> coffee because they both contain caffeine.
能量飲料就像咖啡，因為他們都含有咖啡因。

❹ A is… Similarly, / In the same way, / Likewise, B is…

例 The purpose of TV commercial is to raise people's awareness of a company or product in a positive manner. <u>Similarly, / In the same way, / Likewise,</u> advertisements pay for space in public spaces or airtime, then using the opportunity to deliver a message directly to consumers.
電視廣告的目的是以積極方式提升人們對某間公司或某個商品的意識。相似地，/以同樣的方式，/同樣地，廣告則是付費在公開場合或廣播時段購買某個區間，接著用這個機會來直接傳遞訊息給消費者。

❺ A is as ＋形容詞＋ as B.

例 Working from home <u>is as productive as</u> working in the office.
在家工作這種方式跟在辦公室上班一樣有效率。

(2) 對比相異之處

❶ A and B are different because…

例　KFC and McDonald's <u>are different because</u> they sell different bread-winning products.
肯德基和麥當勞不同，因為他們賣不同的主力商品。

❷ A is unlike / different from B because…

例　Bicycle <u>is unlike / different from</u> scooter because it is an eco-friendly option of commuting.
腳踏車跟機車不一樣，因為它是一種環保的通勤選項。

❸ A is not as / so ＋形容詞／副詞＋ as B.

例　Studying in a public school <u>is not as expensive as</u> it is in a private school.
在公立學校讀書沒有像在私立學校讀書那麼貴。

❹ A ＋助動詞＋ not ＋動詞＋ as ＋副詞＋ as B.

例　I <u>did not arrive</u> at school <u>as early as</u> my best friend.
我沒有像我好朋友那樣那麼早到。

❺ A is more / less ＋形容詞／副詞＋ than B.

例　Being healthy <u>is more important than</u> being wealthy.
健康比富有還重要。

Being wealthy <u>is less important than</u> being healthy.
富有比健康較不重要。

❻ A is ＋形容詞比較級＋ than B.

例　Being honest <u>is easier than</u> telling lies.
誠實比說謊來的簡單。

❼ A...; however, B...

A..., but B...

> 例 Flowers contain seeds; <u>however</u>, vegetables do not contain seeds.
> *花有種子，但蔬菜沒有。*

> 例 Flowers contain seeds, <u>but</u> vegetables do not contain seeds.
> *花有種子，但蔬菜沒有。*

❽ Although A..., B...

> 例 <u>Although</u> fruits are mostly sweet, vegetables are not sweet or very subtly sweet.
> *雖然水果大多是甜的，但蔬菜則是不甜或微甜。*

❾ In contrast to A, B is...

> 例 <u>In contrast to</u> traditional learning, online learning is flexible.
> *與傳統學習方式相比，線上學習是有彈性的。*

Section 03 比較和對比範文解析

　　我們以 Parallel Structure（平行結構）來比較與分析「Traditional Classroom vs. Online Learning」（傳統教室 vs. 線上學習）的相同與相異之處。

第一段 ▶ Introduction（引言）

　　These days, online courses have become extremely popular, as the 線上課程變得流行 COVID-19 has resulted in school closure across the globe. While countries are at different points in their COVID-19 infection rates, 轉折，說明教育的改變 education has already changed dramatically to adjust to the sudden shift away from the classroom. Meanwhile, despite the rising popularity of online education, the 傳統教室試圖創新 traditional classroom is fighting back and trying to adopt newer methods of retaining learners' interest. There are always two sides to a coin: for some individuals, online learning suits their needs better, while others prefer brick-

204

and-mortar education. While these two types of learning method are similar in essence, they differ in regard to the location, interaction, and student performance.

> 主旨句

　　最近，因為新冠肺炎導致全球許多學校關閉，線上課程變得愈來愈流行。儘管各國的新冠肺炎感染率處於不同階段，但教育因應教室內的課堂減少的狀況，已經發生了巨大變化。與此同時，儘管線上教育愈來愈受歡迎，但傳統教室正在反擊，試圖採用更新的方法來保持學習者的興趣。凡事皆一體兩面：對於某些人來說，線上學習更符合他們的需求；而另一些人則更喜歡教室裡的實體教育。雖然這兩種學習方法在本質上是相似的，但它們在學習地點、互動和學生表現方面是不同的。

▸ **第一段解說**

　　開頭就說明了線上課程變得愈來愈流行，特別是因為新冠肺炎導致全球許多學校關閉。While 後面是轉折，說明現在的教育已經有大幅的改變了。Meanwhile 此句回歸到傳統教育，說明儘管線上教育的盛行，傳統的教室試圖要利用新的教學方法找回學生的興趣。後面接著提到凡事皆有一體兩面，對於某些個體來說，線上學習更能符合他們的需求，另一方面，其他人則比較喜歡待在教室裡學習。

　　主旨句說明了接下來的段落會分別說明線上教學和傳統學習的好處。

第二段 ▸ **Subject (1)（要比較的東西一）**

In a traditional classroom, ① students come to campus and attend classes in physical classrooms, and they follow fixed class schedules and durations arranged by the schools. ② Traditional classrooms allow students to interact with one another and discuss with their peers and teachers face-to-face. As students can communicate with their peers or ask questions personally to the lecturer, they could receive valuable verbal and nonverbal feedback from their classmates and the teachers. In addition, they could always cast doubts on the content on the spot. ③ Furthermore, students get external forces from their teachers to put in the effort, and they are more likely to work hard in a course because of peer pressure or encouragement. These factors keep students on task and help those who tend to procrastinate on their studies or assignments.

在傳統教室，學生在來到校園在實體教室上課，遵循學校安排的固定的時程表和課程時間。傳統教室能讓學生彼此互動，也能和老師面對面討論。因為學生能跟同儕溝通或私底下詢問老師，他們可以從同學和老師那裡得到很有價值的口語或非口語的回饋。此外，他們有問題就能當場發問。再者，學生會從老師那裡接收到外部壓力因而努力，他們更可能因為同儕壓力或鼓勵而在用功於課程中。這些因素讓學生能專心在課業上，也能幫助那些傾向拖延學習或寫作業的人。

▸ **第二段解説**

編號①、②、③說明了傳統教育的好處。

好處① 學生在實體教室上課，遵循由學校安排的固定的時程表以及課程時間。

好處② 傳統教室能讓學生跟彼此互動，也能跟老師面對面對談。因為學生能跟同儕溝通或私底下直接找老師問問題，他們可以從同學或老師那接收到很有價值的口語與非口語的回饋。此外，他們一有疑問就能馬上當場發問。

好處③ 學生會從老師那接受到外部的壓力，因而付諸努力。也更有可能會因為有同儕壓力或是鼓勵，而在課程當中用功。這些因素使得學生能專心於他們的任務上，也能幫助那些傾向於延遲學習或寫作業的人。

第三段 ▸ **Subject (2)（要比較的東西二）**

However, sitting in the classroom for a lecture does not meet some
　　　　　　段落轉折
other students' demands. These students find the same classroom, lack
of flexibility, and campus life irritating. First, the class schedule or the
classroom might not cater to their needs. Additionally, campus life, making
friends, and face-to-face interaction intimidate them, and the overwhelming
pressure is a threat to their willingness to learn. Fortunately, technology has
made other options available to these students. ① Compared to traditional
　　　　　　　　　　　　　　　　　本次主題
learning, students need not go to the same classroom day in day out, and
they could take courses online repeatedly and ubiquitously as long as
there is an Internet connection. Lessons could be completed anywhere,

and assignments are submitted online without commuting. ② The similarity between traditional learning and online learning is that interaction is equally important. The students could pose questions or hold a discussion online anytime without worrying that they might interrupt the lesson in progress. In addition, unlike students in traditional classrooms, the participants taking online courses vary greatly with ages and backgrounds. Thus the students could acquire a wide variety of experiences shared by other participants. ③ Another difference is that there is no fixed schedule for online learning. Online classes offer a great deal of flexibility in terms of schedules and learning processes. Students are able to attend the sessions in sections or taking breaks anytime if needed. It is because of this flexibility that students are more willing to shape and organize the learning process of their own.

　　然而，坐在教室上課不能滿足其他一些學生的需求。這些學生覺得相同的教室缺乏彈性，以及校園生活很煩人。首先，課程表或教室可能無法滿足他們的需求。此外，校園生活、交友、面對面的互動讓他們備感威脅。過大的壓力威脅他們的學習意願。幸運地，科技為這些人帶來其他選擇。與傳統學習相比，學生不需要日復一日去同樣的教室，只要有網路，他們就能反覆的線上學習，不受地點限制，任何地點都能上課，不用通勤就可以交作業。而傳統學習和線上學習的共同點就是互動同等重要。學生可以隨時線上發問和討論，而不用擔心中斷課程。此外，與傳統教室的學生不同，參與線上課程的學生年齡和背景變化很大，因此學生可以獲得其他學員的豐富經驗。另一個相異點就是線上學習沒有固定時程表，線上學習在時間和學習歷程提供了很大的彈性。學生可以以區塊分割學習時間，或是需要時可以隨時休息。因為這種彈性，學生更願意去形塑與組織自己的學習歷程。

▶ **第三段解說**

　　線上學習。編號①、②、③説明了線上學習的好處。

　　好處① 與傳統課堂不同，學生不須日復一日去同樣的教室，而且只要網路存在，他們能反覆地線上學習，不受地點與時間限制。任何地方都能上課，不用通勤就可以交作業。

　　好處② 傳統教室與線上學習的相同之處則是互動同等重要。學生可以不用擔心打擾到進行中的課程，隨時都能線上發問或發起討論。除此之外，線上課程中的參與者年紀與背景大不相同，因此學生可以獲得其他參與者各式各樣的經驗。

好處③ 線上學習沒有固定的時程表，線上學習提供學生非常大的彈性，學生可以以區塊分割學習時間，或需要時隨時可以休息。

第四段 ▸ **Conclusion（結論）**

It is obvious to see that there are different benefits to both traditional education and online education offered to students in the modern era. *（重申主旨句）* Regular attendance and schedule in classes help the students interact with other individuals and learn how to be well disciplined. In a traditional classroom, students can pose questions directly and share their views with their peers and teachers during face-to-face interactions. On the other hand, online learning comes along with great convenience, considerable flexibility, and easy accessibility, and all the arrangements will go according to students' schedules. While it cannot be concluded that one method is better or worse than the other, *（總結）* it can be stated that one method will be better for some students than it will be for others. Allowing students to get the most out of the available learning resources and providing them with the opportunity to do it their own way will surely assist the students in reaching their full potentials.

明顯地，在現代傳統教育和線上學習各有不同的好處。規律的出席以及固定的時程表幫助學生與其他人互動，並學習自律。在傳統教室，學生也能面對面直接提出問題和同儕及老師分享觀點。另一方面，線上學習有很大的便利性、彈性、容易取得，並且所有的安排都能配合學生行程。雖然不能總結說哪一種方法比另一種更好或更差，不過可以說某一種方法對某些學生更好，相較於其他學生。它們允許學生可以充分利用能取得的學習資源，並提供他們機會去找到適合自己的方式，確保學生能發揮他們的最佳潛能。

▸ **第四段解說**

重申了主旨句提及的重點：傳統校園與線上學習各有不同的好處。

因為題目並不是要辯論哪一種學習較好，因此總結是：我們很難去下結論哪一種方法優於或劣於另一種方法，但我們可以確定的是某些學生對於其中一種方法更適應。倘若學生能找到最適合的學習方法，不管是在線上或是在實體教室學習都可以獲得最大的成效。

因果關係的文章必須提供給讀者
充分且可信的理由來解釋某種行為、
事件或現象是如何產生的,
也因此,在書寫的過程中,
必須給予事實而非個人意見!

Chapter

06

因果關係

06 因果關係

　　發生事情時，特別是不好的事情時，我們只能大嘆「唉，人生啊！」但寫作時可不能這樣草草帶過。因果關係的文章探討事情是如何發生的（原因），而又會導致什麼（後果）。

　　有時也會利用這類文體探討某個事件、抉擇或情況所產生的後果，或追溯某個狀況的起因或是後續發展。因果關係的文章必須提供給讀者充分且可信的理由來解釋某種行為、事件或現象是如何產生的，也因此，在書寫的過程中，必須給予讀者事實而非個人意見（詳見「你提出的，是事實，還是個人意見？」）來佐證。

　　有些事情的因果關係很好一秒解釋清楚，例如下雨了，導致全身溼透了。原因可能是忘記帶傘，只能淋雨，所以身體濕透了。有些事情則是透過舉例或解釋，才能清楚地讓讀者看見事物的本質。但也正是因為透過我們解釋的過程，讀者能跟隨我們的思維去剖析事物的來龍去脈，理解事情的因果關係。

Section 01 因果關係文章的樣貌

　　因果關係的文章，以五段式文章來說，可以分成兩種寫作方式：

(1) Block Structure（區塊結構：一次只處理同樣的事物）

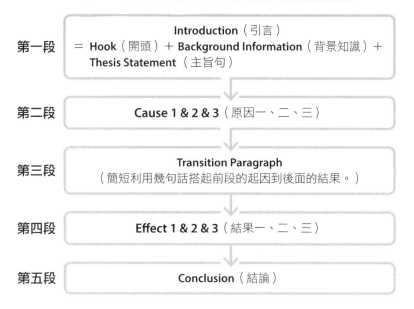

第一段 | **Introduction**（引言）
＝ **Hook**（開頭）＋ **Background Information**（背景知識）＋
Thesis Statement（主旨句）

第二段 | **Cause 1 & 2 & 3**（原因一、二、三）

第三段 | **Transition Paragraph**
（簡短利用幾句話搭起前段的起因到後面的結果。）

第四段 | **Effect 1 & 2 & 3**（結果一、二、三）

第五段 | **Conclusion**（結論）

　　區塊結構的寫法是先把所有原因列出來，中間簡單利用幾句話轉折到下一個塊狀，也就是解釋所有的結果。這個方法能夠清楚地讓讀者一次看到所有的成因和結果，也是最基礎、最保險的寫法，對於使用交叉排列因果論點不太有把握的讀者特別適合。

　　以下以「Why Aren't More Men Taking Parental Leave」（為何沒有很多男人放育嬰假）為題，探討這個主題的因果關係。

第一段 ▶ **Introduction**（引言）

　　Parental leave means time off, either paid or unpaid, for parents to care for their children.
→ Hook（開頭）
In the past, it was usually moms who took the leave; however, modern fathers are more involved in caregiving
→ Background Information（背景知識）
than past generations. Therefore, it's not surprising that more and more organizations are expanding their parental leave policies to accommodate the needs of their workforce. There are several reasons why dads do not take paternity leave.
→ Thesis Statement（主旨句）
Generally speaking, men prefer not to take parental leave ① when company policies implicitly prevent

them from doing so, ② when taking leave violates cultural traditions or ③ because of the concerns for career development.

育嬰假就是父母休假去照顧孩子，不論有給薪還是無給薪。在過去，通常是母親休育嬰假，然而，現代父親比過去幾代人更關心照顧孩子。因此，不意外地有愈來愈多的機構擴大育嬰假政策，以適應員工的需求。父親不休育嬰假有幾個原因。一般來說，當公司政策暗示禁止育嬰假，當育嬰假違反文化傳統，或是顧慮職涯發展時，男人就不喜歡休育嬰假。

▶ **第一段解説**

開頭的 Hook 利用育嬰假的定義來告訴讀者本篇即將要談論的話題。背景知識提及了過去都是母親放育嬰假，但現代的父親比起過去的那一代，更想參與孩子的照顧過程。因此，可以看得出為何愈來愈多公司願意修正他們的公司政策以留住勞動力。主旨句則説明了男人不想放育嬰假有三個原因：① 公司政策暗示不要放育嬰假、② 違反傳統、③ 擔心職涯發展。

第二段 ▶ Cause 1 & 2 & 3（原因一、二、三）：
視情況而定，不一定會有三個原因。

① Some working parents said that their companies have policies that support parental leave. However, there are some parents who complained about a significant gap between their companies' stated support for parental leave and the reluctant attitude they encountered when they requested for a parental leave. Men, in particular, are more likely to experience hard times than women to request time off. ② Secondly, taking leave in some countries violates cultural traditions. Cultural stigmas often damage the reputation and promotion of dads who take parental leave. ③ Last, men have concerns about the damage to their career development when taking time off. They fear that taking parental leave will be perceived to be less committed to their careers. In addition, a temporary absence from their workplace will lead to isolation in the company in the future.

一些職業父母說，他們的公司政策支持育嬰假。然而也有一些父母抱怨，公司表明支持育嬰假和他們申請育嬰假時遇到的不情願的態度之間，有巨大的鴻溝。尤其是男人，更有可能在請假時遭到刁難。其次，在一些國家休假違反文化傳統，社會汙名常常會損害休育嬰假父親的名聲和晉升。最後，男人擔心休假會損害他們的職涯發展，他們擔心休育嬰假會被認為對事業不夠投入，此外，短暫離開職場會導致未來在公司被孤立。

▶ **第二段解說**

原因① 說明了主旨句中提到的第一個理由：公司雖然看似鼓勵大家請育嬰假，但當父母申請時，卻會感受到公司不情願的態度，特別是男性被刁難的比例高於女性。

原因② 指出在某些國家，放育嬰假違反了文化傳統。放育嬰假變成一種會傷害放育嬰假的父親其名聲以及升遷機會。

原因③ 提出男人擔心放育嬰假會危害到職涯發展，因為放育嬰假代表不能奉獻於工作。除此之外，短暫離開公司會造成日後在公司內的疏離。

第三段 ▶ **Transition Paragraph（簡短利用幾句話搭起前段的起因到後面的結果。）**

Various scientific studies have proved that the active involvement of both parents in the upbringing of a child has great social, cognitive, and psychological benefits. Yet, despite legal provisions allowing parents to take parental leave to look after children, many men are still reluctant to take it due to the above-mentioned reasons. These factors, however, have led to some negative effects, both on family life and on society as a whole.

許多科學研究都已證明父母親雙方主動參與帶小孩會產生很大的社會、認知以及心理的好處。然而，即便法律條款允許父母親放育嬰假照顧小孩，基於上述的原因，很多男人依舊不情願放這種假。而這些因素已經對家庭生活以及整體社會產生了一些負面的影響。

▶ **Effect 1 & 2 & 3（結果一、二、三）：視情況而定，不一定會有三個結果。**

① Taking parental leave is not always straightforward because of the cost involved. Despite the increased availability of parental leave, working parents in many countries still find it hard to take time off because of the gap between company policies and practices. The lack of a national policy mandating paid parental leave in private companies for all workers is probably the major concern of working parents. ② In addition, fathers are afraid to be considered less ambitious or not career-driven enough. In many parts of the world, traditionally, men are often expected to be breadwinners and keep their jobs. Some studies do show that taking paternity leave can damage a man's professional reputation and affect his future earning potential. However, if dads do not take parental leave, the childcare responsibility falls solely on mothers, putting a lot of burden and mental stress on women. ③ Furthermore, if the fathers cannot practice hands-on parenthood, highly educated women cannot return to work, which is detrimental to a woman's career and chances for future promotion.

因為請假需付出的成本與代價，休育嬰假並不總是這麼容易的一件事。儘管放育嬰假的可行性愈來愈高，許多國家的父母仍然覺得休假是很困難的，因為公司政策和實行有差距。雙薪家庭主要的擔憂也許是因為缺乏國家政策對私人公司強制命令給予帶薪的育嬰假給所有的員工。此外，父親害怕被認為缺乏野心或不夠有事業心。在世界上許多地方，男人傳統上被認為是養家的人，並必須保有工作。有些研究確實指出放育嬰假會傷害一個男人在專業上的聲望，以及影響他未來賺錢的潛力。然而，如果父親不休育嬰假，照顧小孩的責任就會單獨落到母親身上，加諸女性許多負擔和精神壓力。再者，如果父親不能練習如何當父母，受過高等教育女性就不能回到職場，這不利於女性職涯和未來晉升機會。

▶ **第四段解說**

　　結果① 提到放育嬰假有時候不是那麼一翻兩瞪眼的事情，因為裡面牽涉到了成本。即便放育嬰假的可行性已增加，礙於公司政策與實行上的差距，許多國家的雙薪父母仍覺得請育嬰假是很難的。

結果② 在世界上很多地方，傳統上認為男人應該要賺錢養家，並保有一份工作。然而，如果父親們不請育嬰假的話，照顧小孩的責任就完全落到了母親的身上，因而造成負擔和心理壓力落到女性身上。

結果③ 假如父親們沒辦法練習如何當父母，受過高等教育的女性們無法返回職場，對她們的職涯是種危害，也傷害到了她們升遷的機會。

第五段 ► **Conclusion（結論）**

Creating a friendly environment to support fathers in the workplace isn't just good for men, it's good for the wellbeing of their families. Being able to take parental leave freely is also a necessary step towards gender equality. People in every workplace should have equal rights to better manage a commitment to their careers while supporting their families.

營造一個友善的的環境並不單單只是能支持在工作場所的父親，而是對他們的家庭幸福也有益處。能夠自由地放育嬰假也是邁向性別平等必要的一步。在工作場所的人們應該擁有平等的權利來妥善管理他們對工作的付出，同時也能協助他們的家庭。

(2) Chain Structure（鏈狀結構）

鏈狀結構，顧名思義就是寫完事件的成因之後馬上寫出結果，而通常這個結果跟下一個成因又有關聯，因此成為鏈狀結構。這個方法適用於想要表達一系列的結果都跟前面的原因是息息相關的作者，也因為寫作方式較複雜，需要非常清晰的邏輯，適用於較高階的作者，或是對自己所列出成因與結果有十足把握的作者。

以下以「A Miserable Day」（悲慘的一天）來示範原因與結果如何以鏈狀結構呈現，而這一系列的成因都和結果息息相關。

第一段 ▸ Introduction（引言）

This morning was truly a disaster and a miserable day, and it all started with my bad choice the night before.

今天早上真的是一場災難，也是悲慘的一天，一切都從我前一晚錯誤的決定開始。

第二段 ▸ Cause 1 & Effect 1（原因一和結果一）

I woke up late this morning because I binge-watched my favorite
→ Cause 1（原因一）
TV series till midnight. As a result, I slept through my alarm and had
→ Effect 1（結果一）
to rush to get ready for school.

因為我昨天追劇直到凌晨，所以今天早上我太晚起床了。因此，我沒聽到鬧鐘響，必須匆忙準備趕去學校。

• 方框處為呈現因果關係的詞。

第三段 ▸ Cause 2 & Effect 2（原因二和結果二）

Because I accidentally left my assignment at home and had
→ Cause 2（原因二）
to ran back home to get it, I missed the bus. Consequently, I was
→ Effect 2（結果二）
late for school, and the teacher scolded me for missing my peers'
→ Effect 2（結果二）
presentation.

因為我不小心把作業留在家裡，必須跑回家拿。我錯過了公車，因此我上學遲到了，老師因為我錯過同學的報告而責罵我。

▶ **Cause 3 & Effect 3（原因三和結果三）**

<u>Due to the fact that</u> today was a bad hair day, I was extremely
 Cause 3（原因三）◀   Effect 3（結果三）
grumpy and I shouted at my best friend. <u>Because of</u> my irrational
                                            Cause 3（原因三）
behavior, my best friend left without saying a word. After he left, I felt
              ▶ Effect 3（結果三）   Cause 3（原因三）◀
that this was the day from hell.
       ▶ Effect 3（結果三）

因為今天真的是很糟的一天，我非常易怒而且我吼了我朋友。因為我不理智的行為，我朋友不發一語離開了。在他離開之後，我覺得今天根本就是地獄般的一天。

▶ **Conclusion（結論）**

To conclude what happened today, I would say everything went wrong, and it was a huge mess. I have decided that I will never ever binge-watch any TV series during weekdays to ensure that I will wake up on time in the mornings, and that everything will go accordingly to plans.

要總結我今天發生什麼事的話，我會說每件事情都不順，而且是一團混亂。我已經決定我之後絕對不會在週間追任何一部劇，以確保我會在早上準時起床，以及每件事都能跟著計劃走。

1-1 三步驟讓你搞定因果關係文章

因果關係的架構大多脫離不了解釋問題的起源與結果，或是可能的解決方案。也因為因果關係類的文章並不一定只侷限在討論問題本身，因此有時也可能看到文章要求作者根據各種事件的結果，來推測如何解決問題或提出可能的解決方案。

(1) Step 1：善用各種圖表發想與集合你的思緒

凡事起頭總是難，特別是一件事情的成因可能有許多種，牽涉到的層面又很廣，在毫無頭緒或是不知道如何把各種想法有組織地呈現出來時，可以使用圖表來整理成寫作的大綱。這種方式在大考或正式考試時可以幫助自己快速整理出要寫作的重點，而且不會在時間壓力下亂寫一通。

最基本的方式就是列出一個表格，把因和果都呈現出來，寫出成因時也同時思考會造成的後果為何，如此一來就能有條理的呈現出來。

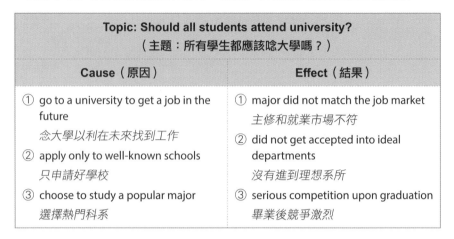

| Topic: Should all students attend university?
（主題：所有學生都應該唸大學嗎？） ||
Cause（原因）	Effect（結果）
① go to a university to get a job in the future 念大學以利在未來找到工作 ② apply only to well-known schools 只申請好學校 ③ choose to study a popular major 選擇熱門科系	① major did not match the job market 主修和就業市場不符 ② did not get accepted into ideal departments 沒有進到理想系所 ③ serious competition upon graduation 畢業後競爭激烈

也可以利用簡單的圖，快速寫出幾個關鍵字，考試時提醒自己不能脫離這幾個關鍵字。我們以「A Flood of Refugees in the Past Few Years」（近幾年的難民潮）和「A Childhood Illness」（童年時的一場病）這兩種題目為例：

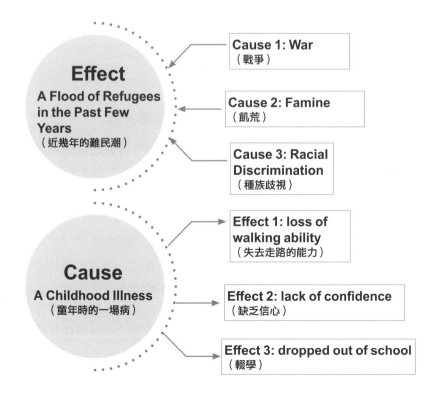

(2) Step 2：大綱很重要，真的很重要！

在寫因果關係的文章時，有時候需要多種原因對上一種結果，有時則是反過來。假如沒有擬個大綱在旁邊時時提醒自己，很容易就會漏掉或是忘了替某個論點舉例。考試前不妨快速寫下幾個當下想到的點子，不需要鉅細靡遺地寫，只需要把當下能想到的論點或可以搭配的例子迅速寫在紙上提醒自己即可。

大綱可以簡單的列出幾點，寫作時要偶爾回頭檢視自己是否有離題或是有遺漏的地方，只要遵照自己一開始設定的大綱，就不容易漏寫重要資訊或多寫了不必要的內容。

例如：

多個成因造成單一結果	一個原因對上多個結果
Causes	**Cause**
① high traffic volume 交通量大 ② investment in infrastructure 基礎建設的投資 ③ pollution 汙染 ④ rise in housing prices 房價變高 ↓	rapid growth in industrialization 工業化的快速成長 ↓
Effect	**Effects**
the need for public transport 對於大眾運輸的需求	① high traffic volume 交通量大 ② investment in infrastructure 基礎建設的投資 ③ boost in economic growth 刺激經濟成長 ④ pollution 汙染 ⑤ rise in housing prices 房價變高

(3) Step 3：為你的因果標上顯眼的記號

找出如何解釋前因後果之後，接著就是要讓讀者能馬上理解來龍去脈。與人打招呼時，最尷尬的就是揮手揮半天但對方根本沒看到自己。寫文章也是同樣的道理，不管內容鋪陳的再好，讀者如果不能讀出你要表達的重點也是白費力氣了。

可以標記因果關係的 15 個動詞			
因→果			**果←因**
affect 影響	produce 產生	bring about 導致	result from 由於……導致
influence 影響	facilitate 促進	contribute to 導致	arise from 源自
cause 導致	trigger 觸發	result in 導致	stem from 源自
create 創造	induce 導致	give rise to 導致	attribute... to 把……歸因於……

Cause（原因）可用句型	Effect（結果）可用句型

• Accordingly, 根據
• For this reason, 根據這個理由
• There are several reasons for…
  有很多理由……
• The main factors are…
  主要因素是……
• The first cause is…
  首要原因是……
• 因 leads to or might lead to 果
  什麼原因導致或可能導致什麼結果
• This often results in 果
  這很常導致什麼結果
• The first cause of… is…
  第一個原因是……
• The next reason is…
  下一個原因是……
• Because of A, B… 因為A，B……
• As a result of A, B… 因為A，B……
• As a consequence of A, B…
  因為A，B……
• because / since / as A 因為A
• to result from A 起因於A
• A results in B A導致B
• to be the result of A 由A所致
• B is due to A B是因為A
• Owing to A, B… 因為A，B……
• B is because of A B是因為A
• B is the effect of A B是因為A
• B is the consequence of A
  B是因為A
	• Before 因 … Now 果 …
	  在什麼原因之前……現在什麼結
	  果……
	• One of the results / outcomes of 因
	  is… Another is…
	  什麼原因的結果之一是……另一個
	  是……
	• A major effect of 因 is…
	  什麼原因的一個結果是……
	• 果 often occurs as a consequence
	  of 因
	  什麼結果常常發生在什麼原因之後
	• The first effect of A is B
	  A的第一個結果是B
	• Another result of A is B
	  A的另一個結果是B
	• As a result, B… 因此，B……
	• As a consequence, B…
	  因此，B……
	• Consequently, B… 因此，B……
	• Therefore, B… 因此，B……
	• Thus B… 因此B……
	• Hence B… 因此B……
	• A results in B A導致B
	• A causes B A導致B
	• A has an effect on B A影響B
	• A affects B A影響B
	• A is one of the causes of B
	  A是B的原因之一
	• A is the reason for B
	  A是B的原因之一

連接各句子可以用的轉折詞	
• Also, 而且…… • too 也 • In addition, 此外…… • Additionally, 此外……	• Thus, 因此…… • Therefore, 因此…… • Consequently, 結果…… • As a result, 結果……

Section 02 因果關係怎麼寫？實用句型報你知

(1) 串聯兩個名詞片語

名詞片語，顧名思義會有名詞，以及修飾它的形容詞。但因為名詞片語本身並不是一個完整的句子，需要動詞＋介係詞串聯起來。

因→果	果←因
• Heavy rain <u>leads to</u> landslide. 　大雨造成土石流。 • Drug abuse <u>results in</u> addiction. 　濫用藥物造成上癮。	• Cardiovascular diseases <u>result from</u> unhealthy diet. 　心血管疾病是由不健康的飲食所導致的。 • The demands for houses <u>stem from</u> higher economic growth and rising income. 　對房子的需求源自於較高的經濟成長以及收入。

串連「果←因」的句型時，也可以善用「is because of」及「is due to」兩個句型來將成因結果解釋清楚：

 The extinction of marine creatures <u>is because of</u> plastic pollution.
海洋生物的滅絕是由塑膠汙染所導致的。

 Depression <u>is due to</u> a chemical imbalance between brain cells.
憂鬱症源自於腦內細胞之間的化學不平衡。

(2) 子句連結子句

　　子句的構成需要主詞＋動詞，有時候也會有受詞。舉例來說：「I ran.」（我跑步）、「She loves you.」（她愛你。）當要連結兩個句子時，必須有標點符號和連接詞一起串聯句子。

因→果	果←因
• Taking Uber is much cheaper, so people nowadays favor Uber over taxis. 搭Uber便宜多了，所以現在的人比較喜歡搭Uber而不是計程車。	• Many people nowadays are addicted to mobile phones because of the prevalence of smartphones. 現在很多人對手機上癮，因為智慧型手機很普及。
• Most Children consume too many sugar drinks. Thus, they become obese. 很多孩童攝取過多含糖飲料。因此，他們變得肥胖。	• It snowed today since the cold air mass hit Taiwan. 今天因為冷氣團侵襲，臺灣下雪了。

(3) 子句與名詞片語

　　把子句和名詞片語串起來的方法就是使用介係詞片語，以及使用標點符號。句子中如果先出現名詞片語，那麼中間就需要一個逗點分開後方的子句。

因→果	果←因
• As a result of smoking, he has developed lung cancer. 因為抽菸，他得了肺癌。	• He has developed lung cancer as a result of smoking. 他得了肺癌，因為他抽菸。
• Due to the tsunami, many people have lost their homes. 因為海嘯，很多人失去了他們的家園。	• Many people have lost their homes because of the tsunami. 很多人因為海嘯失去了他們的家園。

我們以同樣的主題「The Cause and Effect of Genetically Modified Food」（基改食物的因與果）來示範 Block Structure（區塊結構）和 Chain Structure（鏈狀結構）如何寫作。

(1) Block Structure（區塊結構）範文

第一段 ▶ Introduction（引言）

　　Genetically modified food (GM food) is a very hotly debated topic in the modern society. GM food is created by introducing a new characteristic into the DNA of plants or crops, so that the food will be fit for specific demands. GM foods are introduced to the world based on three reasons: ① solution to global starvation, ② the scarcity of seasonal plants, and ③ the need for disease-free crops.

（主題）（定義）（主旨：基改食物的原因）

　　基改食物（GM food）是現代社會中熱烈討論的話題。基改食物是透過引進新的特質到植物或穀物的 DNA 中，以便讓食物更適合某些特定需求。基改食物被引進給世人是基於三個理由：解決全球飢荒、季節性植物的稀有性、以及對有抵抗疾病能力穀物的需求。

▶ 第一段解說

　　開頭點出主題，第二句為基改食物的定義，編號①、②、③則提供了接下來主題發展的順序：基改食物的原因。

第二段 ▶ Cause 1 & 2 & 3（原因一、二、三）：視情況而定，不一定會有三個原因。

　　① Because of the massive increase of human population, many people believe that the rapid growth of the population will soon outpace the global food production. ② In addition, crops and plants consumed by human are usually seasonal, and they will only grow within a certain time period in a year. ③ Last, because of the growing population and the limited seasonal agricultural products available to human beings, farmers cannot afford the loss caused by the pests to crops. Scientists then produce crops and plants that are disease resistant.

因為人口大規模增長，很多人相信人口快速增長的速度很快會超越全球食物的生產量。除此之外，被人類所消耗的穀物和植物通常是季節性的，而且只會在一年當中的某幾個時節生長。最後，因為人口增長及有限的季節性農產品，農夫沒辦法承受害蟲造成的損失。科學家因此製造出了具有抗病能力的穀物及植物。

▸ **第二段解說**

原因① 因為人口大規模增長，很多人相信這種快速增長的速度會超越全球食物的生產量。

原因② 除此之外，被人類所消耗的穀物和植物通常是季節性的，而且只會在一年當中的某幾個時節生長。

原因③ 最後，因為人口增長及有限的季節性農產品，農夫沒辦法承受害蟲造成的損失。科學家因此製造出了具有抗病能力的穀物及植物。

第三段 ▸ **Transition Paragraph（簡短利用幾句話搭起前段的起因到後面的結果。）**

After highlighting some of the main cause for GM food, the following
↳ 說明了前段是成因，而後面一段會著重於結果。
paragraph illustrates the effects of GM food. As genes are mixed from a wide variety of species, this paves the way for unpredictable effects.
預告了接下來要講的會偏向負面的結果。 ◂

在強調了基改食物的某些主要原因之後，接下來的段落會說明基改食物的影響。因為基因是從各式各樣的物種中混合而成，也因此創造了無法預期的效果。

▸ **第三段解說**

這個地方則透過「unpredictable」（無法預測的）一詞預告了接下來要講的會偏向負面的結果。

▶ **Effect 1 & 2 & 3（結果一、二、三）：視情況而定，不一定會有三個結果。**

① With the advances in technology and medicine, they will continue to expand the average human lifespan. As the global population continues to grow, human beings will soon run out of agricultural land since the land will be converted to houses and stores. ② Secondly, GM foods could survive extreme weather, such as droughts, resulting in a higher yield and bringing in greater profits for farmers. On the other hand, in order to grow plants with economic value that survive harsher conditions, existing seasonal species can be overrun by more dominant new species, reducing biodiversity in our environment. ③ Last, there is a growing concern that people are becoming increasingly resistant to antibiotics. Genetic modification builds up plants' resistance to disease; therefore, such trait will make it more tolerant to pesticides. When humans consume GM food, the cells in these foods could affect people's ability to fight against illness.

科技和醫藥的進展將會持續延展人類的平均壽命。當全球人口持續成長，人類很快會耗盡農耕土地，因為土地會被轉換成房子和商店。其次，基改食物可以在像是旱災之類的極端天氣下生存，帶來了更多產量並為農夫帶來更大利潤。另一方面，為了種植可以在惡劣條件下生存的經濟價值作物，更多的優勢新品種作物會超越現有的季節性作物，減少了環境的生物多樣性。最後，大家愈來愈擔心人們對抗生素逐漸增加抗藥性。基改增加了植物的抗病能力，因此，這種特性讓它對農藥更有抗性，當人類食用基改食物時，這些食物中的細胞可能會影響人們的抗病能力。

▶ **第四段解說**

結果① 科技和醫藥的進展將會持續延展人類的平均壽命，當全球人口持續成長，人類很快會耗盡農耕土地。

結果② 新品種植物會較佔優勢，毀滅了原有的生物多樣性。

結果③ 吃了基改食物後，人們對抗生素愈來愈有抗藥性。

To conclude, the causes for GM foods are global hunger and the ➤改寫主旨句 need for mass production of disease-free crops that could survive the harsh condition. When it comes to GM foods' benefits, with the availability of food all year round, world hunger could be solved in the short run. Additionally, the supply of disease-resistant plants and ➤總結優點 crops means that people in some areas will no longer suffer from food shortages, regardless of weather condition. However, creating foods by mixing different types of genes will produce unexpected or harmful ➤總結缺點 genetic changes in both plants and human beings. Furthermore, farmers may favor disease-free plants and crops over seasonal ones; therefore, an imbalance in plants threatens biodiversity in a survival of the fittest scenario. In a nutshell, despite all the positive effects, we cannot overemphasize the necessity of controlling GM food. ➤強而有力的句子作為結論

總結來說，導致基改食物的成因為全球飢荒，以及能抵抗疾病與惡劣天氣的作物的大量生產需求。而提到基改食物的好處，因為一年四季都有食物供應，世界飢荒得以在短期內解決。除此之外，供給有抗病能力的植物意味著在某些地區的人們可以不用擔心因為天氣狀況而面臨食物短缺。然而，創造出混搭基因的食物會對植物與人類造成不可預期或有害的基因變化。此外，農夫會偏好種植能抵抗疾病的植物；因此在適者生存這個情境之下，植物的不均衡威脅了生物多樣性。總之，儘管有這些正面的影響，我們仍不能忽視控制基改食物的必要性。

▶ **第五段解說**

先用一句話換說主旨句，接著用 1 ～ 3 句話來換句話說先前的提到的原因與結果。最後用一句強而有力的句子作為結論。

(2) Chain Structure（鏈狀結構）範文

第一段 ▸ **Introduction（引言）**

Genetically modified food (GM food) is a very hotly debated topic in the modern society. GM food is created by introducing a new characteristic into the DNA of plants or crops, so that the food will be fit for specific demands. GM foods are introduced to the world based on three reasons: ① **solution to global starvation,** ② **the scarcity of seasonal plants,** and ③ **the need for disease-free crops.**

基改食物（GM food）是現代社會中熱烈討論的話題。基改食物是透過引進新的特質到植物或穀物的 DNA 中，以便讓食物更適合某些特定需求。基改食物被引進給世人是基於三個理由：解決全球飢荒、季節性植物的稀有性、以及對有抵抗疾病能力穀物的需求。

▸ **第一段解說**

開頭點出主題，第二句為基改食物的定義，編號①、②、③則提供了接下來主題發展的順序：基改食物的原因。

第二段 ▸ **Cause 1 & Effect 1（原因一和結果一）**

Because of the massive increase of human population, many people believe that the rapid growth of population will soon outpace the global food production. However, the advances in technology and medicine will continue to expand the average human lifespan. As the global population continues to grow, human beings will soon run out of agricultural land since the land will be converted to houses and stores.

因為人口大規模增長，很多人相信這種快速增長的速度會超越全球食物的生產量。然而，科技和醫藥的進展將會持續延展人類的平均壽命。當全球人口持續成長，人類很快會耗盡農耕土地，因為這些土地會被轉換成房子和商店。

原因① 因為人口大規模增長，很多人相信這種快速增長的速度會超越全球食物的生產量。

結果① 科技和醫藥的進展將會持續延展人類的平均壽命。當全球人口持續成長，人類很快會耗盡農耕土地，因為這些土地會被轉換成房子和商店。

第三段 ▶ 第 Cause 2 & Effect 2（原因二和結果二）

In addition, crops and plants consumed by human are usually
→Cause 2（原因二）
seasonal, and they will only grow within a certain time period in a
year. Yet, GM foods could survive extreme weather, such as droughts,
→Effect 2（結果二）
resulting in a higher yield and bringing in greater profits for farmers.
On the other hand, in order to grow plants with economic value
that survive harsher conditions, existing seasonal species can be
overrun by more dominant new species, reducing biodiversity in our
environment.

除此之外，被人類所消耗的穀物和植物通常是季節性的，而且只會在一年當中的某幾個時節生長。然而，基改食物可以在極端天氣生存下來，例如旱災，導致產量增加，農夫的獲利也會變多。但另一方面，為了要能夠栽種具有經濟價值且可在艱困環境下生長的作物，現存的季節性品種會被占優勢的新品種超越，因而毀滅環境的生物多樣性。

▶ **第三段解說**

原因② 被人類所消耗的穀物和植物通常是季節性的，而且只會在一年當中的某幾個時節生長。

結果② 基改食物可以在極端氣候生存下來，例如旱災，導致產量增加，農夫的獲利也會變多。但另一方面，為了要能夠栽種具有經濟價值且可在艱困環境下生長的作物，現存的季節性品種會被占優勢的新品種超越，因而毀滅生物多樣性。

Last, because of the growing population and the limited seasonal
　　　　　▶ Cause 3（原因三）
agricultural products available to human beings, farmers cannot afford
the loss caused by the pests to crops. Scientists then produce crops
and plants that are disease resistant. Nevertheless, there is a growing
　　　　　　　　　　　　　　　　　　▶ Effect 3（結果三）
concern that people are becoming increasingly resistant to antibiotics.
Genetic modification builds up plants' resistance to disease; therefore,
such trait will make it more tolerant to pesticides. When humans
consume GM food, the cells in these foods could affect people's ability
to fight against illness.

　　最後，因為人口增長及可提供給人類的有限的季節性農產品，農夫沒辦法承受
害蟲造成的損失。科學家因此製造出了具有抗病能力的穀物及植物。然而，有一股
逐漸增長的擔憂，那就是人們對抗生素愈來愈有抗藥性。基改食物會增加植物對疾
病的抵抗性，因此，這樣的特質會使得植物對殺蟲劑更加具有耐受性。當人類吃進
基改食物時，食物內的細胞會影響人類對抗疾病的能力。

▶ 　第四段解說

　　原因③ 因為人口增長及有限的季節性農產品，農夫沒辦法承受害蟲
造成的損失。科學家因此製造出了具有抗病能力的穀物及植物。

　　結果③ 但有一股逐漸增長的擔憂，那就是人們對抗生素愈來愈有抗
藥性。基改食物會增加植物對疾病的耐受度，因此，這樣的特質會使得
植物對殺蟲劑更佳具有耐受性。當人類吃進基改食物時，食物內的細胞
會影響人類對抗疾病的能力。

第五段 ▶ Conclusion（結論）

To conclude, the causes for GM foods are global hunger and the
　　　　　▶ 改寫主旨句
need for mass production of disease-free crops that could survive
the harsh condition. When it comes to GM foods' benefits, with the
availability of food all year round, world hunger could be solved in
　　　　　　　　　　　　　　　　　▶ 總結優點
the short run. Additionally, the supply of disease-resistant plants and

Chapter 6 因果關係

crops means that people in some areas will no longer suffer from food shortages, regardless of weather condition. However, creating foods by mixing different types of genes will produce unexpected or harmful genetic changes in both plants and human beings. Furthermore, farmers may favor disease-free plants and crops over seasonal ones; therefore, an imbalance in plants threatens biodiversity in a survival of the fittest scenario. In a nutshell, despite all the positive effects, we cannot overemphasize the necessity of controlling GM food.

總結缺點

強而有力的句子作為結論

　　總結來說，導致基改食物的成因為全球飢荒，以及能抵抗疾病與惡劣天氣的作物的大量生產需求。而提到基改食物的好處，因為一年四季都有食物供應，世界飢荒得以在短期內解決。除此之外，供給有抗病能力的植物意味著在某些地區的人們可以不用擔心因為天氣狀況而面臨食物短缺。然而，創造出混搭基因的食物會對植物與人類造成不可預期或有害的基因變化。此外，農夫會偏好種植能抵抗疾病的植物，因此在適者生存這個情境之下，植物的不均衡威脅了生物多樣性。總之，儘管有這些正面的影響，我們仍不能忽視控制基改食物的必要性。

▶　**第五段解說**

　　先用一句話換說主旨句，接著用 1 ～ 3 句話來換句話說先前的提到的原因與結果。最後用一句強而有力的句子作為結論。

words, words, words 好的選字
讓你的作文高下立見！

Chapter

07

佛腳給你抱：
寫作秘笈大公開

佛腳給你抱：
寫作秘笈大公開

> "Propositions show what they say: tautologies and contradictions show that they say nothing."— Ludwig Wittgenstein, Austrian philosopher
>
> 「觀點說明了人們想要說的東西：冗詞贅述與矛盾顯示了他們什麼都沒說。」
> ——奧地利哲學家路德維希·維根斯坦

　　在寫作時，礙於時間限制，和腦容量被各種想法和資訊淹沒的情況下，很容易會寫出重複的字，或是涵義過於廣泛的字。而要能夠在上戰場時有足夠的功力替換字詞，除了在日常閱讀時多留意作者如何描述，也可以利用英英字典，或是一個非常好用的網站 www.thesaurus.com，只要輸入想查詢的單字，就可以快速看到同義或反義詞喔！

Section 01　超NG！過度濫用的字就別再寫了！

　　你是不是碰過這樣的困擾呢？單字背了很多，但寫來寫去就那幾個，整篇寫完後發現自己明明會的單字很多，用字遣詞看起來卻很貧乏。我們來做個練習：請在看完以下的中文單字後，立刻寫下你所想到所有能相對應的英文單字。

炎熱	友善的	驚奇的	走路	跑步	解釋	懶惰	大的

　　寫完之後請對照，在剛剛那個當下，你是不是只寫出這些單字呢？

炎熱	友善的	驚奇的	走路	跑步	解釋	懶惰	大的
hot	friendly	amazing	walk	run	explain	lazy	big

好的寫作會善用適合文章當中的情境所需要的字詞，才不會看起來過於初階或者不夠精準。這個時候叮以考慮使用 synonym（同義詞）替換：

hot 炎熱	heated, sizzling, roasting, scorching, burning
friendly 友善的	affable, amiable, sociable, warm, affectionate
amazing 驚奇的	astonishing, astounding, surprising, stunning, spectacular
walk 走路	stroll, amble, trudge, plod, dawdle, hike, tramp, march
run 跑步	race, rush, dash, hasten, hurry, scurry, scamper
explain 解釋	describe, explicate, clarify
lazy 懶惰的	idle, slothful, shiftless, inactive
big 大的	large, sizeable, considerable, immense, enormous, massive

從替換過後的字可以發現，原本無趣的又過度使用的單字，居然可以在替換一個詞之後就變得精準又生動。下次在寫作時，不妨考慮在寫完後花個幾分鐘的時間再次瀏覽，更換掉不夠有活力的單字吧！

其實跟中文一樣，英文裡也有各種同義詞，例如以「喝」來說，「啜飲」叫做 sip，「牛飲」叫做 gulp，為了更能貼切地描述事物，必須善用同義或反義詞來讓讀者了解我們要陳述的事物具備何種狀態。

以下請你試著寫出這些單字的同義詞與反義詞：

單字	同義詞	反義詞
kind 好的		
exciting 刺激的		
new 新的		
rough 高低不平、崎嶇的		
loud 大聲地、響亮地		
develop 發展、成長		
belief 信仰、信念，看法		
clumsy 笨拙的、不靈活的		

單字	同義詞	反義詞
carefully 小心地、仔細地		
old 老的		
smart 聰明的		

並對照以下表格內的單字，這些單字你是否都認識且會用了呢？

單字	同義詞	反義詞
kind 好的	• amiable 和藹可親的、親切的 • charitable 仁慈的、寬厚的 • compassionate 富有同情心的 • considerate 體貼的、周到的 • friendly 友好的、友善的 • kindhearted 好心的、善良的 • loving 有愛心的 • sympathetic 有同情心的 • thoughtful 考慮周到的 • tolerant 寬容的 • understanding 善解人意的	• cold 冷淡的、冷漠的 • cruel 殘忍的、殘酷的 • harsh 嚴酷的、嚴厲的 • hateful 令人討厭的、可惡的 • inconsiderate 不體諒別人的、不為他人著想的 • indifferent 冷淡的、無動於衷的 • thoughtless 不為他人著想的、粗心的 • uncaring 冷漠的、無同情心的 • unfriendly 不友好的、冷漠的
exciting 刺激的	• exhilarating 令人極度興奮的、使人興高采烈的 • inspiring 鼓舞人心的 • interesting 有趣的、引起興趣的 • intriguing 非常有趣的、引人入勝的 • mind-blowing 令人印象深刻的、 令人驚奇的 • stimulating 有啟發性的 • thrilling 令人激動的 • zestful 充滿狂熱的、充滿熱情的	• boring 煩人的、乏味的 • dull 枯燥的、乏味的 • moderate 溫和的、不過分的 • unenthusiastic 不熱心的、缺乏熱情的 • uninspiring 不令人感到興奮的、不能引起興趣的 • unpromising 前景不好的、沒希望的
new 新的	• brand-new 全新的、嶄新的 • cutting-edge 領先的、最新的、尖端的 • latest 最新的、最近的	• antiquated 陳舊的、過時的、老式的 • old-fashioned 老式的、過時的、老派的

	• modern 現代的、新式的 • novel 新穎的、新奇的 • state-of-the-art 最先進的 • up-to-date 現代的、包含最新資訊的	• outdated 過時的、陳舊的 • out-of-date 過時的、陳舊的
rough 高低不平、 崎嶇的	• bumpy 顛簸的 • coarse 粗糙的、不光滑的 • rocky 多岩石的、崎嶇難行的 • rugged 崎嶇難行的 • stony 布滿石頭的	• flat 平坦的 • gentle 不陡的、平緩的 • smooth 光滑的、平滑的
loud 大聲地、 響亮地	• deafening 震耳欲聾的、聲響巨大的 • ear-splitting 震耳欲聾的、極響的、刺耳的 • resounding 響亮的、洪亮的	• quietly 安靜的 • silently 寂靜地、沈默地
develop 發展、 成長	• advance 使進步、使發展 • establish 建立、創立 • evolve 逐步發展、演變 • expand 擴大、增加 • flourish 茁壯、蓬勃發展 • foster 促進、培養 • grow 增多、增長、成長 • progress 進步、改進、進展 • thrive 茁壯、興旺、繁榮	• cease 停止、中止 • circumscribe 控制、限制、抑制 • decline 減少、衰落、降低 • decrease 使減少、下降、降低 • discontinue 停止、中止 • halt 使停止 • lessen 減少、降低、減輕 • narrow 使變少
belief 信仰、信 念， 看法	• concept 概念、觀念 • creed 信條、信念、教義 • doctrine 政治或宗教的信條、教義、學說 • faith 信任、信心 • principle 原理、原則 • tenet 信條、宗旨、原則 • theory 理論、學說	• disbelief 懷疑 • doubt 懷疑、疑慮、疑問 • proof 證據 • reality 現實、實際情況 • skepticism 懷疑論

clumsy 笨拙的、 不靈活的	• blundering 跌跌撞撞地走、踉蹌地走 • bumbling 糊塗的、笨手笨腳的 • bungling 笨手笨腳地搞砸 • butterfingered 拿東西不穩的 • ponderous 行動遲緩的、笨拙的 • ungainly 笨手笨腳的、舉止不優雅的	• adroit 敏捷的、靈巧的 • agile 敏捷的、靈活的 • athletic 擅長運動的 • coordinated 動作協調的 • dexterous 敏捷的、靈巧的
carefully 小心地、 仔細地	• cautiously 小心地 • discreetly 謹慎地 • gingerly 謹慎地、小心翼翼地 • meticulously 小心翼翼地 • prudently 小心翼翼地	• carelessly 不小心地 • incautiously 不小心地 • thoughtlessly 輕率地
old 老的	• ancient 古代的、古老的、年代久遠的 • decrepit 破舊的、年久失修的、老朽的 • elderly 年老的、上了年紀的、年紀較大的 • senior 比其他成員年長的、資深的	• contemporary 當代的、現代的 • current 現時的、當前的、現行的 • modern 現代的、新式的 • new 新出現的、新興的 • recent 最近的、最新的 • up-to-date 現代的、最近的、包含最新資訊的 • young 年輕的
smart 聰明的	• brainy 有才能的、聰明的 • bright 聰明的 • brilliant 有才氣的、聰穎的 • intelligent 有才智的、聰穎的 • resourceful 機敏的、足智多謀的 • shrewd 明智的、精明的 • wise 有智慧的	• clumsy 笨手笨腳的 • foolish 愚蠢的、傻的 • ignorant 無知的、愚昧的 • naïve 天真的、幼稚的 • stupid 愚蠢的 • unintelligent 缺乏才智的、愚蠢的、無知的

濫用字也是語言癌

　　請看以下的句子，想一想有哪些是你在讀了之後覺得很無聊或重複性過高的字，並寫出你覺得可以怎麼改善這個過度濫用字的情況。

1. Dave was very excited about his girlfriend's visit, but he also felt very overwhelmed.
   戴夫對於女朋友的到來感到興奮，但是他也感到不知所措。

   → _____

2. It was very cold the day my grandmother left; I was very worried about her.
   祖母離開那天非常冷，我非常擔心她。

   → _____

3. Mark's eyes were very blue; his hair was very white.
   馬克的眼睛很藍，他的頭髮很白。

   → _____

4. The glass bowl was very full, so I made sure to walk very slowly.
   玻璃碗是滿的，所以我確保我走得很慢。

   → _____

5. My dad said that he was retiring; my mom said: "Finally! About time!"
   我爸爸說他要退休了，媽媽說：「終於！是時候了！」

   → _____

6. Our boss says that we are too inexperienced for the project; I want to say that we're not.
   我們老闆說我們對這個案子很沒有經驗，我想說並不是。

   → _____

7. Without saying too much, Megan says that she must leave immediately.
   沒有說太多，梅根說她必須馬上離開。

   → _____

8. Justin glanced at me and said he hated me. "Okay," was all I could say.
   賈斯汀盯著我並說他討厭我。「好吧！」是我唯一能說的。

   → _____

9. Basketball last night was exciting. It was a good game, and we had good seats.
   昨晚的籃球超讚。是個很棒的比賽，而且我們有好位置。

   → _____

10. When asked if he had a good day, James replied, "Well, I sat down in a café and had a good cup of coffee."
    當問他說是否那天過得不錯，詹姆士回答：「嗯，我坐在咖啡廳並喝上一杯好咖啡。」

    → _____

參考答案

以下提供修飾這些句子更好的寫作方法：
1. Dave was **extremely** excited about his girlfriend's visit, but he also felt <u>rather</u> overwhelmed.
2. It was **freezing / icy** cold the day my grandmother left; I was <u>deeply</u> worried about her.
3. Mark's eyes were **quite** blue; his hair was **extremely / rather** white.
4. The glass bowl was **extremely / fairly / pretty / quite / completely** full, so I made sure to walk **particularly** slowly.
5. My dad **declared** that he was retiring; my mom **murmured**: "Finally! About time!"
6. Our boss <u>claimed</u> that we are too inexperienced for the project; I want to <u>defend</u> that we're not.
7. Without **divulging** too much, Megan **asserted** that she must leave immediately.
8. Justin glanced at me and **shouted** he hated me. "Okay," was all I could <u>comment</u>.
9. Basketball last night was exciting. It was a **competitive** game, and we had <u>front</u> seats.
10. When asked if he had **an eventful** day, James replied, "Well, I sat down in a café and had <u>an excellent</u> cup of coffee."

　　有些時候在寫作時，學生會反應説怕字數不夠，或是描述不夠完整，所以會一直想塞字進去文章裡。但往往塞到最後，批改者看的不但有過度濫用的字，還有許多不必要的細節，讀起來就變成很多廢話塞在文章裡。

　　請先試著閱讀以下的文章，並在你覺得是不必要的地方畫底線：

The moment when I drove through the dry desert, my heart grew more and more depressed. Deep in my mind, I knew I should have never left, but I was tired of the lies and the arguments. I could still hear my family's loud screaming in my head, and my hand trembled.

It was getting late, and I knew I should take a rest. I saw some broken ruins, so I stopped the car to watch the evening sunset. Seeing the scene, for the first time, it came to my mind that I was fully and completely alone. My first priority had always been my family, but none of them felt grateful for my dedication. Now it was time I put myself first and made plans for myself. First and foremost, I needed to get away from my family and stop giving in to their constant demands.

I stepped out of the car, hoping to get some fresh air, but all I breathed in was hot air. I locked the car securely and noticed a flickering shadow. It was then that I realized that I wasn't alone. There was a stray dog lying weakly on the stone with no food or water. With caution, I personally approached it in close nearness.

I made a noise as I approached the dog in order to signal my arrival because I didn't want to frighten the poor creature. However, it didn't even move at all. When I was close enough, I let out a whistle, but again it didn't move; it kept on remaining still as if she were made of stone.

　　接著我們來逐段閱讀潤飾後的文章！

潤飾後的第一段：

The moment when I drove through the ~~dry~~ desert, my heart grew more and more depressed. Deep in my mind, I knew I should have never left, but I was tired of the lies and the arguments. I could still hear my family's ~~loud~~ screaming in my head, and my hand trembled.

當我開車穿過沙漠時，我的心變得愈來愈沮喪，在我心深處，我知道我不應該離開，但是我厭倦了謊言和爭吵。我仍能在腦海中聽見我家人的尖叫，我的手顫抖著。

▶ **第一段解説**

① desert 本身就已經是乾燥的地帶，加上 dry 沒有任何意義。

② screaming 這個字一定是分貝比較高的，不需要加上 loud。

潤飾後的第二段：

It was getting late, and I knew I should take a rest. I saw some ~~broken~~ ruins, so I stopped the car to watch the ~~evening~~ sunset. Seeing the scene, for the first time, it came to my mind that I was ~~fully and~~ completely alone. My ~~first~~ priority had always been my family, but none of them felt grateful for my dedication. Now it was time I put myself first and made plans for myself. First ~~and foremost,~~ I needed to get away from my family and stop giving in to their constant demands.

很晚了，我知道我應該休息。我看見一些廢墟，所以我停下車並觀賞日落。看到這一幕，我第一次覺得我真的是獨自一人。家庭一直是我心中第一位，但是他們沒有一個人感激我的付出，現在我該把自己放在第一位，並為自己計畫了。首先，我必須離開我的家庭，並不再向他們持續的要求讓步。

▶ **第二段解説**

① ruins 指的是廢墟，所以加上 broken 是多此一舉。

② sunset 只會出現在傍晚，所以不需要加 evening。

③ fully 和 completely 是同義詞。

④ priority 已經帶有優先的意思了，不須再加 first。

⑤ First 和 foremost 是同義詞，不用重複使用。

潤飾後的第三段：

I stepped out of the car, hoping to get some fresh air, but all I breathed in was hot air. I locked the car ~~securely~~ and noticed a flickering shadow. It was then that I realized that I wasn't alone. There was a stray dog lying weakly on the stone with no food or water. With caution, I ~~personally~~ approached it in close ~~nearness~~.

我走出車外希望得到一些新鮮空氣，但我只吸到熱氣。我鎖上車，並注意到一個閃爍的影子，就在那時我意識到我並不孤單，有一隻流浪狗沒有食物也沒有水，虛弱地躺在石頭上，我小心翼翼地接近牠。

▶ **第三段解説**

① locked 表示已鎖上，不用再加 securely（牢固地）這個字了。

② I 就是你自己了，不需要再加 personally。

③ close 代表靠近，不需要再加 nearness。

潤飾後的第四段：

I made a noise as I approached the dog in order to signal my arrival because I didn't want to frighten the poor creature. However, it didn't ~~even~~ move at all. When I was close enough, I let out a whistle, but again it didn't move; it kept on ~~remaining~~ still as if she were made of stone.

我靠近那隻狗時，我出了聲以示我的到來，因為我不想嚇到這可憐的東西。然而牠卻一動也不動，當我靠得夠近時，我吹了聲口哨，但牠還是不動，好像牠是石頭做的。

▶ **第四段解説**

① even 跟 at all 都是強調沒有，擇一書寫即可。

② keep on 跟 remain 是同義詞。

　　從粗體字可以看出，在寫作時，假如同樣的內容用不同的字重複敘述，看起來不但很多餘，而且在正式寫作中也是不正確的用法。因此，在寫完後務必要快速瀏覽過，在內心默念文章，檢查是否有重複書寫之處。

Section 03 為什麼不能說Merry Birthday？搭配詞的重要性

　　你是否曾經在寫作時被批改的老師下了評語說使用的介係詞或是動詞是錯誤的呢？或是曾經有過懷疑為何某些單字或片語就只能搭配這個介係詞或動詞呢？這是因為在英文當中有「搭配詞」，是約定俗成的用法。就像我們只能說「Happy Birthday!」、「Merry Christmas!」而不會隨意轉換「Merry Birthday!」、「Happy Christmas!」。

　　現在可以回想一下，你在學習 have 這個單字的時候，除了「有」這個意思之外，是否還知道其它意思呢？

　　例如：

- have lunch 「吃」午餐
- have a bath 「洗」澡
- have a rest 「休息」
- have a meeting 「舉辦」一場會議
- have a haircut 「剪」頭髮
- have a drink 「喝」飲料
- have a good time 「度過」美好的時光
- have a relationship 「有」一段感情
- have a holiday 「享受」一個假期
- have a problem 「有」問題
- have an argument 「爭吵」

以上這些搭配詞就是文字的魔力，藉由結合兩個單字，讓詞的發展更多元，而這也是中文跟英文很不一樣的地方。

我們接著以 interest（興趣）這個單字為例：

(1) 要表達「極大的、強烈的、濃厚的」興趣：可以使用 considerable、deep、great、intense、keen、strong

> 例 She always has a great interest in the contemporary art.
> 她對於當代藝術總是有著極大的興趣。

(2) 要「表達」興趣時：可以用 express、show、take

> 例 My friend expressed an interest in seeing where I work.
> 我朋友有興趣想知道我在哪裡上班。

(3) 提到「激起」興趣：會使用 arouse、kindle、spark、stimulate、stir up

> 例 The government failed to arouse any public interest in the new pension reform plan.
> 政府未能激起任何大眾對於新的年金改革計畫的興趣。

(4) 「發展」興趣：可以使用 develop

> 例 While in prison, the ex-con developed an interest in Chinese calligraphy.
> 在獄中期間，這名前科犯發展出了對書法的興趣。

如果我們想要用介係詞＋ interest 變成一個介係詞片語的話，我們可以使用：

(5) 好奇問問：out of interest

> 例 I'm asking purely out of interest.
> 我只是單純好奇問問而已。

(6) 感興趣地：with

> 例 They listened to the program with interest.
> 他們興致勃勃地聽著節目。

接著來簡單做個練習，當你想到 disease（疾病）這個字的時候，你會想到那些可以搭配的詞呢？請先快速瀏覽中文，並寫下答案，再來核對英文答案。

形容詞＋ disease	
	• common disease 常見的疾病
	• rare / obscure disease 罕見的疾病
	• dangerous disease 危險的疾病
	• serious disease 嚴重的疾病
	• chronic / acute disease 慢性的／急性的疾病
	• deadly / fatal / killer disease 致命的疾病
	• curable disease 可治療的疾病
	• preventable disease 可預防的疾病
	• communicable / contagious / infectious disease 傳染性的疾病
動詞＋ disease	• have / suffer from disease 罹患疾病
	• catch / contract / get disease 得了、感染疾病
	• die from / of disease 死於疾病
	• cause disease 導致疾病
	• carry disease 帶有疾病
	• spread / transmit / pass on disease 傳染疾病
	• prevent disease 預防疾病
	• treat / cure disease 治療疾病
	• combat / fight disease 對抗疾病
disease ＋動詞	• disease＋spreads 疾病散播
介係詞＋ disease	• with a / the disease 有這樣疾病的……

做完這個練習之後，你是不是發現自己對於可以搭配的字詞，寫來寫去總是那幾個？所以在日常閱讀時，可以有意識地去留意文章當中的每個字詞之間的搭配，學習起來會更有效率喔！

3-1 提升文章層次的搭配詞

以下是寫作時常用的搭配詞及例句，可以根據寫作需求適時加入文章當中，會讓你的整體程度更加提升，看起來更道地喔！

❶ do an experiment / a research 做實驗／做研究

例 We are doing an experiment to test people's reactions to the new vaccine.
我們正在做一項測試人們對新疫苗的實驗。

❷ do damage 造成損害

例 The earthquake did some damage to our house.
地震對我們的房子造成損害。

❸ do exercise 做運動

例 It is suggested that people should do exercises on a weekly basis.
人們被建議應該要每周運動。

❹ do harm 造成傷害

例 According to several studies, air purifiers used in confined spaces, such as an elevator, may do more harm than good.
根據一些研究指出，空氣清淨機使用於密閉空間，例如電梯，可能會弊大於利。

❺ do someone a favor 幫忙

例 Could you do me a favor and pick me up some groceries from the supermarket?
你可不可以幫忙去超市買點東西？

❻ do the laundry 洗衣服

例 I'll do the laundry after work.
下班後我會洗衣服。

❼ do your best 盡力

例 All it matters in your life is to do your best.
人生當中最重要的就是盡力而為。

❽ break a habit 改掉壞習慣

例 Psychologists estimate that it takes roughly 60 days to break or form a new habit.
科學家估計大概要花上 60 天來改掉或形成一個新的習慣。

❾ break a leg 祝好運

例 I heard that you are going to give a public speech. Break your leg and knock them dead!
我聽說你今天要公開演講，祝你好運，希望引起觀眾廣大的迴響！

❿ break a promise 違反承諾

例 This app broke a privacy promise to its users by sharing more data with a renowned social media website.
這個應用程式因與知名的社群媒體網站分享更多資料，違反了對使用者隱私權的承諾。

⓫ break the ice 打破僵局、打破冷場、緩和緊張氣氛

例 He started the meeting with a couple of jokes to break the ice.
他用幾個笑話來為會議起頭，以便緩和緊張氣氛。

⓬ break the mold 打破常規

例 The company is breaking the mold in its new advertising campaign.
這間公司在他們新的廣告活動中打破常規。

⓭ break the news to someone 告訴某人不好的消息

例 I didn't want to be the one to break the news to my best friend.
我不想把這種消息告訴我最好的朋友。

⓮ have a break 休息，小憩

例 Let's have a break when you finish this part of the exercise.
你完成這部分的練習後我們就休息一下。

⓯ have a conversation / chat 對話、聊天

例 The hardcore fans were hoping to have a chat with their favorite singer after the fan meeting.
鐵粉們盼望著有機會跟他們最喜歡的歌手在粉絲見面會後小聊一下。

⓰ have a look 看

例 The executive is having a look at this quarter's sales figures.
行政主管正在看這一季的銷售數字。

⓱ have a try / go 嘗試

例 I never tried bungee jumping before but I'll give it a try / go.
我從沒試過高空彈跳，但我會試看看。

⓲ have an argument 爭執

例 I am tired of having an argument with you about your spending every time the credit card bill comes in.
我對於每次你的信用卡帳單寄來時，要為了你的花費跟你吵架深感厭倦。

⓳ have difficulty 做……是有困難的

例 The trainees had difficulty understanding what to do.
實習生對於要做什麼覺得很難理解。

⓴ make a change / changes 改變

例 The new principal is planning to make some changes.
新校長正在計畫要做些改變。

㉑ make a choice 抉擇

例 It is very difficult for parents to make a choice between their career and family.
對父母親來說要在職涯與家庭間做抉擇是很困難的。

　　關於搭配詞查詢的網站，可以參考 Online OXFORD Collocation Dictionary of English（線上牛津搭配詞字典）、Cambridge Dictionary 的 Collocation 功能或 Merriam-Webster 的 Collocation 功能。

請先運用直覺圈選出能搭配後面字詞的單字，核對答案後如果有疑問，建議平常可以整理屬於自己的搭配詞筆記本，以及多使用字典增加自己對搭配詞的熟悉度喔！

1. The lecture was almost two hours so it was really hard for the students to <u>give / have / pay / keep attention</u> all the time.
   這堂課大概兩小時長，所以學生很難無時無刻保持專注。

2. This public crisis is difficult to <u>make / keep / hold under control</u>.
   這個公關危機很難被控制住。

3. It took us all day to clean up the house after the party – the guests <u>did / made / had a terrible mess</u>.
   我們花了一天才清乾淨開派對後的房子，而客人弄得一團糟。

4. I don't think we should <u>hold / make / create a decision</u> before we get the whole picture.
   在我們全盤了解之前，我覺得我們不應該做決定。

5. Only 10 percent of the students who <u>made / took / wrote the exam</u> passed it.
   只有百分之十的學生通過考試。

6. We should look for a new business partner since the one we have at the moment <u>makes / causes / increases us too many problems</u>.
   我們應該要找一個新的商業夥伴，因為我們現有的這位給我們造成太多問題了。

7. Many companies offer their employees free on-the-job training programs but not many people <u>do / use / take / make good advantage of it</u>.
   很多公司提供員工免費的在職訓練，但並沒有很多員工運用。

8. Our professor is leaving temporarily next month as she is <u>making / expecting / waiting for a baby</u>.
   我們的教授下個月起會暫時請假，因為她懷孕了。

9. I guess we can <u>exactly / safely / accurately assume</u> he didn't work hard as the test result was pretty poor.
   我猜我們可以有把握地說他並沒有努力，因為考試結果滿差的。

10. The antibody test, a blood test to check if you have had COVID-19 before, is not <u>fully / widely / completely available</u> yet.
抗體測試，也就是一種能檢測你是否曾得了新冠肺炎的血液測試，目前還沒有廣泛地可供使用。

11. You must <u>fully / wholly / exhaustively assess</u> the situation, including analyzing the scale of the problem, as well as its cause and effect, before you make the final call.
在你做最後決定前，你必須全面性地評估情勢，包含分析問題的規模，及其成因。

12. The young man just sits at home all day playing online games, and he has no friends and no job. He really needs to <u>get out / get started / get a life</u>.
這個年輕人整天就是在家玩線上遊戲，而且他沒朋友也沒工作。他真的應該要找點事做振作起來。

13. My husband is learning coding because he <u>got over / got started / got the sack</u> from his job last month and he needs to learn new skills.
我先生正在學寫程式因為他上個月被解僱了，而他必須學習新的技能。

14. My wife passed away two years ago, and I have never really <u>gotten off / gotten over / gotten down it</u>.
我太太兩年前過世了，而我還沒有真的走出來。

15. The surgeon coming to give the seminar is <u>the front / winning / leading expert</u> in cardiovascular disease.
要舉辦這場研討會的外科醫生是心血管疾病的頂尖專家。

參考答案

以下提供修飾這些句子更好的寫作方法：
1. **pay**（pay attention：專注）
2. **keep**（keep under control：控制住情勢）
3. **made**（made a terrible mess：弄得一團糟）
4. **make**（make a decision：下決定）
5. **took**（take the exam：參加考試）
6. **causes**（cause someone problems：給某人帶來麻煩）
7. **take**（take advantage of something：利用、運用、佔便宜）
8. **expecting**（expect a baby：懷有身孕）
9. **safely**（safely assume：有把握地說）
10. **widely**（widely available：廣泛地可供使用）
11. **fully**（fully assess：全面性地評估）
12. **get a life**：找點事做、振作起來
13. **get the sack**：被解雇
14. **get over**（get over something：忘卻傷痛、走出來）
15. **leading**（leading expert：頂尖的專家）

英文中的正能量、負能量以及保持中性的意涵

　　我們都知道，文字帶有力量，否則就不會有筆誅墨伐、妙筆生花這些成語來形容文字可以帶來的正面或負面的能量。使用文字時往往也會帶有情緒和含意，在華人世界，「很瘦」是一句讚美別人的話，但換成英文 skinny 的時候則帶有貶意，表示某個人瘦得很不好看。也因此，從中文思維轉換到英文寫作時，必須要留意英文單字的正負面以及中性意涵，才不會因為誤用而冒犯到他人。

This toy is really cheap.	字面上的意思：玩具很便宜。
	實際含意：玩具做工不好、很廉價。
He is a talkative person.	字面上的意思：他很喜歡講話。
	實際含意：他講太多話了，很吵。
She wore a plain dress.	字面上的意思：她穿了一件很素的洋裝。
	實際含意：她穿的洋裝很普通而且不好看。
He is inexperienced at work.	字面上的意思：他還沒累積什麼經驗。
	實際含意：他很菜。

　　從以上的例子可以看的出來，使用文字時，必須考慮到這個字在英文當中可能會讓讀者意會錯我們原本要表達的意思。

多樣化的形容詞

請在下方單字下格分別標上「＋」（正面）、「－」（負面）以及「 」中性。

1. 形容使用金錢的態度

thrifty	cheap	economical

2. 形容說話的能力

communicative	talkative	chatty

3. 形容對事情的態度

obsessed	preoccupied	focused

4. 形容對事情的態度

nosy	curious	inquisitive

5. 形容有自信

proud	self-assured	arrogant

6. 形容有年紀

old	elderly	mature

7. 形容氣味

smell	stench	aroma

8. 形容有創意

creative	crafty	resourceful

參考答案

1. 形容使用金錢的態度

thrifty 節儉的	cheap 廉價的	economical 節約的
＋	－	△

2. 形容說話的能力

communicative 交際的	talkative 多話的	chatty 愛說話的
△	－	＋

3. 形容對事情的態度

obsessed 著迷的	preoccupied 全神貫注的	focused 專心的
－	△	＋

4. 形容對事情的態度

nosy 愛管閒事的	curious 好奇的	inquisitive 好奇的
－	△	＋

5. 形容有自信

proud 自豪的	self-assured 自信的	arrogant 自大的
△	＋	－

6. 形容有年紀

old 老的	elderly 有年紀的	mature 成熟的
－	△	＋

7. 形容氣味

smell 氣味	stench 臭味	aroma 芳香
△	－	＋

8. 形容有創意

creative 有創意的	crafty 狡猾的	resourceful 機智的
＋	－	△

　　轉折詞看似簡單，但卻是寫作中很重要的一環。有些轉折詞可以幫助我們表達意見、提出證據、反駁對方、串起各個論點之間的關係，或是下結論等等。妥善運用轉折詞，可以讓讀者更快速掌握文章重點，並能更流暢地閱讀。

表達時間或先後順序	**(1) 首先**	
	• first	• first of all
	• to begin with	• to start with
	• in the beginning	• in the first place
	• at first	
	(2) 接下來	
	• next	• then
	• and then	• secondly
	• thirdly	• shortly after
	• after a while	
	(3) 最後	
	• last	• lastly
	• finally	• in the end
	• eventually	• to sum up
與論述有關	**(1) 此外**	
	• furthermore	• moreover
	• what's more	• in addition
	• additionally	• besides
	• similarly	• apart from this
	• aside from this	
	(2) 換句話説	
	• in other words	• to put it differently
	• to put it in another way	
	(3) 最重要的是	
	• above all	• most importantly
	• on top of that	
	(4) 事實上	
	• in fact	• actually
	• as a matter of fact	• to be honest

	(5) 如上述所言 • as I have said earlier • as I have mentioned earlier • as have been shown
舉例	**例如** • for example • for instance • Take… for example. • such as • like • just like
說明	**基於這個理由** • for this purpose • for this reason • with this in mind • in the event that • to this end
反駁或提出相反論點	**(1) 然而／儘管** • yet • however • nevertheless • despite • despite the fact that… • regardless of… **(2) 雖然** • although • even though **(3) 相反地** • on the contrary, • on the other hand, • in contrast **(4) 有些人可能會說……** • Some might say that… • Some might argue that… • People might hold different opinions that…
提出結果或下結論	**(1) 因此／結果** • consequently • as a result • as a consequence • hence • thus • therefore • accordingly **(2) 簡單來說／總而言之** • in brief • in conclusion • to put it simply • in summary • in a nutshell • to sum up • to conclude

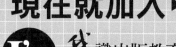

國家圖書館出版品預行編目（CIP）資料

最強英文寫作指南： 風靡全球的萬用寫
作法,五大類文體完全適用! / 楊舒涵著. --
初版. -- 臺北市：我識出版社有限公司,
2021.03
　　面； 公分
ISBN 978-986-99662-5-2(平裝)
1.英語 2.寫作法
805.17　　　　　　　　　110000138

最強英文寫作指南
Powerful English Writing Techniques for All Purposes

風靡全球的萬用寫作法
五大類文體完全適用

書名 / 最強英文寫作指南：風靡全球的萬用寫作法，五大類文體完全適用！
作者 / 楊舒涵
發行人 / 蔣敬祖
出版事業群總經理 / 廖晏婕
銷售暨流通事業群總經理 / 施宏
總編輯 / 劉俐伶
執行編輯 / 謝有容
品牌顧問 / 路易思
校對 / 張汝萍、楊易、劉婉瑀
視覺指導 / 姜孟傑、鄭宇辰
排版 / 謝青秀
圖片 / tw.pixtastock.com
法律顧問 / 北辰著作權事務所蕭雄淋律師
印製 / 金漬印刷事業有限公司
初版 / 2021年3月
初版七刷 / 2023年8月
出版 / 我識出版教育集團——我識出版社有限公司
電話 / (02) 2345-7222
傳真 / (02) 2345-5758
地址 / 臺北市忠孝東路五段372巷27弄78之1號1樓
網址 / www.17buy.com.tw
E-mail / iam.group@17buy.com.tw
facebook 網址 / www.facebook.com/ImPublishing
定價 / 新臺幣349元／港幣116元

總經銷 / 我識出版社有限公司出版發行部
地址 / 新北市汐止區新台五路一段114號12樓
電話 / (02) 2696-1357 傳真 / (02) 2696-1359

港澳總經銷 / 和平圖書有限公司
地址 / 香港柴灣嘉業街12號百樂門大廈17樓
電話 / (852) 2804-6687 傳真 / (852) 2804-6409

2011 不求人文化

2009 懶鬼子英日語

I'm 我識出版教育集團
I'm Publishing Edu. Group
www.17buy.com.tw

2005 意識文化

2005 易富文化

2003 我識地球村

2001 我識出版社